M000031952

Panoramic Diaries

Bill O'Neill

RED MOUNTAIN PRESS

© 2020 William O'Neill

Cover photograph and design © 2020 Susan Gardner

© Author's photograph by Susan Gardner, 2017

All rights reserved. No part of this book may be reproduced in any form, by any means, electronic or mechanical, without permission in writing from the author, except for brief quotations for the purpose of reviews.

This book is a work of fiction. Names, characters, places and incidents either are products of the author's imagination or are used fictitiously. Any resemblance to actual events or locales or persons, living or dead, is entirely coincidental.

ISBN 978-1-7326501-5-2

Printed in the United States of America

RED MOUNTAIN PRESS

Santa Fe, New Mexico
www.redmountainpress

For Jack O'Neill

September 7, 1920 – November 16, 2014

My secret weapon, always

More is asked of us than just being swept along…

—Rainer Maria Rilke

CHAPTER 1

It's actually quite easy—hopping a freight—especially if you have experience. Back to my days of self-exploration, before I joined the world—workaday, that is—and the affirmation in a paycheck. Boxcars are the stereotype, of course, and that's where I am now (eyeing the massive steel door, making sure it's secure). But I prefer the undercarriage of a truck trailer, even if it means I'm directly exposed to the wind. It's no problem leaning up against the large tires, and the underbelly of the truck chassis provides plenty of shelter.

It doesn't matter if I've forgotten most of their names, the state prisoners who came to us at Hope House. They gave my life meaning because I found my place in the world as their advocate. They were full of color and sadness, and there are some I could never forget. Maestas, with his Easter basket, walking down the quiet Sunday street for an early-morning dish shift. Mary Lou's proud clay rendition of herself after she was hit in the face with a fire poker. Samuel's tears streaking his African profile. Ernestine's overall accusatory way. Lewis's con-man laugh. All of them adding up to a chorus of lament. Their dinner prayers were memorable, sincere, especially in the face of the turbulent and menacing forces that awaited them outside.

I couldn't live it anymore, plain and simple—I just got to *that point.* Still, how can I forget that original bunch, my fabulous five? No problem with *those* names.

It shouldn't be surprising that they come back—that initial group was special. And I, first-day alert, consumed by the strangeness of their turbulent worlds. I was the representative or emissary from the *straight* world, receiving their apologetic accounting for what they'd done. How I remember waiting for the buzzer in the hot county lockup. Mary Lou had uneven teeth, some missing, but she was still pretty, with her clear blue eyes. She was crying inside the brick facility, telling me what had happened to her.

"Chief, it was horrible," she said. "Bullets flew. And Bucky was too high … I guess I'm going back now, right? Can you keep my stuff for me?"

"Of course we can," I answered.

"I know I let you down, Chief." This kind of conversation always seemed skewed, misplaced—Mary Lou was the one in the orange jumpsuit, not me. Had I let *her* down?

"Yes, I am sad, Mary Lou. But you're the focus here."

"Can somebody cover my dish night?"

"Don't worry about that."

"Okay," she replied.

"What happened?" I said. "You know you made Channel 3 News?"

"Did I?" she brightened slightly. "Well, Bucky's crazy. I should've known better. Guess I'll never get my kids back now."

The tears resumed. "I was just *there,* Chief. I wasn't doing anything wrong. I was scared. The police were shooting at us."

"You're lucky you didn't get killed." I had to state the obvious.

"Chief, it's not because you aren't running a great house. It's *my* fault."

"Please, Mary Lou, just worry about yourself. I mean, we're talking new charges here. Not a parole violation."

"I know."

"You'll always have a place at Hope House as long as I'm in charge."

"You're the *Chief.*"

"Damn right." We didn't say anything else at this point, both of us probably realizing that her days in our household were over. Freaking meth.

Next were her desperate but somehow also cheerful letters from the lockup a county away. Asking for photos of her kids, apologizing again for missing her dish night, asking about the household, and always misspelling Chief. The endearing wiring of my rookie household—*that* bunch, even after they'd individually and collectively fallen into their familiar disappointments, with their urgent and apologetic messages. Ernestine's ironic distance."Can you come get me, Mr. Murphy? I'm sorry to ask. I don't even *like* this drug. Why am I doing this? I'll be waiting on the corner if you can." Ernestine often reflected on her behavior with distance, as if it belonged to somebody else, and she had her Twelve Step slogans memorized, like talismans meant to undo the bad spell of her entire existence. I retrieved her from the city corner that night and returned her to her safe and newly secured apartment—and the long odds of her new life.

I lived the craziness with them, and I was sympathetic, of course, but I came from wildly different circumstances, with no cape or power to heal. At best I was an upbeat older brother or uncle, as dazed as they were by the malevolent forces in their lives. But I could invariably summon the hopeful countenance or anecdote, my role as the somewhat-prepared professional and the fact that all of them were unaccustomed to actually being listened to made it work. That's why I'd receive their messages, I suppose, long after they left Hope House, often after the authorities had become involved.

How fitting to be out here again. I'm a different person now, or at least I hope I am. There have been big changes. My father died, and for all the tension that existed between the two of us, it feels strange not to have him glaring at my bewildering decisions from a thousand miles away. My mother passed on too. I have no one to rebel against now. So, if I'm always to be a child, which it seems is my role in this life, it comes with a hollow feeling that nobody's watching. At least I'm in the world now—which would please the both of them (sort of)—earning a paycheck, though its meager size wasn't something that either could ever understand, especially my father. And working with *ex-convicts,* for Chrissake? But they definitely approved of my relationship with Kit; to them it represented a normalizing influence. When we first met up North, I'd talked Kit into joining me on the freight trains.

How on earth did I pull *that* off, convincing a beautiful, complicated young woman in her mid-twenties to abandon her life in Crystal Point, Idaho, and join me in my search? I suppose it was incremental, one choice leading to the next, culminating in her willingness to follow me into the workaday world and down to this desolate Southwestern city. It makes sense. Our issues have always mirrored each other—rebellion against family, an uncertain place in the world, privilege. So we continued to pursue the puzzle of our respective lives together—unmarried, of course, as a symbol of our defiance, but no reflection on our commitment to each other. Such conventional choices we left to others. We were fine with that. Kit couldn't make a strong enough case to stay in Montana, which had become a kind of theme park for both of us, characterized by being white in the fullest sense of the word. We were still together, she pursuing her painting (which she'd totally hidden from me for the first eleven months of our relationship) and I with the discovery of the nonprofit world (nonprofit was not a term I even knew when I graduated from college). We even have a house together—with her studio in the back—and two dogs in this desert city that would never be confused for the snowy pines of the Northwest. But we were still West. That was a categorical imperative for both of us, coming from what we came from.

Chapter 2

Is it the smell of creosote in the noonday heat that brings it all back? My adventures up North? I'm staring for miles down the silent tracks, engine activity in the distance, the sound approaching. Entering this world and escaping the other. If nothing else, it'll be an interesting morning anecdote. On the court, at my upscale gym, in between games, winners dibbed, "I swear ... he took off on the trains. No lie. Nobody's heard from him. Chapman always was weird."

One day, not *that* long ago, I'd tried to snap Lewis out of his crack-induced daze in one of those motels on the worn-out avenue. I was new on the job and motivated, before the dark energies kicked in. It was never a good thing to give up like this, I'd tell him, "Come on, fella, let's get *out* of here. I'll give you a ride." Lewis disassociative, but always with that ready laugh of his. "It's silly, isn't it?" He smiled. "Here I *am.*"

These pep talks would become so familiar to me—a miscast evangelist. "We'll get you some of that tea," I told him hopefully. I was naïve, maybe, but I was choosing this worldly wisdom on purpose.

So I bought Lewis a car painted a shade of blue that made me think of hope. He assured me, *swore* that he would pay me back, and because he was a skilled, college-educated professional I had some reason to believe him. Laws of equilibrium or physics. Once off track, the momentum of decisions takes over. The point was to have them, all of them, imagine their own normal, law-abiding lives, right? Like with young Maestas and the promise of a road trip North once he got off paper, back when I had my European sport convertible—oxidized but functional—before it too became a casualty of Hope House. And then that particular plan evolving into, and including, his heroin buddy and future fellow resident Cortez. The three of us would take that trip, *someday,* North, in my doomed convertible, into the land of no ethnicity.

The idea was to loosen the reins of deprivation a bit, to have them actually *participate* in this surrounding world, to present the prospect of a valid adventure and give them less of a reason to shoot up.

Even if these travel plans were remote, it became important to sustain all variations of futurity that we existed upon, both staff and residents. *If* I could get my car back from the barrio, and *if* Maestas could return from heroin land, *then* we could spring Cortez from rehab and actually do the trip. No robbery or felonies, instead a legitimate road trip. And maybe if that had happened, I wouldn't be out here again, alone on the freight trains.

With Lewis, however, it was more a question of pumping up his earning potential—the hourly anchoring skill that he went to school for, that his professional license, once retrieved, would present. Or the reference to his wife and three children who perhaps could be reclaimed as well, though *that* situation was much more complex. I became a spokesman or ambassador for ways that I myself either resisted or did not fully understand. I had discovered the nonprofit sector and consequently hunkered into it, finding a home, getting paid.

Kit was good about understanding all of this—we both had grown in that way—though she didn't appreciate how consuming this paycheck world would prove to be, especially with the astounding needs of my parolee population, the way their lack of life skills made me feel like an adult, but always the sincerity of their wanting to know. "Chief," they'd ask, do I need an I.D. in order to cash my paycheck? And when I get out on my own, how do I get my own phone? Do I have to get my car insured? And how is that done? How do I open a bank account?

Much harder for Kit were the late-night phone calls, when Ernestine or Mary Lou or Cortez or Maestas or Lewis would need immediate attention—or money—in order to prevent the dreaded relapse. It's not as if I had had any training in this regard, being a liberal arts casualty, and of course the parole authorities were wondering what to make of me, especially in our initial months of operation. *Do-gooder. Enabler. Did I understand the importance of rules?*

But hardest for Kit were the visits made inappropriately to our newly purchased house. They would pull up in the front driveway, battered old cars and no shortage of tattoos, the neighbors wondering. These situations would present themselves, and all I knew was that the stakes were high and the consequences of bad decisions were very real. She would look at me. "*Again?*" she would say, in that soft voice almost like music, her sincere brown eyes searching. Wanting to know. Her curly hair tomboyish. I never had much of an answer for her, as I too was trying to navigate the newness of it all.

Samuel is probably dead by now. He comes back to me full on. I remember his suicide attempt on the same bleak avenue Lewis inhabited, and their shared cocaine expeditions. That was, of course, well after they had been ejected from Hope House. Lewis had rescued him and stopped the gas in the dingy motel room. They were a reluctant duo who didn't particularly care for each other, though they had much in common besides being black.

Samuel and his grief, the silent tears as he stared into "the afternoon of his life," as he liked to call it. And on our house outing, to the bargain movies we'd go, Samuel's cynical comments. "What, is Porkie's Amusement Park next?" he said. "Is this high school? Or a halfway house?" And then, at times, suddenly militant and sullen. "Chief, you are singling me out. And I know why." And toward the end, after I brokered his honorable release from our residential contract, and of course covered him to parole, I learned that he was *everywhere* before prison—Vietnam, Alabama in the early sixties, San Francisco. "Chief," he said to me, a fugitive by then in our supermarket aisle, "I just want to go home." Again this alternating current of hope and the evidence to the contrary (his file *was* a thick one). Did he find his home later? After his warrants had expired? Had they stopped looking for him? Employment at that particular hospital worked for a stretch, I remember, and his burly doctor was enthusiastic. Then one day Samuel slipped out the door and disappeared into the desolate afternoon.

I remember the looks that the group of us would draw; we were always a motley bunch. The cashiers would stiffen, warily eye Lewis and Samuel and Maestas as they searched for some decent clothes at the chain clothing store—until I'd appear, white guy in the oxford shirt—and then the immediate change in the given clerk's demeanor, immediately respectful, even solicitous, though still confused about our particular association. Only a discount store on the avenue and these three residents with no attention span, already stretching me and our limited charitable budget (Samuel wanted *two* suits), their collective bad history, and our resulting mission of redemption.

Samuel hated what he called his slave name, Sam, but he used it nevertheless, on occasion. Expert phone salesman until the boss hurt his feelings, great hospital floor waxer until he slipped and broke his ankle, excellent household resident until I couldn't ignore any longer the smell of vodka on his breath. And then there was the evening when everyone was high on their substance of choice, suspiciously giddy laughter in front of the assembled church volunteers bringing dinner. Mary Lou with those gray-skinned friends of hers. Lewis nodding his head like a blind musician, Maestas way too alert. Who else? Ernestine, furious at the whole scene, looking at me, accusing. "I can't stay sober in this house," she said to me more than once.

This group, they were my teachers. And at least they didn't become progressively thinner like that *later* group, gathered around the table with the church volunteers. The household was losing weight together, in true collective spirit—on their substance of choice—and all would ultimately be violated by the parole authorities.

But not my original five, at least not all at once. They were fighters, determined to prove everyone who'd ever been in their lives wrong.

CHAPTER 3

The distant engine's light is approaching now, midday and still this heat—for sure much hotter down here than up North. The approaching train is heading West, so why the heck not climb on this one? I'm feeling that excited hint of the future, like I used to up in Montana—this is my familiar realm. There are so many reasons to be out here again. One reason for every state prisoner who came to Hope House, for example. This isn't an overstatement; each of them wore the evidence of how this world doesn't work for everyone. Their names come back to me as I await this slowly approaching freight train, those beyond the aforementioned original five. Eppie, with his sailor's cap and walkie-talkie, graduating from us to the city streets, and always dapper. Boris, who spoke of the iron cages and regarded his own anger with awe, swift on the fast break like the Lakota champion he was in high school. Briana, with her hurriedly sewn-up face, petite with her one eye before the heroin regained control—chocolate sundae running down her blouse, nodding off in the parole officer's presence, and off to the lab for a urine test.

So many to be resurrected, the ghosts of their striving pulling me out of my own grievance, the drama with my Board.

But the first one, our all-star household, keeps coming back to me. That radiant Saturday afternoon, for example, with our raffle tables, ready for the families. Bringing in money for our unconventional family, alert for public uneasiness with my increasingly trained eye.

But I'm on the train now, and it was easily done, my favored piggyback stopping conveniently within twenty yards of my isolated spot in the city freight yard. I've been warned that catching a freight on the Union Pacific is much different from what I experienced up North on the Burlington Northern. Down here, I'm told, they arrest you on the spot. Not an issue this evening—the train's gathering speed as I lean up against the tires, a nice shelter from the blustery wind. I remember Lewis standing at the east entrance of the supermarket.

"Chief, we're doing most impressively this afternoon," he said, punctuating his statement with a laugh. Now, does this cash help you at all? Feed the monkeys, I mean?" Again that deep laugh of his. "You know, those certain Board members who wish you gone?"

"Yes, in fact it does," I replied. "But it's not that bad. What're your hours this weekend?"

"Let's see, I believe the usual," he answered. "Oh, and Chief, I need you to write that letter for me so I can be reinstated. I would be so grateful."

"Sure, I can do it. How long before the panel decides?"

"That's a good question," he laughed again. "It sure would be mighty fine if they responded quickly, don't you think? But Tillie the Chair don't care for this negro."

"Are you sure?"

"Most definitely. So I'll probably have to appeal. Meaning that night shift will probably remain for a while. Have you heard anything about the other job?" At that point a woman came through the automatic doors. Lewis and I stopped talking.

"Excuse me, Miss?" Lewis began. "Would you be interested in saving the life of a desperate soul such as me?" She stopped, uncomprehending. "I am talking, Miss, about a program profound in its scope and righteous in its purpose."

"It's a halfway house for parolees," I interjected. "We're selling our raffle tickets this afternoon."

"Yes," Lewis continued. "And this gentleman is the prince among men who runs the operation."

"How much are the tickets?" she asked, approaching the table. "Do you have anything in writing?"

"Oh yes, Miss," Lewis replied, handing her a brochure.

"And the tickets are quite inexpensive for all of the wonderful donated prizes you stand to win."

"One for five dollars," I said. "Or three for ten."

"I'll take three," she said, resting her purse on the table.

There are *so* many reasons to be out here again. Creating with Kit an enclosure to keep the wrong influences out, or at least muted, at an adult cost. Late bloomers we were, both of us, living an extended adolescence. She warned me one night early in our courtship, referring to her troubled childhood and crazy family and that kind of stuff. But did I listen? Of course not. I had a different version of the same thing, and both of us ended up in the same place. *Estranged.* I was the prodigal, the rebel, the one absent from the table. Her family situation was similar. How could we resist each other? We had some things to work out.

Before I left our house—which was not an easy decision, by any means—Kit handed me my old journals that she'd fished out of a back closet, from our courtship days. I had room in my familiar duffel bag, so I figured why not take them with me? There's certainly plenty of time for reading out here.

Here is one of my first entries.

June 4, 1987

I have some time now to clarify the events of the past week. Writing a diary's kind of weird, I have to admit—it seems to belong to another time, another age. Should I begin each entry with *Dear Diary?* PLEASE.

But reflecting on the past does seem to help with these troubles. It began after college, with my saying no to what my fellow classmates were doing, as they followed their appointed scripts — Wall Street, Law School, Grad School, The Family Business. I had no idea which direction to go, and certainly no burning desire to be a stockbroker or a lawyer, and of course there was no way could I work with my dad.

It kicked in when my brother roped me into being his best man, assuming I knew the various responsibilities involved, commandeering the assembled room, coming up with witty toasts, pretending I felt like a part of this strange world of convention. It was the tinkling of the glasses, and that moment when Frederick handed me the microphone and I truly had nothing to say. It felt like a big lie, me being in this role, as if the weight of ceremony and the festive banter represented a direction I was supposed to embrace as well. I kept looking out over the audience, speechless—like in a dream where you forget your lines, have no idea why you are on stage—I couldn't do anything about it. Finally, mercifully, one of the bride's more animated brothers came to my rescue, made a kind of light joke about my being too brainy for such a role, and took over the moment with some kind of Asian cheer, not *bonsai,* but close.

Wow, that wedding was tough. So embarrassing. And a foreshadowing of what was to come. It was kind of an *aha* experience at age twenty-three, like a megaphone in my ear. *You're on a different path, pal.*

My current circumstance warranted a response, a reason that led me to this—especially as virtual strangers and donor prospects would go on indignantly about me not returning their phone calls. My role was to raise the money, to keep Hope House solvent.

And then there's Kit's undiagnosed illness—adding *that* to my equation—how she would look at me, with fear, determination, and hope in her eyes. Not a rational play, never even a straight line, but this final darkening twist made it even harder. I hit my own limits of being her best possible partner.

So I left our house in the mesa sun, and the animals, to depart for this ghost-world of the freights. Kit needs my help, and I would do anything for her—anything that I could provide, anything she would accept—but with us it also means that she's alone, like we both had always been. It's an honest alliance. Her beauty had me when I first saw her. And her voice, even if her manner could draw unwelcome attention, especially when we first met. This was one of our scenarios, the reassurance of my dramatic exit and her encouraging words. Kit's alone now with her uncertainty, while I sort out my personal disappointments, trying to make sense of the world.

As to my other situation—the one I experienced at work—now I can ponder *that* within the sanctuary of this piggyback flatbed car. Competing with those uniformed children as they sell home baked goods for *their* cause. "Let's see, which raffle table do we visit? The Girl Scouts? Or the parolees?" A glaring example of our insignificant and doomed devotion, no matter how sincere, to our important cause. Of course I couldn't chase them off, though they and their parents were already frightened by our tattooed presence. So we packed up our raffle tables and went home.

Where were my peers at this point, anyway? My fellow classmates from college. Certainly they weren't in a supermarket entrance with ex-convicts, competing in charity sales with Girl Scouts. My parents were right about me. I could've done better with my life, if that was the measure. My peers were elsewhere, and for good reason—attending reunions, weekend golf games, shopping at some upscale supermarket. In submission to the calming order of things.

We all make our choices. I have no problem with that. If I have felt a burning need to reject what I was born into since I can remember, and if my father especially was not exactly down with my choices, why should this be some kind of turbulent mystery? There're such deeper burdens on the scale of things, and certainly the years with my ex-felons have put my own family drama into perspective.

CHAPTER 4

I look into the future and nothing registers except the length of empty track in both directions, which *could* represent a measurement of my love for Kit. I am here before a vast expanse—like a gray ocean from a beach—thinking of our interlocking sorrow. And defiance. We made a pact that might be doomed in a world like this but whatever happens, we will always have the memory of our union.

Their disapproval brings me out here as well, the adults of my life—starting with my own father—his certitude always puzzling me. My choices were not meant to offend anyone. Certain individuals are wired a certain way and should be left to roam outside. This is not something that can be easily relayed over breakfast to my naturally curious donor prospects.

So what have the past seven years been about? Becoming some kind of protector of convention? To be allied with what's real, whatever that is? As if the law-abiding and conventional life message to the ex-cons is the solution to everything? Will somebody please say something real, I'd think to myself as I waited for my turn to pitch Hope House, our worthy endeavor, at the early morning civic club, or the Chamber of Commerce lunch, or the United Way gatherings. So much is possible. In a different world. It all seemed so paltry. Certainly in comparison to the startling reality of our various troubled residents. How did they accept their own circumstance in life, in between the bus rides and a world turned amiable, this sudden and unexplainable welcome presented by the existence of a Hope House?

Our employment safaris were adventures, to say the least. "Chief," Lewis would say, "if only I could regain my professional license, we could leave these problems behind us, couldn't we?" *We?* He was too much. Lewis would laugh and roll his head, there at the stoplight with his newly applied Jeri Curl, my letter of support nicely typed in my suit pocket. "She doesn't like me, Chief," he said in reference to Tillie, the licensing supervisor. "She gave me a chance once before, and I did not reciprocate."

"Lewis," I replied with impatience, gunning the car into fourth gear for emphasis. "You should have told me that before I wrote this stupid letter. I didn't know about a previous chance."

"Well, she's been known to look kindly too. And I did pray about this."

"So tell me again about your fantastic slide," I said, changing the subject. "What on earth happened to you, anyway?"

"It was the drugs, bro," he sighed. "Seriously."

"Yeah, but what was *underneath* that? You had this fine life, right? Or at least a normal one. Up until that point?"

"I've got too much history in this town." He sighed, looking out the car window.

"Is your wife talking to you yet?" I asked. We pulled into the licensure office parking lot. "Maybe this *isn't* a complete exercise in futility," I continued. "Would it help if I went in with you?"

“Chief, that would be very fine. You know,” he continued as we exited the car, “some of this is not unlike what I've witnessed you go through. With your own Board, I mean.”

“It's just the president. She doesn’t like me.”

“My point exactly. We have to figure out a way to feed everyone. You know, enough so they are distracted from *us*.”

“You mean like the monkeys?” I replied. We both laughed.

“The monkeys,” Lewis echoed, almost manic at this point. “They just need to be *fed*.”

“Okay. Game time, right? Let's go.”

The supervisor in question was formal, courteous, and of course justified in whatever she would ultimately decide. There were concerns, justifiable concerns. Lewis was familiar to everyone, which was not necessarily a good thing, and his situation would need to be discussed with the rest of her Board.

Our days passed like this, as we went about the solemn business of reclamation. Whether it was Lewis with his array of revoked licenses, Maestas with his well-documented juvenile anger, or Ernestine with unreceived valentines (Mary Lou, in contrast, had way too many of those). And Samuel, preoccupied with the purchase of his next suit. The household went on like this in its stormy way, featuring regular visitations from skeptical parole officers and giddy church volunteers, and I was expected to be the leader. My ensuing education was sincere in its dark quality. I can say that I tried my best. That I was not, in that role, what anyone had anticipated, including myself. And I can say that I was entirely consumed. Other areas of my life suffered. Like my relationship with Kit.

This was a world I didn’t know. The world of Briana with her sewn-up face, Boris with his extreme rage, and Callahan, the wiry and gentle ex-con emeritus (oh my God, *Callahan)*, with his murdered victims weighing relentlessly somewhere, but not on us—that was not our focus.

CHAPTER 5

Here we go.

June 8, 1987

> Our group has multiplied. I've got a nice spot here under what I guess is a cottonwood tree. Timothy's gone to hoodwink the clerks at the Mohawk County Courthouse—some business about his car title. Rodney's spending the afternoon with someone he just met named Shawna. And I'm here by the river, trying to figure things out. Like what my next step should be. We're all supposed to meet later in the west end of the railyard. The deal is that if Timothy manages to sell his car, then Rodney will escort him, via rail, to the nearest big city, probably Seattle.

So, this is a relaxed railroad town, with no fence around the yard, no axe-blade signs reading Beware. And the yard is big enough that all the freights stop, if sometimes only to change their crews. Mohawk has its share of healthy, happy young people; it must be a resort town. Everyone seems to be my age. Usually I avoid these places. It's easier that way. But such a posture has its demands. The relentless effort to keep things out, the securing of some kind of shell, protection. Learning what to avoid is an art like everything else.

Maybe that's why I end up on the freights. As Rodney says, you can't get much lower (other than maybe the Otis Hotel). And there's no need to explain yourself to anyone. Plus, you have the illusion of motion, of progressing from one point to another. But how conscious is it? The alternatives shrink, or vanish entirely, and I end up out here. It's not so bad. I like being alone with my thoughts ... and the noise. Night is the best, when the escape is the most convincing. Anything rehearsed from an open boxcar, into several thousand tons of shaking steel, is guaranteed never to find its audience. Private revelations are the richest—but you must guard them with every ounce of cunning you possess. Like Timothy says, who's going to understand? Who's going to see you for what you are? I wish I wasn't so cynical. I wish the past didn't weigh this much. Seems strange to be so young, twenty-six, and have this kind of heaviness in my psyche.

No one can touch me now, in this waking life. I'm free to roam this high-plained expanse interrupted only by the junkyard cities. Reading my old diary makes me want to interject, *Dude, stop whining. Get over yourself.* Yet here I am again, on the freights replaying workplace indignities with my flashlight pen, ink on paper. The ecstasy of not caring, bouncing wildly along the tracks.

Workplace betrayal should be expected—I would've known that if I'd had more experience actually working for a living in the conventional sense. The Murphy birthright is one of optimism, the better self which will ultimately triumph in any reasonable situation. The gift of my mother, and my dad, in his dark way. Part of growing up in the rural Midwest? Alliance, Iowa. Friday nights, the town assembled, under the lights, another touchdown run. The appreciative nod of my history teacher as she returns our papers. Invisible abundance and, more important, an unquestioned feeling of safety. So naturally I'd seek out its opposite, right?

What else? My father's understandable absence—his work—his inability to understand my life hasn't been easy for me, but understandable. My mother's complete misreading of the boy entrusted to her, the off-limits realms of terrifying feeling to be managed or handled. The scrapbook of charged moments not enough to carry this authentic family. Instead, my father's of little assistance to his puzzling son, mesmerized—justifiably—by his own loving reflection in tall glasses of bourbon. His attention to surface caring, nicely done. And my mother's effort almost enough to compensate. Authentic questions, bedside notes, pancake breakfasts for my teammates. Actually it *was* enough, more than enough—so heroic on her part, a solo act carried out with inspired and polite detail. Ours was *the* house for sleepovers.

The problem, though, was when the complexities came, neither parent was around to help. But then, in comparison to *anyone* in my parolee household—Maestas, Ernestine, Mary Lou, Samuel—my grievances were completely ridiculous.

Seven years back and I'm still drawn to this journal.

June 15, 1987

I'm sitting in the mouth of a triple-tiered gondola car. I have it to myself—no automobiles, no tramps. Rodney and Timothy are on a grain car, leagues back. It's been dark for several hours, which must put it close to midnight. I have this pen with a tiny light attached to its dorsal side. Rodney gave it to me. Where he found it I'll never know. It suits my purpose, spotlighting the page as I write. Because of the bouncing of this particular freight, I'm all over the page (we're talking wide margins). I have my earplugs, but the noise comes through anyway, sometimes loud enough to give you a headache. You get used to it, like everything else.

Well ... I have to admit that there's a whole bunch of stuff that I'll never get used to. Such as lying on this cold, greasy, steel floor, staring into a tunnel of empty automobile carriers. A hollow organism screaming through the moonlit countryside. Arid, rolling hills and an occasional barnyard lamp; crossings with no one there to hear the ringing bells. The exciting meter of a speeding train, the rhythm of your own thoughts. Minimal shelter from the ancestral wind, which tugs at your sleeping bag and threatens to steal anything not tied down. I wish it'd make off with what I am thinking right now. Sweep away the memories that seem to grow more distinct and vivid with each passing night, blending into whatever's going on with me, as if they belonged there.

I'm thinking about my family. The events of the past few days. I'd rather not. I'd rather get up and walk forward, through this segmented tunnel into a new life, one confined entirely to the present. But the bitter wind disappoints; it won't be my ally. Instead I find a familiar, finely twilled tablecloth. It's my turn to light the candles. Mother enters the dining room, and we remain standing until my brother gets her chair. Father sips his bourbon, wanting to know how my day went. Fine, I answer. Coach put in some new plays for our next game, plays that are designed to get the ball to me. My feet search for Charlie, our dog who loves to lie underneath the table on the oriental rug. Father asks how my ankle is, whether it will affect how many times I carry the ball on Friday night. I explain how the trainer has rigged up something with an elastic bandage and adhesive tape. My younger brother Nathan asks if Mother could please pass the rolls. Mother answers that she will if he can remember to keep his elbows off the table. Underneath, our dog stretches his legs. My mind is elsewhere, specifically on how to best disguise my nerves when I call Phoebe after dinner. I need something witty, a spontaneous lead-in to smooth my wooden training. She will be surprised, possibly embarrassed at this sudden declaration of interest. Maybe I won't call after all. I finish my lamb chop, then ask to be excused. It's Nathan's turn to wash the dishes. Mother asks me how come I do not want dessert—butterscotch pudding being one of my favorites—and I say that I have a lot of homework to do. Father returns to his couch next to the fireplace and his half-finished evening paper. I go upstairs to my room, deciding not to call Phoebe after all.

What was so great about those days? Belief wasn't an issue. Sanction came from every corner of my tiny college town. Alliance, Iowa. I became a product of the prevailing winds, mesmerized by my own name in the sports section. The fleet-footed, breakaway threat; two yards or sixty, depending on the tilt of the moment. Awash in the smiles of girls whom I could never know. Fan mail, even—how weird—concern over my diet. It was warped, but how could I resist it? And I wasn't even as good as Frederick, my older brother. How can I forget that Friday night roar as the herd of burly farm kids tried to catch me from behind? The crowd was cheering for *me.* I was loved. And now, here I am on a freight train.

CHAPTER 6

Seven years later, an empty automobile carrier—I'm in its vented belly with a quilted drifter at the other end who's ignoring me, thankfully. I used to joke with Boris, our Hope House brave warrior, that we could've run into each other on the freights, especially as he was Lakota and knew the Burlington Northern routes well. This was before I'd ever heard the term *iron cages.* It's different down here in the Southwest, though. Fewer transients. Easier to claim your personal space. Plus, I don't want to talk to anybody. I don't have the curiosity that I had years ago, up in the Northwest.

But how's anyone ever fully equipped for a life—Maestas, Boris, *me*? Maestas had his incarcerated adolescence, gleaning what he could from the program's movie night, alert to the other random teachings that came his way. Mary Lou came home to her family's padlocked front door after school one afternoon, parents gone, no note. Ernestine was suckled on gin at age one. Samuel was a product of segregation and social upheavals. Lewis had his narcotic-induced madness when faced with the onset of approaching middle age. And *Cortez,* holy moly, nothing like stabbing your own father dead on Super Bowl Sunday to remember each night.

The first bunch was a foreshadowing of what was to come for me, I suppose. It's had an impact on me, and why wouldn't it? I sought the opposite in all things and this is what I found. The succession of imprisoned lives and the sincerity in their failure. Certainly I was in over my head. I could be of assistance, maybe more than I realized, but it seemed to always revert to my predictable, upbeat, *Don't get discouraged.* And so on.

June 22, 1987

> I, Chapman Murphy, son of privilege. At least this existence is one of my own making. These greasy blue jeans are mine. And so is that rip there on my thigh. No one expects anything from me. I lord over this domain, as relieved as any fugitive. I've successfully avoided all forms of responsibility, both real and disguised. In my defense, I go the whole route with this rebellion stuff. I haven't had any contact with my family for what … two years? My older brother, Frederick, the stockbroker and former star athlete, maybe thinks I'm gone, to some kind of invisible world. Or at least that I'm troubled. He isn't alone in that view. I support myself and have done so for a couple of years or so. I get odd jobs without much trouble: dishwasher, waiter, tree planter. If I plan on staying awhile in a given town, I do what I can to line up restaurant work. It demands some level of social ease, but I can pull that off, and tips are cash in your pocket.
>
> I don't pretend to be above money. In my head I know my real situation. My family doesn't understand it, and what kind of explanation can I offer? The whole business seems to

invite a strange judgment. I toy with the notion of giving away my inheritance, whatever the sum might be. (Frederick has the account in his office, I'm sure.) Seriously. I could divide it among those who are more worthy, the types that I run into out here, for instance. That's it. I could be a philanthropist of the freight trains. But I suppose that's not very practical. All I'm left with is to simply behave as if my background doesn't exist. Sometimes I do get an overwhelming impulse to phone my brother, as I did when Timothy was explaining his monetary predicament. But how can I do that without blowing my cover? If I knew, maybe I would. Shouldn't the money that's supposedly mine go to someone who could appreciate it? Someone other than myself. Somehow, at a young age, I got the idea in my head that money was a less-than-ideal thing. When it began to flow into our home more easily, as Father's business expanded, I could feel it begin to take over. It made people treat me differently in our small Iowa town. It made my brothers disappear—to prep schools and summer camps. It spread us out within our own home, which kept expanding. It made Father drink more.

It's hard to admit a sentiment like this. How ridiculous, to be complaining about abundance. It probably invites some weird kind of curse. Giving these thoughts concrete form makes me nervous. But in my defense, my feelings are genuine. In this, as in other areas, I'm simply unable to see the whole picture. I should be thankful to have had the opportunity to attend college, to go on those family vacations. Can I help but look around in the yards, and in the lobbies of fleabag hotels, and wonder what I'm doing? Am I trying to prove something to somebody?

The times I feel the best are when I don't care what happens. There's wisdom in not caring; a fellow can probably sleep better. A fellow would not be out here unless that was the case. People don't belong out here. There's an insult in the accumulation of sharp angles, in the cold metal. Could I exist in the mainstream, without being inundated by the strange music inside?

I remember that stupid locker-room banter in the trainer's room, getting my ankles taped. Or in the shower after practice. All *that* ever made me feel was lost. Nick used to say I take all of this too seriously. Dating made me nervous, for sure. But not as nervous as a group of linebackers lathering up, winking, joking about a girl named Ellen. All of these assumptions, as if all men thought the same way.

What I hear now, out on the freights, goes down a little easier, perhaps because of the circumstance. No flashy swagger here. Transients have other things on their minds. There's solace in the cross-eyed man. Or in Rodney's description of his own failure to settle down. I sensed from our first meeting that he was onto something, that his philosophy of relationships contained the commendable urge for purity that I aspire to. The difference is that his is grounded in reality, in experience.

CHAPTER 7

It became harder to pull off the contradiction that defined my life as the months, years, went past in my workaday world — a weekend in the churches, same weekend in the bars. Hawking the tickets, insinuating ourselves into the unwitting world of the churchgoers, tactical happenstance for the worthy endeavor. That priest who wouldn't let me near his granite podium, himself wired seamlessly, the lighting just right, and his predictable following afterwards, a long line seeking affirmation in his eyes. The deacon who mocked my delivery, who wanted to hear more about Jesus, and in response my own growing anger, which is probably not the best way to sell raffle tickets.

The Masses would incite my thirst, and the well-meaning chatter would do the opposite—sincere quiet within the rituals, a gathering of families promises of virtual belonging. Neither one a settling place, temporary, the many different selves to be reconciled—or set aside for the ultimate, unifying honest one.

Maybe *that* is why I'm out here again. Some exercise in rolling truth, how the infinite parallel track promises something, and why not a righteous epiphany? I'm out here because it became unworkable—the enveloping, increasingly bad-spirited world. I realized one interminable, dry afternoon that they *do* expect to have their calls returned, these donor prospects, that they're not in on my joke of an ill-fitting world.

Was there a modesty to the conventional ways that I never fully embraced? Card games might have had a calming effect, provided a respite from my perpetual unease. Such a pace would have been welcome—Kit's family had it, despite what she said. But then her affluence came from the success of her grandfather's board game invention, so certainly there was an unspoken respect for the intimacy such activities provided. I'd had it that summer they shocked me with the trophy at the New England summer camp. But that was before the complexity set in, which clearly had something to do with adolescence.

The whole thing became ill-fitting, my experiment in the workaday world, especially after the accumulated years of Hope House. These forced apologies on my end as they truly wanted to know why their calls were not being returned, the gathering lie of my life being slowly revealed. And then problems with Kit as she didn't understand why I was so *absent.* Just give me time, I'd say, I'm under a lot of pressure. All of this is new. And then the morning brotherly ritual in the basketball gym, close enough to truly belonging as my pickup team holds the court. Finding myself later that evening on the second-story patio bar, trying not to return a look, the signal of who I'm not, though down there quite willing. *I am in a relationship.* Haunted always by these other lives, those of my teammates—the small problem of their masculine voices and the confidence with which they carried themselves. We'll sit there until the bar closes, alert for the opportunities.

This ceremony of the freight trains is simply a polite response to all of the above.

CHAPTER 8

June 25, 1987

We're on a different train, not sure of the exact route, but heading westward. Stunning scenery—high up, arid on the railroad embankment, the majesty of some northern river, close to Canada, heading toward Seattle. I want to record the conversation we just had before I lose it. The three of us, while motionless on a siding for an indeterminate length of time.

"But you two guys!" Rodney had begun, irritated. "You act like you're the first ones to get caught up in complicated situations. A sensible person handles it, then goes on when it's over. Don't take it like some kind of judgment from up there." Rodney pointed toward the sky.

"Specifics," Timothy replied. "Details that illumine."

"Well," he answered, softening. Pensive. "I mean, I was talking mainly about Chapman. He's got some years on you. His case is different."

"Gym teachers rate as much."

Rodney looked at me for translation.

"I think Timothy wants to hear your advice."

"Okay, like to the level of this rail bed we're traveling on?"

"Calisthenics. I do them," Timothy continued. "Why shouldn't others?"

"What do you mean?" Rodney answered. "You're on the frail side. You just don't seem that athletic."

"Not in that way," Timothy said, annoyed. "Stretching the *mind*. A leap—" He waited for Rodney to finish his thought for him.

"Look, conversing with you two is fun, I admit. All I can say is that it must be a comment on the educational system to have y'all ending up out here."

"Mary Kay lived down the street. She invited me in one day to see her rock collection. Things began to escalate."

"I imagine her folks kept a pretty close eye on you, eh?"

"After the fire, they did."

"What fire?"

"My poetry fire. After Mary Kay suggested I go out for basketball."

"Well, kid, it seems to me like it's for the best."

"I didn't feel comfortable in those surroundings."

"Soon you'll be in the big city, drinking that fancy coffee. And talking about them ideas of yours. You won't have to explain yourself no more. Yeah, you get yourself a position waiting tables at some high-class café. Meet a woman who smokes imported cigarettes. More on your level than Mary Kay. I wish I'd seen what you see now when I was nineteen!"

"What I see makes no sense. Swirling, entwined, lacking direction."

"Yeah, but you're only *nineteen*. Take Chapman over there. He's got at least five years on you."

"At least," I replied.

"And he's still confused. Right, Chapman?"

I wanted to reply that Rodney's spiel reminded me of certain pep talks, the ones we were subjected to on Saturday afternoons before the game in college, our coach's neck veins bulging. We lost despite his efforts, that fumble of mine not helping. My college, the doormat of the Ivy League. Instead, I shrugged and told him that I couldn't see my own situation too clearly. That I didn't have much in the way of objectivity.

"Ya'll have read a whole bunch of books between you. And I respect that, for sure," Rodney said quietly, exhaling the smoke from his cigarette. "That's a fact. But you can't let your education get in the way of your … education. Especially when it comes to living your life. I know it sounds trite, but why think too much?"

"What?" I replied. "I take myself too seriously? Is that what you mean?"

"That's not what I'm saying. That's the way it should be, a conscious existence and all that. But you have to realize what other folks are going by."

"You don't think I know that?" I replied defensively.

"I'm not sure what you know. I just mean that the whole endeavor is not tainted. Worth giving up on."

"Okay, I hear what you are saying."

"And a person has control. Choice is real. Don't you see that?"

"But why bother, like Timothy says? If in the end you know you'll be disappointed?"

"How do you know that?"

"For you, I guess … but with me, things happen the same way."

"How's that? Give me some evidence."

"I don't know … Take my word for it."

"Aw, come on."

"I don't want to go into it."

"Come on!"

"Uh, if anything would come back … it'd be more toward the beginning." I noticed Timothy had moved near the open door of the boxcar. From his pack he'd pulled a box of cattle markers. "I don't know if I want to get into this." Timothy was drawing something on a steel panel of the boxcar.

"Why not? We have to pass the time somehow."

"I don't know," I replied. "I was thinking the other night I might be dwelling on this stuff too much. I think I want to move on."

"If you wanna get through it, you should play it out. Be extreme and whatnot."

"I'm not so sure … but say I do? What do you want to know?"

"How 'bout this gal you are getting over … what's her name?"

"Athena."

"Oh, come on. That's her name?"

"I swear to God."

"She was older than you, right?"

"Yes. And I don't want to go into that all over again. I don't think it's honest. I mean, it wasn't that bad. I learned a lot. We had our good moments. Though they seemed to all be in the first week."

"Question is, how come you let that throw you off course? Put you in a shame spiral or whatever. It's not like *she'd* want that."

"I seem to need a lot. It gets out of control."

"That happen to you a bunch of times?"

"Once."

"You're too much."

"Really?" I answered facetiously.

"And you'd chuck it all based on that?"

"Have you been in that situation?"

"Not like you, I figure. But close enough. I don't see how people can go on like that."

"Are you religious?" I asked, sort of out of nowhere.

"Me? No. But I do believe in some things." I waited for him to continue. When he didn't, I asked him what he believed in. "Just what I pick up along the way. I damn sure don't believe *this* is all there is," he said with emphasis, addressing the inside of the freight car. "Those folks who go strictly by what they see—they got it wrong. I'm not sure who or what's pulling the strings. But somebody's at the controls. I don't buy that randomness business."

"Did you know primitive cultures don't have a word for chance?" Rodney looked at me blankly. "I mean, everything's meaningful. There's no such thing as chance."

"Yeah? It don't surprise me none. It don't take much to figure that we're just pawns in some larger carnival. Like there's probably a reason for us being together on this train right now. Maybe we were brothers in a past life?"

"So you believe in reincarnation?"

"I don't know. I understand it, but I don't figure I can explain it."

"Do we always come back as a human?"

"Unless you fuck up royal. That's the way I got it."

"What would be classified as fucking up?"

"Oh, killing your mother. Killing your father. Stuff like that."

Reading this excerpt makes me cringe—especially the reference to "killing one's father." That occurrence has new meaning for me since Cortez came into my life. And why I was so keen on divining important answers from Rodney Mills is beyond me. But then, I was raised in a family where there was no such thing as a bad question—that message coming mainly from my mother, of course. Speaking of family, my goodness, I was fortunate to be born into the Murphy Clan. I was taught to believe in myself, that anything was possible, that the world was fundamentally a welcoming place.

June 26, 1987

We just crossed what I think is called the Raccoon River. The train's accelerated again, which means that you can hardly hear yourself think—probably a good thing on the whole. Decisions are looming. Rodney wants to visit an old girlfriend in Crystal Point, Idaho. He guesses the town is about an hour away. He can't be sure, though, because no one has a map. He maintains that there's a 50-50 chance the train will stop of its own accord. If we're lucky, we can make Crystal Point just as another freight is pulling onto the bridge—either from our own direction or from the west. The problem's if our train doesn't stop. Then we're faced with the decision of whether or not to jump. Rodney's assured us that our train will be going at a slower pace, because of the bridge.

June 27, 1987

We survived jumping off the moving freight train, though Timothy's been complaining about scraping his knee. We're in what appears to be a fairly large railroad yard, especially for a small town. Rows of vacant sidings extend to the tree line. We've stashed our packs in the bushes nearby and we'll head into town soon. The boundaries of the yard extend to the manicured fairway of the local country club on one side, and to the shore of the vast, glacial lake on the other. According to Rodney, the lake's responsible for the town's reputation as a place for leisure. He explained how Crystal Point used to be a flourishing railroad center—since it marks the intersection of the two main freight routes—but things have changed. "At least there aren't any railroad detectives here anymore," he said, after we crossed the footbridge that separates the yard from the town.

Timothy and I take a bench while Rodney's finding a pay phone. On first glance, this looks like a European resort town with sundeck cafés, yellow umbrellas, old-style architecture. Rodney's dismissed all this as a cutesy send-up of some foreign notion of elegance. "It's on the circuit, sure enough," he sighed. "Beyond gainsay. And I guess that's why we here." From where we sit, you can tell the bridge has been recently constructed as part of a larger shopping mall complex—you can still smell the pine tar. Glass everywhere, piped-in Bach. A beaming young woman just walked past with a baby strapped to her back. She glanced in our direction, then pretended to ignore us. I found my reflection in a nearby glass panel; there's grease on my face. I can see Rodney grinning into the pay phone receiver several blocks away, holding it like a pro. (He did tell me once of his stint as a phone solicitor.) It's nearing six o'clock. I imagine cocktail hour has some meaning in this town. Rodney's taking a while on the phone. A group of men and women just came by—actually, they were skipping by—when one of them broke away. She came over to Timothy and me.

> "Would you care to join us?" the young woman asked. "We're celebrating Wednesday evening."

I waited for Timothy to answer, but he didn't. "Um," I started, "where are you going?"

"To drink champagne. In glasses, with those little cherries bobbing up and down. Are you new to our town?"

"Yes."

"Well then, we're going just a little ways up the street. It's a bar called Trifles. A cute place—"

"*Cute?*" erupted Timothy, his tone making me uneasy. "What does that mean?"

"Pardon me?" the young woman managed. Someone reached out to pull her back into formation.

"Who will do the translations?" Timothy continued. "Who won't turn traitor when it comes time to stand in line? Enjoy your shower while you can."

"Hey, Timothy, calm down."

"When blood should be flowing in the gutters?"

"Why'd you go scaring her like that? She was just being nice."

"Nice?" Timothy sneered. "Nice? People like that . . ."

Rodney returned to us with a bouquet of flowers, adventure in the air. "We're in luck, fellas!" he exclaimed.

We'll see.

I remember how great Lewis looked in his white tennis shoes and jeans when I spotted him on the drug avenue walking in a hurry, preoccupied, after he'd officially relapsed and vanished into the system again. And after my visit with him in one of those motels where the plan was to bring him back into the universe of rules and sane choices. Before the authorities became involved, as they inevitably did. Lewis kept staring out the window of his room. Whatever attention he had left was on an imminent phone call.

"Lewis," I stated emphatically. "You've *got* to get out of here." It was toward the end of his Hope House stint.

"I know, I know …" his voice trailed off. "But Chief, she is so sweet. I need to protect her."

"You can call her from the house."

"Just give me a few minutes."

"There's no point, guy," I continued. "Look, you still have your job. You can get that tea you can buy. And you can get back on track."

"I know." He sounded weary, still largely absent. "It's just that the will … becomes diminished. And the Lord's assistance has its limitations."

"Lewis, why are you caving in like this?" I said. "You've worked hard to get your license reinstated. It's not too late."

"I need to protect her."

"Okay. You're putting me in a bind," I said. "It's on you, guy."

At least with Maestas and Cortez I was never so blatantly in the do-gooder costume—they kept their activity hidden. It'd go in the same general direction, though, my last-chance pep talk, noticing how thin they'd become. There was that stretch where each evening at dinner the majority of our residents would be slimmer and slimmer, and our volunteers would comment, "My, how *trim* everyone looks." That look they had, their eyes and skin.

All of it was previously unknown to me. We had our own small-town versions of seeking oblivion in Iowa, though not on this level, not with needles. Maestas and Cortez were a duo, and they sometimes mentioned how they'd saved each other, alternating resurrections, ice treatments after too much heroin. All of this was revealed to me later, of course, when being out of the program made shop talk possible. Sometimes I could space out on their tattoos, sometimes witness their crying—Cortez especially, remembering the father he'd stabbed to death. Maestas preferred humor, at least when he wasn't agitated about the dark manipulative forces out to get him. They both deserved a road trip, and it was a gift I could give them from my world, but my convertible had to be fixed first.

Lewis, on the other hand, was into me deep, and personally. They all were. I didn't have the best boundaries. Lewis actually convinced me to help buy him that gleaming blue Jeep on the sunlit lot. "Chief," he kept saying, "I'll pay you back *immediately,* I promise. Remember, I'm a skilled professional."

"It does look like it's in great condition."

"I've been walking past it for days," Lewis continued, "to the bus stop. It'd bring everything together. *Everything.*"

"How much is it?"

"Only twelve hundred. See that radio?"

"I don't have that kind of money."

"I know. Just help me with the down payment. I get my first paycheck tomorrow."

"You have to keep this confidential."

"You're a good man."

Then the retrieval of that once-proud vehicle after it'd been abandoned on the drug avenue. Melted wires, cellophane peppermints in bulk, the radio gone. A disturbing smell emanated from under the hood, hinting of fire. Absolutely no sound when I tried to start it. And before this, when Lewis wasn't officially on the run, I'd tried to coax him to see his parole officer as scheduled. There we were, in my car, outside the parole office.

"What're those police cars doing here?" Lewis asked me nervously.

"They're always here, Lewis. It's state parole."

"Not like that. She probably called them here."

"You don't know that."

"I know more about this than you do."

"Okay," I agreed. "All I'm saying is, if you don't go in, then you *are* in trouble."

"She has it in for me," he said quietly.

"Tell her you made a mistake. That you're back on track now. You're okay with our program, you have your job, et cetera."

"She won't give me a chance. She's given me one already."

"What choice do you have? Lewis?"

"I can go to Colorado. I have friends. The Jeep will get me there."

"That's a great car." We both nodded. "Or it was when you got it."

"I'll pay you back, I promise."

"Don't worry about that." I answered. "This situation is what matters."

"Maybe I could shift my parole to up there."

"That's ridiculous. You'll be a fugitive. Technical parole violation."

"I can't go in there."

"It's up to you. What kind of life would it be, in Colorado? Looking over your shoulder?"

"I can't go back to prison."

"You're not going to go back. They give you a hearing, you know?"

"Will you come to that?"

"I'll be there," I assured him. "But I'm saying it's not necessarily going to go in that direction."

"All right. I suppose I should go into that building."

"That's the spirit."

He did walk in, but exited through the other door immediately after I'd left. We missed him around the dinner table, especially when it came to saying grace for the benefit of our volunteers. He'd go on and on, and other residents might roll their eyes, but our elderly company loved it, and they loved Lewis. These situations had their similarities, undeniably. Like with Cortez and the methadone clinic. Early mornings, medical personnel behind the bulletproof glass, the beaten-down waiting room. An aroma of disinfectant, a positive spin by the nurses, and the puzzling rose-colored liquid in question. I was there in my suit, searching for anything similar in my background, but coming up blank.

"Does this stuff work?" I asked Cortez, who was visibly pale and shaking.

"Not really, man." I always had trouble keeping my attention away from one of the more suggestive tattoos on his forearm. "But it helps with the craving. And I'm okay if I use a little on top of that."

"But doesn't that defeat the purpose?" I asked innocently.

He laughed and then replied in a quiet voice, "This shit makes my bones ache. You know it eats your bones?"

"You mean literally?"

"Yeah. And these assholes here piss me off."

"Why? They seem nice."

"They'll only give you enough for one day. Each time you sign these fucking forms."

"Well, there's a reason for all that."

"I hate this place," he replied, looking around. "Maybe I can get clean again and stay out of here."

"Look, Cortez, these are the choices that you made. The nurses behind the glass are not the reason you're here."

"I don't think they're *real* nurses. How come they aren't wearing caps and shit?"

"I don't know what they are," I said. "But I'm sure they're licensed medical professionals of some kind."

"I hate this place."

"Then stop fucking using."

"Easy for you to say. Ivy Leaguer and shit."

"This isn't about me. It's about the kind of life you could have. You know you can have it."

"I had that stretch at Hope House."

"I remember," I answered. "That's why I'm here with you, moron. Even if you're out of the house now. You were doing great."

"It's just hard to stay away from the heroin. It creeps up on you."

"You have so many skills that other residents don't possess," I said. "You must've learned a lot from your father." I shouldn't have mentioned his father. "Or someone else," I said quickly.

"My uncle taught me how to do upholstery. My dad was real good with cars."

"That's what I'm saying. You have marketable skills. People like you. Mr. Diaz would hire you back in a second."

"It's not so easy."

"I'm not saying it is," I said. "Just try to get back on track, and good things will happen. You're off parole now. You're doing this on your own."

"We could take that trip you keep talking about!" he said, brightening slightly.

"Damn right. We just need to find your buddy Maestas. Get him on track too."

"Not hearing good things about him."

"No matter. He's like you, minus the vocational skills. But he's a hard worker. "

"And we'll go to Montana and shit?"

"Exactly. But you need to fix my car first, right? Like how you told me? But not too low-rider, okay?"

"You wait and see. You won't believe it's the same car."

"Well, restrain yourself there, okay? I like my sports-car look."

"No worries, Chapman. I'll take care of you."

"You can have a great life. Trust me on that."

"It's just this methadone," he said, surveying his grim surroundings. "It eats your bones and shit."

June 30, 1987

It's been an intense couple of days. It all started with Rodney's enthusiastic framing of the situation.

"Betsy's looking forward to meeting you both," he said. "Though I warned her you ain't got much sense, either one of you. She don't care, as long as you show some remote knowledge of manners. That stuff means a lot to her."

"Is she coming downtown?" I asked.

"Well, it'll be a while yet. She lives in this fancy house on the lake. And her folks are entertaining tonight. Last time I was through, they weren't around. You should see this crib. It's got a big fireplace, all stone. And a yard that goes straight up to the water. Anyways, she's gotta help with the food and other things. Truth is, she likes that:, dressing up, being hostess."

"So where do we go from here?" I asked. "Back to the yard?"

"Hell no. We in *town* now. I was thinking we could go up the street to this bar. Not spend a whole lot of money or nothing. Just stay long enough so we can use their bathroom in good conscience. Heck!" he exclaimed, running his fingers through his hair. "It's some kind of crud that gets in there. I hate being dirty like this."

We went to the tavern. Rodney holding court, growing sharper with each shot of tequila. Laughter, smoke, and the animated interest of others. We sit at the bar, Timothy glowering at the tans, the calculated casual wear, pieces of conversation adding to his incendiary internal narrative, "How was the sailing today?" "Did you hear about what they're doing down the road? Aren't you glad we have zoning?" "I love it here." We're sticking out again.

Betsy appeared in the doorway of the bar. Rodney gladly abandoned this dialogue, springing off his stool to help her in the door. "Hey doll, you're looking fine tonight!" Betsy wore a full-length evening gown, and her blonde hair fell shining to the small of her back.

"Why, thank you, Rodney. You are such a dear. I would have been here sooner, but I simply had to help Mother with the deviled eggs. We made over two hundred of them, can you believe it?"

"Sounds like a genuine wingding. You invite the entire town?"

She laughed and said, "No, not entirely. But we do have a position to maintain. Certain individuals do get offended if they are left off the list. But, oh, Rodney, I was the only one under forty! I did my best to be witty and gracious. Do stop me from going on about myself. Who are these two handsome friends of yours?"

"You mean these sorry-ass fellows? You'll take that back once they open their mouths."

"Oh, Rodney, I know you're kidding."

"Don't say I didn't warn you. When they start talking weird, just keep in mind that it isn't their fault. They're educated. Like you."

"Hey, Rodney. These are friends you're talking about."

"Speaking of friends, did you get in touch with either of your gal friends?"

"I tried and tried, but no one was home. I am awfully sorry, but maybe I can try again later. Oh, Rodney, I simply cannot believe that you are here! And by *freight train,* no less."

"A body's gotta get around somehow."

"Yes, but isn't it terribly dangerous?"

"Nah. There ain't a lot to it. Can't be if these two guys can do it. Oh, by the way, this here's Chapman. And the delicate-looking one is Timothy."

"Pleased to meet you," I said.

"I'm charmed. My name is Betsy." Timothy grunted something incomprehensible. "But Rodney, what was that you said about having to jump off?"

"It ain't nuthin'. If it be moving slow enough, like it was. Hardest thing was convincing these fellows they wouldn't die."

"If he does understand electrocution," Timothy suddenly interjected, "he shows no sign of it. Do you know the dance too?"

Betsy looked bewildered. "Why, I ... can't say."

"I warned you," Rodney said flatly. "I been listening to this nonsense for days."

"Now, Rodney, don't be rude.

"Pardon me, baby, but it's true."

"Well, no wonder! He's clearly *creative.*"

"When he ain't bumming around with Chapman and me."

"That's wonderful," she exclaimed, facing Timothy again. "What is your preferred medium?"

"The wind," Timothy replied.

"He's a poet too. I forgot to tell you."

"Oh, how ... poetic!" she exclaimed, addressing Rodney. "Of course I can't be sure what he's talking about. Artistic people speak a different language. But I bet he does good work. And he's so young."

"That's right," Rodney echoed. "Only nineteen years old, and already a bona fide social outcast. A rebel."

"Well," she added, "you know what they say about the suffering artiste. And what can you tell me of the shy one sitting next to him?"

"Who, Chapman? He's just your standard confused motherfucker."

"Rodney!"

"Sorry. It's just a habit, I guess. Chapman here is searching for some answers, like most of us. Only he has the good sense to keep it to himself. He's wise that way."

"But how did you ever end up in the company of someone like Rodney?" she asked, looking directly at me.

"Oh, I don't know," I answered. "Life, I guess."

"Aw, we're not that different. I got a lot of the same questions, you know. We just come from different highways is all."

"And the milieu does kind of throw us all together," I said.

The conversation had turned once more in my direction, and I cursed myself for telling Rodney about my own background. Betsy was visibly impressed with where I had gone to college. She began to speak at length about her illustrious grandfather and where he had graduated from college.

One answer to Rodney's question began to congeal, however, as the night progressed. Manners were high on the list as far as Betsy was concerned. And Rodney observed to the letter all rules of decorum with which he was familiar. Another revelation came when she suddenly exclaimed, "Oh, how I wish I were as free as you boys! I would quit my job," she added wistfully, "and simply leave town." I could see in her more than just rumblings underneath. She appeared to be ruled by the fear that she was missing out, that maybe, just maybe, the rules she clung to were hollow and outmoded. Her instinct insisted upon the possibility. To Betsy, Rodney was an outlet, a propitiatory offering to that side of her that urged, "Get out of here. Get out *now*." Someone once told me never to underestimate the vicarious (it could have been Chief White Owl). With Rodney, she could indulge without paying the consequences. He was only passing through.

CHAPTER 9

It's increasingly difficult for me to stop reading this old journal—just passing the time out here, stopped on a siding, motionless. I know it's coming up to an important moment, encountering for the first time the woman who would essentially change my life. Happily, first impressions don't rule the day if you don't give them that level of influence—and what kind of issue-laden, strange young man did I present to her in that Idaho bar?

July 1, 1987

> "Hey, buddy, you *can* change the music!" The voice came from my immediate left in the tavern, where an animated short-haired woman was addressing the bartender.
>
> "Okay, Kit. Whatever you want to hear," he answered.
>
> "The one about hurt. Play the one about hurt!" She leaned over the bar to make sure of his selection, spilling at least

two glasses. "Whooops. I'm sor-ree," she said in the direction of two men who seemed to know her.

"Do you ever slow down?" asked one of them, half-teasingly.

"Fuck you, asshole," the woman shot back, her eyes flashing. "Give me a reason to slow down, and I might."

"Hey, Kit, I was only kidding."

"That's all the men do around here. Kid. But don't take it personally, honey," she said, tickling his ear. "I'm feeling good tonight." A dance floor pose, a shake of the hips. "Owwww! I just smoked the most outrageous—" She stopped talking when she spotted our table. Timothy, Rodney, and I each received the once-over. Then she strode up to Betsy and said, "Here she is, Queen of the Mountain." Betsy sank into her seat, visibly embarrassed. "There I was, honing in on first place. Feeling *bad*. When some guy taps me on the shoulder and says some other chick had a better time."

"The snow was fast," Betsy answered modestly. "I had a good run."

"Cut the demure act, sister. You beat me, fair and square."

"Kit here is referring to the downhill skiing contest this spring. Up on the mountain." Betsy clarified.

"Why is there always a mountain?" Timothy sighed. "In towns like this?"

"You walked off with the trophy," the woman continued, "but it's okay with me. I know all about losing."

"There is always next year. As they say," said Betsy.

"I might be good for another year in this town. Are you going introduce me to these three hunks? Or do you want them all to yourself?"

"Oh, excuse me! I should have introduced you earlier."

"Better late than never."

"Now then, this is Rodney. We met last summer. And these are his two friends, Chapman and Timothy. Men, this is Kit."

"Pull up a chair," Rodney said, scooting over to make room. Before sitting down, Kit gyrated a last time to the tune now blaring from the barroom speakers. Her jeans were tight.

"What that song says! What I would do to that little singer boy! If I could get him alone." She looked at me again. "What did you say your name was?"

"Chapman."

"My God, your eyes are blue."

"Aw, look at that," teased Rodney. "He's getting red."

"A shy one, huh? I don't mean to put you on the spot, honey. I just think your parents ought to be congratulated."

"I'll uh, pass that on … next time I see them."

"You do that. And what about this boy over here?" she asked in reference to Timothy. "Can he possibly be of drinking age?"

"Well, you know how it is in these western towns," Rodney interjected. "They relax the standards. Let all kinds of bodies in."

Timothy eyed both of them with contempt. "As if age means anything."

"Oh, a serious one, eh?" mocked Kit.

"One battle matters. What takes place between the hemispheres of the brain. Who are you?"

"I'm a bonus baby," she answered quickly. "One of many in this town. Though I'm the only one who'll come straight out and tell you." She closed her eyes, bobbing her head to the music. Suddenly, they opened wide, as if at some private surprise.

"Does it have to do with trophies?" Timothy asked. "Or the currency people can see?"

"Uh oh," Rodney said. "This could be getting metaphysical again."

"It has to do with money," Kit answered. "Having lots of money. It's given to you because you happen to be born into a certain family. It's like getting a Christmas bonus each month. It's a lot of fun. And people treat you nice."

"Where are you from?" Timothy asked.

"Where it's flat," she replied. She started to sing, *"I'm a bonus baybee, fed on rice and gravy."*

"Did you go to school back East?" Timothy asked, in an unusual display of attention.

"School?" she answered scornfully. "Are you kidding? My family was into games. Board games. Masterpieces of entertainment. You'd probably recognize some of them. There's money in games. And I'm the living proof."

"So you didn't go away to private school?" Betsy queried.

"Hell no. Like I said, it was games in my world. That's how you measured up in my clan. With how wild of a game you could come up with. My old man had a lot of pressure on him to live up to Grandpa, his legendary standard of creativity. He'd milk our brains if it got real tense. I was named after a street on one of his board games."

Betsy excused herself from the table, apparently for a visit to the women's room. She seemed threatened by Kit's high-powered performance. Rodney was as captivated as Timothy with the ravings of this petite creature. Kit sensed her growing audience and decided to remain at our table. She had a formidable, cutting wit. "Go ahead, baby!" Rodney urged, slapping his thigh at some off-color remark she had made. "You gots the floor." She shot him a look to remind him that she needed neither advice nor encouragement—especially from a man who would be with a woman like Betsy, and from the South, no less. She took it personally, as I found out later.

"I just got this heavy déjà vu," Kit said out of nowhere. "I like your friend Chapman." I flinched at the sound of my name. "He's devastatingly handsome. And I have a weakness for shy men."

Rodney laughed, then patted Timothy's shoulder. "Looks like you're out in the cold, kid."

Timothy shrugged. "So what?"

Meanwhile, I'd been gauging the implications of Kit's stated preference. It surprised me. The fact was, I liked her. I liked her because she seemed to be honest. She was also very pretty—lithe, tomboyish—and she clearly had a quick mind. She knew men well, or at least had an intuitive sense of what we respond to. The way she moved, for example; there was an authority in her gait, in her gestures. She didn't wear makeup, except for a touch of eye shadow. Silver slivers of moon for earrings. It had been a long time since I slept with a woman. Or it seemed so at least.

Betsy invoked the image of worried parents soon after her brush with Kit. Although she and Rodney had to maintain a chaste posture in her parent's home, Rodney didn't seem to care. He was going to get his shower. Timothy went along with them. The plan was to meet at a local diner the following morning for breakfast.

So Kit and I were left alone at the table. She ordered another drink.

"What you said about your financial status." I began. "Did you mean that? Like how people respond to you? Their resentment?"

"Is that what I said?"

"I guess that's a … paraphrase."

"You must be a college boy. Taking liberties with my conversation like that."

"Well, it must be difficult to have a lot of money."

"Are you *serious?"*

"Definitely. I mean to be the object of envy."

"Oh, it's sheer torture," she replied facetiously. "Beyond beyond."

"Well, it must affect how others see you. I mean, you're pretty straightforward about it."

"Hell, why should they care? It just makes me more popular. They want in on the action. Don't you?"

"Not really."

"Look, I come from where it's real flat. Growing up there kind of levels out the brainwaves. I like to ski. I like to party. Careful not to mistake honesty for lack of imagination."

"Still, you could be more secretive."

"Why?"

"To protect yourself. But it's like you'd rather have others know right off the bat."

"It's simpler that way," she said, shrugging her shoulders. "Everybody's got an angle. It's a way of letting them know that I know. So these pretty boys won't think that they're getting away with something." Kit reached out to stroke my hair, then whispered, "I don't have a curfew tonight."

I tried to act calm, to buoy the implications of her inviting smile, the assumptions weaving themselves into an intriguing pattern. A question rolled out of my mouth, something like, "What do you mean, everybody's got an angle?"

"Are you kidding?" she replied.

"I mean, it's a kind of dark view of humanity."

"How old are you?"

"Twenty-six."

"You don't act like it."

I didn't know how to respond. What came out was, "Am I that bad?"

"Where's your pacifier?"

"Wait a minute. I don't see how you can equate maturity with cynicism."

"I just did. Two plus two equals four."

"But there are people who have been around for a long time. Who aren't cynical."

"Then they're stupid."

“So it’s all self-interest? The whole thing?”

“Any game that matters is. I didn’t need my grandfather to teach me that. Mother made it clear enough .”

“I think it depends on who you meet.”

“Does it, now? Well, this guy *said* he was a biker. He was much worse.”

“How young were you?”

“Young enough. But who wants to go into all that? Let’s go to my place instead. See if we can find a way to get back into the present.” Her hand found my thigh. The inside of my thigh. “I bet we might come up with something.”

So there we are. I follow her lead the way I’m meant to do. She gives me the keys to her car. Languid in the front seat, she issues the directions. I pull into her reserved parking place and then leave the car running longer than necessary. Then we head up her front stairway. She delicately finds the right key, her head on my shoulder, and pushes open the door. She shows me where to put my coat. And then a quick tour of what was purchased with her grandfather’s money. I buy time at the icebox, settle for another can of beer. She’s behind me now, massaging my neck.

“I am quite giving,” she says quietly.

“I … don’t doubt it.”

“I want to give to you only because you’re so nice.” I turn around like I should. She kisses me, her tongue pushing its way between my teeth. My response is awaited. The details, the only thing that remains at issue—what will distinguish me from the rest. Impassioned groping. Jazzed-up. She suddenly turns passive, goes limp in my arms. She wants me to take over now, and I do. I hold her hand through the living room and into the bedroom. We collapse onto the giant mattress. Her arms go up, and I once again respond on cue. Off with the sweater, off with the bra. "I must visit the bathroom now," she says, squeezing my hand. "Don't go away."

Go away? Where to? Sounds from the tiled bathroom. Nonlinear, random. The underlying gesture toward caution, and the finality of a faucet being shut off. She's back, awaiting my unwavering, resolute embrace. I want her, but will I want her two minutes from now? Perhaps. The real issue is whether I can get what I want in spite of what I want. She has my pants off. I'm already rehearsing my opening statement. Reluctant maneuvers and a slow-breaking revelation. She removes her hand. I recognize this.

"I'm sorry. I guess I'm just a little tense."

"That's all right." Too brightly, too quickly. "We don't have to do anything. We can just … cuddle."

"Maybe if we just slow down a bit … I might relax."

"You must think me a hard woman. But it doesn't bother me."

"It's not like I don't like you or anything," I reply. "I mean, you know I find you attractive."

"You don't have to explain."

"It's just that I am not very good at being casual."

"I think it's neat."

"It doesn't feel neat."

"What I mean is, I think it's to your credit. That you won't leap into bed and ravage me with impunity."

"I guess I need a little bit more time." Pretty noble. "I should be more aware of my limitations." You should. "I guess I need to be reminded sometimes." You do.

"You mind if I have a cigarette?"

"Not at all."

"Listen, Chapman," she says, digging into her purse. "I'm serious. I like you a whole lot better because of it." Great. "I mean, you got some depth that I should have picked up on earlier. You're not just another pretty face."

"Yeah?" Look appreciative. "Well, I still can't help but wish … that it were easier."

"Let's talk," she says.

"What about?"

"Tell me about yourself."

"It's not as if I want to get into this. I mean, I … think I understand things a little better these days. I don't think it helps to review past mistakes."

"So it's happened to you too, eh?"

"What do you mean?"

"You've been hurt. Badly." There is recognition in her voice, a certain sadness. Her beauty is growing on me. I want her. "There was someone in your life. I know how it feels."

"Is it that simple?" I ask.

"For me it was."

"It happened a long time ago. I should be over her by now."

"It takes time."

"Not this long."

"What's long? What do we know about eternity?"

"You don't strike me as the spiritual type."

"I'm not. Mother took care of that."

"Then what do you mean … *eternity*?"

"Oh, it's just something I picked up from Sunday morning television. I used to get up real early on Sunday, roll myself several joints, make a pitcher of Bloody Marys, and watch those religious shows. It was a real kick."

"How long did that last?"

"A couple months. It was a lame winter, the mountain nothing but ice. No powder. No face-shots."

"Do you ski every day?"

"Damn right. If it's white, I get on it."

"Must be a good way to stay in shape."

"We're getting off the subject. You were going to tell me about yourself."

"You mean why I'm—"

"I bet you've had plenty of women in your time. You shouldn't be so hard on yourself."

"I don't think I'm exaggerating."

"Oh yeah? If you say so. What about that guy Rodney? What are you doing with him?"

"How's that?"

"He's not exactly on your wavelength. If you know what I mean."

"I've known him for a little over six weeks. He's smarter than you think. We have great conversations. There's always plenty of time to discuss things on the trains. But it's rare to find someone you can talk to. I like him. And he knows the Hi Line."

"Yeah, but what are *you* doing?"

"I don't know," I answered defensively. "What are you doing?"

"Me, I'm having fun. 'Life's a party, life's a gas—give me a bad time, and I'll bust your ass.'"

"You are so assertive."

"Are you making fun of me?"

"No." Yes.

"I was gonna say you're awfully nice." Awfully. "What are you doing riding freight trains? You don't belong doing something like that." Where do I belong then?

"It's not that bad. Maybe you'd want to try it."

"Come on. Me? You can't be serious."

"You meet interesting people And they don't care how rich you are."

"I don't get where you start thinking that's a problem. If I didn't have money, nobody would give me the time of day. Around here, at least."

"Whatever. But what have you got going here? I mean, of any substance?"

"You can't be serious. You *are* serious. Take a look around you. Why should I leave this? I think I've got it pretty good. So would most people."

"That isn't the issue, and you know it."

"What're you trying to sell me?"

"Nothing. I'm just saying that you need more. That's all."

"How do you know that? I keep telling you I don't have any complaints."

"It's all over your face. In your silent moments."

"Oh, I get it. You're one of these people who's found it. And now you want to share it with me. Out of the goodness of your heart."

"No, that's not what I'm saying."

"That's what it sounds like to me."

"What I'm doing is … kind of reminding you what you already know. That you don't belong. Can't belong, even if you try. Here or most anyplace else. So why pretend you can? Or do?" There, it's done. Now change the subject.

"What're you doing? Trying to mess with my head?"

"I usually don't speak like this to someone I just met. I don't understand why I'm doing it now."

"So tell me how come I don't *belong*?"

"It's, um, a combination of things. Just who you are. I think a lot of it has to do with your money."

"What should I do then, give it all to you? Or whatever cause you're hooked up with?"

"I don't want it. And I'm unaffiliated."

"You are damn near saintly, aren't you?"

"Why not consider leaving town with us?"

"On the freight trains?"

"Why not? What else do you have going?"

"You're too much."

So here I am, on this rotting wooden flatcar at the back end of the Crystal Point railyard. The clouds, floodlit by the moon, tell me that rain is a possibility. I am using my flashlight pen again, because I can't sleep. If it rains, maybe I'll go back to Kit's condo. Or find cover in that grove of trees down by the lake. There's that shelter on the distant golf course fairway—I'd have to clear out by morning, though.

The twenties, my salad days. My salad days have been a complete washout. I don't know how it happened, but it's nobody's fault other than my own. I obviously misread some signals as I went through the ordained steps. There was an emptiness ... that's all I know for sure. I felt that emptiness, the same way I feel the nail heads sticking up through the rotting wood of this flatcar. At the family dinner table. In the football locker room. At the university library. The parties. It just took me a long time to wise up.

What exactly is my problem? It's undeniably strange that I'm out here mixing it up with hobos and troubled individuals such as Timothy. My college classmates are living different lives, that's for sure. Me, I guess I had to go this extreme, looking around and seeing nothing in their lives, or anyone else's, that spoke to me enough to hold me in the fold.

I'm definitely *not* in the fold. It probably begins with Father. He's always bewildered and puzzled and yet vaguely curious about the choices I make, and certainly being out here in the rain on this railroad flatcar would qualify. It was just a delayed rebellion on my part, I suppose—when it came time to sign up, after college, I balked. And it's continued unabated.

There continues a deep expectation of something different, as if I could discover the desired reality for myself by continuing this irrational defiance wherever it leads, or a life largely defined by what's rejected. No to marriage. No to family. No to what my peers are doing. No to the family business or whatever it is my father expects from me that he unfortunately neglected to impart. No to my position as a *Murphy,* which in my rural Iowa town is a big deal.

And then the accumulating refusals begin to assume their own momentum, yes, like a freight train slowly gathering speed as it leaves the yard (which is a beautiful, tactile experience). The assumptions that people operate from become stranger and stranger, more difficult to comprehend—especially as I was supposed to be a part of all this—and yet I never quite got the message. Much to the frustration of Father and Mother, and even my brothers. "He is out West, trying to find himself." I can hear their pained summary over the cocktail banter.

CHAPTER 10

Talk about cringe-worthy. I want to shake my twenty-six-year-old self and shout, "*Dude!*" Relax, for Chrissakes. Just acknowledge that you need more when it comes to intimacy. Is that such a bad thing? Hell no. I don't know what I was measuring myself against at that time in my life. I think all of that self-doubt and questioning had its inevitable side effects, or manifestations, in unexpected ways. In a perfect world I'd have been mentored into these carnal matters—the soft voice of reassurance from an older brother or an uncle or even father, a voice I could trust. Instead I was surrounded by the wrong messages—wrong for me at least. And yes, an undeniably traumatic experience at too young of an age. But I don't want to think about that.

Here's the deal with sleeping outside, as I'm about to do, on the outskirts of this freight yard—somewhere in Arizona, near Flagstaff, maybe? It's not that big a challenge, as there's plenty of space, it being the *outdoors*. The absolute key of course in this situation is to avoid any meaningful contact with one's fellow transients; it's not in the spirit of superiority, let the minutes reflect, but basic personal safety. Plus, I'm rather weary of people, not keen on initiating conversations. The casualty of the past seven years with Hope House. Instead, I'm aware that it's nearly dark, and my headlamp is starting to flicker, and I could use a new battery for my trusty flashlight pen. I prefer sleeping next to a wall of some kind, and I see a spot as the light fades. It looks like it's still railyard property, which can be problematic—especially down here, as opposed to the rural yards of the Northwest; here they'll arrest you immediately, at least that's the word, no tradition of warnings, a harsher financial presence on the part of the railroad company. Trespassing is against the law. Once situated against that stucco wall, I'll be fine. And there's nothing like waking to the sound of train engines and the boom of steel. Or sleeping through it, for that matter.

My thoughts drift back to my days at Hope House. Give us a Sunday morning or late afternoon in summer, when the A Crew's been assembled, and watch us generate some revenue. Door traffic cased, an art like anything else, and Lewis at the main table. I sit with Maestas because of his anger—so easily ignited, but not in predictable ways. His wire rims make him almost appear calm. Mary Lou more than capable at the third door. It's difficult, meeting the public head-on, but after an enthusiastic introduction by the priest or minister or whomever and my three minutes at the lectern, we're ready.

My A Team was *good.* They were talented at being attentive to opportunities. There's that universal human impulse to assist, the unhappiness with the given world, felt to differing degrees, of course, along with the parallel belief in something better. You still can't convince me that people, for the most part, have ever truly accepted our world as it is. If given half a reason, people will cast it aside for something better.

But what do I know?

"Chief, can I go get a pop now?" Mary Lou held up the wad of bills with pride. "I told you I could help out."

"That's great, Mary Lou. Sure, go ahead."

"One guy wanted to take me out, kept pressing me for my number. But I told him no. I'm part of a household and will not be taken lightly."

"Good job, Mary Lou," I replied. "Hey, do you know if Ernestine is back at the house?"

"How should I know?" Mary Lou replied.

"That's fine. Just mindful of house morale is all."

Our weekends would pass like this, supermarkets and churches and department stores, the public hurrying past until we could distract them. And we needed the money, especially in those first years, simply to pay the utility bills. Pitching the idea of a second chance, with the actual persons invoked in attendance, selling the tickets. Everyone feeling their best on Sunday morning, promise inhabiting the chapel with the sunlight streaming though stained glass.

These were good times.

July 2, 1987

> I woke up this morning to a light drizzle that's been quietly soaking my sleeping bag. It's stopped now. This rusting flatcar is becoming my new home, and I'm totally okay with still being in Crystal Point. Just now a threesome waited to tee it up on the eleventh hole (I can see the pin flag). The hole is a dogleg with a wicked-looking bunker, dead-center fairway. They seemed uneasy, perhaps surprised, to find a spectator on the back nine. They tried to remain aloof, but I caught their nervous glances. Contempt, maybe, in their eyes, birdies on their minds. The first guy shanked one to the

right, deep into the railroad yard. He took a mulligan, then sent the next one straight up into the air. He cursed under his breath, then sent a nasty look in my direction. The next guy duffed a low grounder fifty yards up the fairway. A forced, tense laugh as he slammed the club back into his bag. The last guy looked straight at me right before his last warm-up swing. Then he whacked the ball a good distance. An excellent drive, if not for the abrupt left hook that left him deep in the trees. They resumed their positions on the cart, then motored quickly away.

I'm left to regard the day. What now? A visit to town? Should I try to get in touch with Kit? What will her attitude be in the sardonic light of a Sunday morning? Enough of this. I'm slightly cold and not exactly dry, and, as Father would say, it is time to get up and get with the program—whatever that might be.

July 6, 1987

So, *Dear Diary,* it's been an eventful few days (& the Fourth of July no less). I suppose most of my entries qualify as *eventful*, it being my only life and all. But here is how it went.

Later that Sunday morning I stood on a corner of downtown Crystal Point, next to their glass-enclosed mall. It took them nearly an hour to make it in from the lake. Kit was either not at home or not answering her phone. The plan was to eat breakfast at a local restaurant. I noticed my appetite was strangely absent when Betsy pulled up in her expensive foreign car. I climbed into the back seat with Timothy. Betsy knew of a place a little ways out of town. Rodney was smiling, no doubt feeling quite full of himself. He turned and looked at me, his expression one of hopeful curiosity. When I didn't respond, he returned his attention to Betsy. I could've given him a simple thumbs down—a concise summation of my evening with Kit—but my mind doesn't work that way. "I don't care if it's a lousy day," Rodney was saying. "I'm one lucky motherfucker."

"Rodney!" reprimanded Betsy. "Your language."

"You'll have to excuse me. I forget sometimes, baby. But as I was saying, I'm one lucky guy. We all are. If you think about it."

"How so?" I heard myself ask.

"Well, here we are ... in the company of a lovely woman. Who, by the way, keeps on talking about paying for breakfast. We riding for a change, instead of walking. And Sunday is spreading out before us like a field of okra."

"Just because you got to take a shower," I replied, "doesn't mean—"

"Hey, I'm telling you. It's all in how you look at things."

Betsy tightened her grip on the steering wheel as she pulled into the restaurant parking lot. There was little conversation during breakfast. What dialogue there was centered on Betsy's prospects for a new teaching job in another town. "I should get out of the house," she said. "Out of this town." She seemed visibly relieved that Kit was absent, though she was as curious as Rodney about how things had gone between us the other night. She also seemed anxious to divulge what she knew about Kit—perhaps to even up the score from that same night—but she caught herself. More than once. Timothy was preoccupied and laconic. Just then I noticed Betsy's expression change as she glanced out the window. Rodney looked at her inquisitively and was about to ask a question, when I heard an intrusive, newly familiar voice:

"That's right. Go ahead without me. After all, I *did* finish in second place. Though it was my skis."

"Well, hey there, Kit!" Rodney said. "What a surprise. This guy led us to believe that you were indisposed."

"That's not what I said." My ears were turning red.

"I had some things to take care of this morning," she answered. "But that does make me feel better. That he phoned, at least."

"Pull up a chair," I said too eagerly.

"He's a gentleman, isn't he?" she said, squeezing my arm.

"I tried to teach him a few things." Rodney sighed.

"Oh, shut up," I said curtly.

"See? He ain't got it right yet."

"Well," Kit began, "I'm not giving up. I'd be a stupid woman if I gave up on the likes of him." She gazed at me meaningfully. Embarrassed, I asked if she wanted something to eat.

"No thanks. I've already eaten a huge breakfast. I do that right before I'm ready to go on a trip."

"Where you going?" asked Rodney.

"With you guys," she answered.

Rodney laughed. "You're coming with *us*?" Betsy didn't look pleased. "Well, I'll be damned. This boy must be one smooth cat." He winked in my direction. "Like, to get a fine woman like you to come out on the trains? No one ever done that for me." Ouch. I found myself looking at Betsy.

"Maybe he could teach you a few things," Kit replied shortly.

"Kit … are you sure you want to come?" I asked, trying to conceal my anxiety.

"I'm sure."

"But … I don't even know what my plans are. And these guys … I'm not sure what they're doing either."

"Hey," interjected Rodney. "Don't worry about me and Timothy. We all going our separate ways anyhow."

"Well, where are we going?" I asked him. "Today. for example?"

"We gotta get a ride down the road, to Spokane. Found out yesterday, westbounds don't stop in this town no more. Betsy was saying she could haul us all down there, but she don't have to."

"I have a car," Kit offered. "I could just park it somewhere."

"What is this for you?" asked Rodney. "Like, do you know what's involved with this kind of thing? It's no summer outing we're talking about."

"Fuck you," Kit bristled. "I was trying to help. That should be enough, shouldn't it?"

"We're going take the trains to the coast. Seattle, right?" I asked Rodney. "Or, I mean, you are?"

"That's my agreement with the young man over there," he said, motioning toward Timothy. "Ain't no reason why you and Kit can't come along too. The whole ways, if you want."

"These ... *definitions,*" pronounced Timothy with utter contempt. "What good are they?"

"Yeah," muttered Rodney, searching Betsy's face for clues. "How you doing, babe?" His hand was on her thigh.

"Oh, I'm fine. I was only thinking that it sounds terribly confusing. Everybody taking off every which way. Who's going with whom."

"Well, it'll get clearer once we out there. After a couple of days on them damned trains."

"I suppose it will. And here I am, having to teach school tomorrow."

"Come with us," Rodney said flatly.

"You know very well I can't," Betsy said angrily, her temper flaring. "Rodney Mills, how unfair of you to ask me that question!"

"Shoot, babe ... I don't always know what you can and can't do."

"Well then, you should at least have an inkling of what my responsibilities are. I can't simply ... fly off—"

"We ain't flying."

"Or, shall I say, *hobo-off*? To some godforsaken place. And leave my parents. My students."

"Call in sick."

"Rodney, stop it! Some of us don't have that kind of freedom." There was a pause, and Kit shifted impatiently in her seat. Only Timothy seemed to be enjoying himself—exploring the tributaries of his own private reality. "Besides,"

Betsy continued, "I thought you were going to stay on an extra day."

"You know I would. But like I was telling you last night, we only got so much money between us. And I have to be getting to the coast, where I can make some more."

"I don't see how one more day will do any harm."

"But what about these other folks?" he said, looking around the table. "It isn't just me involved here." Another pause.

I was thinking of a way to delicately address some of the more vivid doubts I had about this emerging plan. I had enough trouble with the daily dilemmas of where to eat and where to sleep and when to move along. Did Kit expect me to take care of her out there? Would I have to fend off leering intruders at every depot?"

"Kit," I began, "are you sure about this? I mean, that you want to do it and all?"

"I told you once. Yes. I couldn't sleep all night, thinking about what you said. I need a change. Something drastic. This is drastic."

"Yeah, but … we don't even know each other."

"So what? We'll have plenty of time to get acquainted."

"That's not the issue."

"Look. You were giving me a hard time about being a cynic, right? Well, what do you think is going on now?"

"I'm trying to figure it out."

She rolled her eyes. "Faith, sucker. Isn't it what you want to see? You don't think I have it in me. I say let's just roll the dice and find out."

"I never said that."

"You implied it."

"Nobody's questioning your faith. At least I'm not. What I am wondering is whether you realize what it's like."

"How is somebody supposed to know until they try?"

"Yeah, but it's not as if I belong out there either."

"Come on, Chapman," inserted Rodney. "You've earned your stripes."

"Maybe so," I replied, wishing he would shut up. "But I still don't belong out there."

"Who does?" Shut up, Rodney.

"You see?" Kit added. "And if something dreadful comes up, we'll protect each other. You've got to be pretty far gone not to taste the romance in that. Plus, I can be scary, too. You know what they say about us rich bitches."

"I wish you wouldn't talk like that," I replied. "So how long can you be gone for?" I continued.

"I'm gone."

"What about your condo? Or whatever it's called."

"I cut a lot of ties. Sometimes you have to do that."

"What about your financial obligations?"

"You mean my money? That's the whole point, isn't it?"

"I guess so."

"You were a hell of a lot more adamant last night."

"I get that way sometimes."

Cortez appeared at my door one morning, in a better, earlier time, when he was still under the general guidance of our program, but off-site. Tearful, alarmingly early.

"The car, it's *gone,* man!" meaning my British convertible.

"What do you mean, it's gone?"

"They stole it." He was very upset. "I been so careful. Wouldn't let anyone go near it." He pounded his fist on our front porch wall.

"Are you *sure?*"

"Bad things always happen when I'm involved." He looked at me, stricken. "I'm sorry, man."

"It's okay," I said calmly. "It's only a car."

"I didn't hear nothing, nobody trying to start it. Damn." He hit himself.

"Well, maybe it's around? Let's go look."

"I'm just bad news."

"Let's go. Come on in while I get dressed." He came inside briefly as Kit emerged from the kitchen, giving me that familiar look.

It was always like this—these variations of trauma, the old scars often awakened in the early morning. The history of impulse is a long and extensive one. Mercifully, in his case, the car *did* turn up several blocks away, with only minimal damage. I waited for Cortez's spirits to improve, but something deep within him had been provoked; the dark moments were taking over, I could tell. Daily events in his life would assume the status of omens, forecasting his inevitable doom.

"Hey, it's *my* car," I finally said to him. "Aren't you going to appreciate how lucky we are to have it back?"

"I was so careful … I arranged my bed so I could keep my eye on it out the window."

"We should probably keep it in a garage."

"I'd waste whoever took that car," he said evenly, without drama.

"There's no need for that," I replied hastily. "We got it back."

"They're lucky I didn't wake up."

"Looks like you're making progress," I said, looking at the vehicle in question, trying to change the subject.

"You won't recognize it when I'm done," he said. At least Cortez was starting to come around. "I've been wanting to show you the catalogues." Still not his usual enthusiasm about the car, still shaken.

"Let's go look."

There were other moments with him. The gym outings at my club—our group of ex-cons in the lobby, standing out. My basketball pickup guys were polite, knowing the context, knowing me. Things went well on balance, basketball being a universal language, and our residents had talent, even if they were raw and unschooled. I hated the player who was guarding me, a young newcomer. Building tension around my particular fashion of defense. One more time this kid claimed wrongdoing.

"I didn't touch you," I protested.

"Fuck you. You fouled me."

"Asshole," I replied.

"Don't call me an asshole." The ball rolled in the other direction as we squared off.

Cortez came between us, speaking quietly to my nemesis. "If you mess with him," he nodded in my direction, "I will *kill* you." Again, evenly and without emphasis, my opponent muttered something inaudible, and understandably let it go. Play resumed, situation over, my foe quiet the rest of the game. Eventually we stopped going to the club as a program, not because of problems like this, but mainly because our entrance to the club invited stares. Stereotypes, always stereotypes. And our residents often lived up to the bad outcomes that were expected of them.

Eppie usually had an urgency in his voice, calling my name as they all did, in their netherworld zone. *Chief!* The glue that Eppie had sniffed in his youth didn't help matters. Small and childlike, he was also full of accusation and unafraid at our marathon household meetings. Group therapy with a facilitator (did we *do* that?). His particular antagonist that night was hardened, to say the least. They all knew each other's crimes. I was surprised to see him back down from Eppie, his muscular frame in defeat, sinking into the marshmallow couch. There was always tension like this under the surface at our house, though arriving with their code made it all workable. Unspoken rules, clearly understood, a secret culture.

This hidden world was revealed to me—gradually—in the early weekend mornings when I would come by to do paperwork. The kitchen was either too clean or not clean enough, the heat sometimes raised to a sauna level. There was the vacant bed, the trouble of a locked room, the collective giving up of no information. I could feel the craziness, and I did my best as the miscast enforcer of the rules. I'd get close to it, these concealed layers of secrecy, but only in glimpses.

It was manageable, barely, when Solomon was pulled out of his room through the small window by our hatchet-wielding neighbor. I'd get calls like that on weekends at the office, though by then I was off-site. Our neighbor spoke of irreparable harm, his wife the siren. Furious, he said, "I will shut you down. I'll make it my purpose in life if you don't get down here immediately. I'll call the newspapers. I've had enough of you people."

And there I was, consoling a shaken Solomon, the embarrassing magazines on his bed, him up against the neighbor's undisputed version. "I wasn't *looking* at his wife," Solomon said quietly, guiltily. "I was, you know …" he looked in the direction of the magazines, " doing *that*."

The officers arrived and we retired to a more private room, where I produced Solomon's file and suggested his possible innocence. They responded with a skeptical but hyperbolic version of his particular criminal type—methhead—which could only further inflame our aggrieved neighbor if he were to find out. Solomon had to go, but he wouldn't be arrested. I gave him a silent, reassuring ride to the wrong side of town.

Emergency meetings characterized the next week, as we prepared for the torches that happily didn't materialize. Solomon's injuries were never seriously considered—the neighbor hit him with a shovel—so the incident ultimately became just one of those things that happen. I felt bad for Solomon, I probably could've defended him more adamantly, but there was no other viable choice in the matter. Our community standing was key; we were fortunate to have found a neighborhood that would accept us.

My judgment served me well when I was visited by Briana and Sylvia. Alone in my desired satellite office—always on a weekend—in these two would come, separately, with their scant outfits, the desperation of addiction informing the room. I know there'd been at least one bet during my early days, to see if Mr. Murphy could resist. But despair is anything but erotic, and I'd never abuse my authority in such a fashion.

July 7, 1987

It was a quiet two-hour drive to Spokane. I'm not clear on Timothy yet. The way he clenches his hands seems authentic enough. His eyes are brown and luminous, almost childlike. Two prominent veins stick out in his forehead when he becomes upset, which seems to be a lot of the time. What does he think of our new companion, Kit? Will Seattle do him any good, as Rodney maintains? I'm also not too clear on where Kit and I stand. Sitting together in the back seat, tentative hand in tentative hand. She liked me. But she made me nervous, posed a threat to the routine I've come to value so highly. Things are complicated. Whatever happens, happens. That's my attitude now

We took our packs out of Betsy's trunk, then said goodbye. Familiar broken glass and broken teeth, the stoned wonder of men with grease on their faces, ubiquitous transients. We stepped over them, me watching Kit for signs of fear. None yet. Maybe she wasn't so terribly locked into privilege. Still, it could be just another adventure for her. Another expedition, or stunt. This time slightly offbeat. Not to be found in any catalogue.

We walked the desert walk on the three-pound stones. The cast-iron behemoths were there, promising to take us away. But not without some surprise. A long freight train without a single empty, for instance. Or nabbing a southbound that veers north, confusion on the low grade. Kit could probably handle any of this, I reasoned. But could I? She looked like a boy from a distance—the short hair, the quick step. Rodney knew the yard, knew where to position us. And whom to ask. He studied the evolving configuration of what was being locked and unlocked, chopped up and fed back. What we wanted — a groaning, segmented creature going nonstop to the Coast. A brakeman gave Rodney an ambiguous smile, then pointed in a direction he didn't bother to look.

As long as we were with Rodney, he could make the decisions, shoulder some of the weight of Kit's presence. After all, I'd never been here before. Not in this urban yard. And he knew more anyway. Still, I could see the emerging alliance, could see it forming in the bend of a train as the engineer slowed for the curve. Rodney and Timothy. Kit and me. Our separate ways, but not yet. Rodney placed his bet on a train that looked dead to me. An empty boxcar, one door open. Timothy complained about the lack of light. Rodney praised the opportunity in the winds and pointed to the cardboard lying in the corner. Kit grabbed my arm and pulled me up. She said this could be the right situation for her to finally quit smoking.

"Yes, but what are you going to substitute instead? asked Rodney. "We got nothing but time out here."

"I didn't bring a pack with me." There's a determined, petulant quality about her.

"A lot of these derelicts will happily oblige you, if you know what I mean." Rodney winked. "But a gal like you don't need to be told that. Most of 'em are harmless anyways."

"Then why are you telling me?"

"Because I'm challenged. In certain ways." Rodney looked over at Timothy. "At least I know I have these limitations."

"You're so humble," Kit said. She could be very cutting.

Rodney laughed. "I'm glad you came along. I didn't think you had it in you. I stand corrected."

"A fellow as *challenged* as you should be accustomed to surprises."

"You're right again. Only thing is, I can't divine what you see in Chapman over there. They do say love is blind."

"Who says we're in love?" Kit fired back.

"Hey, I'm not rushing to no conclusions."

"Thanks. I think that'd be a benefit to us all."

"Rodney," I began, "are you sure … this is the train we want?"

"Hell no, I'm not sure. If I had that power, I'd be real popular out here."

"There will be no art today," Timothy pronounced, as if in conclusion to a discussion we'd been having. "No art."

"If it isn't this one," Rodney continued, "the right one will come along soon enough. It don't make sense to be in a hurry. Hell, you know that. How about breaking open that can of tuna? Sunday's the time my appetite kind of wells up." I noticed Kit, who by then had realized there was some doubt over whether this *was* the correct train. She started to say something, then caught herself. I pulled out the can opener.

"Without light," Timothy continued, "the mind shrivels. We could live in a world without light. Are there reasons not to?"

"Timothy," interjected Kit, "what is it you plan to do in Seattle? Find employment? Go to school?"

"I will change my shirt. Polish my toenails on the mud-caked sidewalks. Chirp outside your window."

"So you don't plan on staying there?" Kit replied, unfazed. "Oh."

"If someone don't give him a crayon quick, he'll be like this the rest of the day."

"They are not *crayons*," said Timothy with contempt. "As if that's what they are!"

"Didn't you hear what he said?" echoed Kit. "About there not being enough light?"

"You know," Rodney replied, "these here doors can slam shut pretty quick." He looked at Kit. "In the event of a sudden stop."

"Why are you telling me that?"

"Because a girl like you should have all the facts. That's why."

"What do you mean, a *girl like me*? What do *you* know about *me*?"

"You said a lot of stuff the other night, remember?"

"What is this? Go ahead, scare me. I'm terrified."

"You have me wrong. I'm not trying to give you a hard time. Honestly."

"Then watch your assumptions, buster. They're not appreciated."

"Well, think what you will about me."

"I think you're a jerk, that's all."

"Fine. I won't take it personal."

Eventually the train began to move. Tug, jolt, the delayed reaction. Kit looked even younger than she did in the bar. Rodney leaned back against his bedroll, a country boy with a weed splitting his teeth. After several minutes of slow rolling, we had yet to escape the barbed-wire kingdom, the realm of rust and machines. Then we stopped. Kit looked at me for an explanation. I deflected her question to Rodney. The train started backing up.

"Like I said, this might not be the right one."

"Apparently," replied Kit, irritation showing. "Isn't there any way to be sure?"

"What's your rush, girl? You're on the trains now."

"It's just a little too uncertain for my taste. It sounds as if you simply plop yourself down on any old empty train. And hope for the best?"

"That's about right."

"He's baiting you, Kit," I said. "There's more to it than that. I mean, like, he asked around."

"Shouldn't somebody ask again?"

"This might be the one," I said hopefully. "We'll know soon."

CHAPTER 11

I've felt like an interloper throughout most of my thirty-three years. The sense is that I'm crashing a world where I don't belong, the small Midwestern town where I grew up, the nonprofit world I tried to make my vocational home, and of course this hobo realm that I periodically return to. The only exception might be the athletic fields or basketball courts. Possessing whatever talent I've had in that area, from an early age I was always picked when teams were being divided up. I wasn't ridiculed, teased in that way, forced into a corner to grapple with my own sensitivity. I was at home in the huddle, or in calling winners for the next pickup basketball game.

When I entered into the workaday, nonprofit world, I immediately stood out. What is *he* doing here? I remember one corrections professional confessing to me three years into my Hope House employment that she had a bet with her colleagues that I wouldn't last six months. And she was not even referencing the oddity of someone with *my* background inhabiting the reality of boards and church volunteers and raffle tickets and an annual salary that my father found ludicrous.

Yet it was directly from him, and my mother, of course, that I got the confidence in myself to continue down this odd path that called to me so loudly. I was taught that all things were possible, including the notion of finding my adult life. If this exploration went on way past when it was supposed to expire, for years, so be it. This adopted vocational path unraveled for me, but I gave it a good try at least.

The green light in the distant twilight promises escape into a timeless, anonymous realm—soon the pounding movement will carry me away. I guess I am going to California. I can go into the details of my Hope House departure later, but I can say that there was stamina involved, or lack of it, which would apply to my relationship with Kit as well. I told her that she was tough, that she was a survivor, but she heard something different when I said that—we were struggling at this point—and understandably her visits to the doctor were of increasing importance; the imminent verdict of an x ray was her pre-occupation—and matched my own with Hope House. We were quite a couple.

One thing I should make clear. When I speak of joining the workaday world, I mean the *salaried* work force—the language my father and others would understand—as I've been no stranger to the hourly wage. Planting trees, picking apples, washing dishes at fancy cafés. The secret's been to keep my expenses low—cheap monthly hotels, the boarding house with the bathroom down the hall. All with the intention of distancing myself from the family money. I could continue my rejection of all things Murphy simply by supporting myself. I suppose it was my secret, but I'm not sure if I fooled anyone, if that was the point.

Of course, everything changed with my job at Hope House. Not that it ever counted with my father, as he couldn't fathom my paltry annual wage, or the notion that I was working on behalf of ex-convicts, but even he in his distant home must have sensed some change in my situation. Or maybe my brother Fred explained it to him in the romantic language of money that they both understood, allowing, of course, for the special rules that apply to one such as myself, an exemption I receive for my noble endeavor. No doubt Fred and my other brothers would become interpreters for my parents about the strange life choices I would continually make.

But Kit's health was of increasing concern, and she was very private about it—it was in her nature to be so, anything but to look for sympathy or unwanted attention; her anger flashed randomly, consistently, the signature of her daily outrage. This thing that we have in common—a code, a secret rite within our difficult walls, the world outside becoming the ultimate enemy. "You are *not* listening," she'd say with her accusing stare. "I can't talk to you about this. We need separation. Or counseling." Furious, she'd exit—she was always decisive, and a fast walker. I'd follow behind her at times, my own voice echoing down the street.

Nevertheless, she *would* want me out here on the trains, if it made me happy, which it does, even if my absence has made her life more difficult. And our future together is uncertain. She's always been fiercely independent, not one to speak of herself in terms of *we,* the way other couples do. And I liked that.

This grain car is as good as any, and it's ready to take me out of here—it's sheltered, sort of, but riding over the wheels isn't pleasant, which is why I have earplugs.

This situation was set up as it became harder to fulfill the obligations of my conspicuous salaried life, the noontime reminder in my teenage foe's surprise, "You're *how* old? Running like you do, and that shot of yours?" Exactly when did I become one of the older guys in the gym?

Basketball. Sprinting to nowhere, the momentum carrying me farther away, less easy banter as a private emptiness wanted its time also. Pretending to want the ball, to take my shot. I wanted simply to escape on a daily basis.

Who can explain the promise of this momentarily silent train, my grain car stopped now on a siding? East to the fading municipalities, west to the high plateau and California, north to the pine mountains. Any direction represents an answer, like it did seven years ago up North.

My real tribe, my adopted one, had problems that unfolded on a different level, Samuel with his decaying jaw; Maestas, the sailor of early death; Mary Lou, lost in meth;

Ernestine needing that valentine or off she goes into a relapse; and Lewis with his cocaine habit. Cortez, killed his father and consequently rates his own special category. All these assorted folks did the best they could when I was Chief, as I would ultimately fall back on encouraging words meant to counter my own ambivalence about adult life. Still, it was a good effort on my end, wringing from the present any workable lie.

I think that's what happened. Everything became so *tactical* for me. Tending to the whims of the capricious donors for the common good, meditating on the surrounding nastiness to keep the household afloat for another month—always the worthwhile enterprise for a yearly salary. Will the morning paper bring the neighbors out with torches? Will my Board President's overall irritating manner drive me and others away? What'll she use against me at the next Board meeting? What should I conveniently omit in my next report to them?

These became the rules — omission, flattery, the set charitable conversations like cocktail banter, and the haunting sincerity of our criminal residents. Then the surprising ill favor toward me bloomed, on her part, and as she was Board President, it had ramifications. Lewis, because he was of the professional class, was the first resident to pick up on the obvious tension, and he didn't hesitate to pull me into what I didn't want to hear.

In the Board's defense, it must have been unsettling to have a boy in charge, especially given the nature of our work. Of course, it's easy to understand these criticisms, because they were right. I was too lenient. This was a serious program. But I had my own defiance to contend with. Fiercely alone in the trance of my existence, I had nevertheless found a point of entry into the surrounding, visible world; this had become my livelihood, what I could tell others, including my family, when they asked what I did.

This played out in a difficult way, at least emotionally, my searching for the tenuous second home and the belonging that it would bring. Attend to the financial sustenance of Hope House, keeping our scrawny but sufficient compound in business—two identical three-bedroom houses anchored by an expansive gravel lot, and a shack-like third building that served as my office, at least before the conflict. Always the relentless needs of our residents.

I just grew weary and had to act. And off I went to the freights. Again.

July 8, 1987

> So, there we were. An hour must've passed, maybe two. Our train showed all the signs of having died. Kit glared at Rodney. Bad blood. Eventually she calmed down, began inching toward the resignation that can characterize people out here. Way out here, in the slumping afternoon. The bold embrace of free time. Kit reached for my hand. Rodney couldn't suppress a smile. "Like I said, you're good for each other."
>
> "Who asked you, cowboy?" Kit replied sharply.
>
> "It's in the air."
>
> "I don't get the feeling we're on the right train."
>
> "It's always easy to criticize."
>
> "I thought you were the guide for this expedition."
>
> "My mama always used to say that folks who hurry through life hurry to their own death."
>
> "Wow. That's profound."
>
> "Stick around," I nudged Kit. "He's full of such things."
>
> "I figure it's my duty to share what I've learned."
>
> "And you," replied Kit, "take it upon yourself to save others?"
>
> "Decency isn't foreign to me."
>
> "Lacerate the face," Timothy interjected, to no one in particular, "and the stupor is no longer—"

"I'm not trying to save anyone," Rodney continued. "I damn sure don't go 'round thinking I know more than your generic transient. But I just can't believe my eyes sometimes. Ears too. I don't know why I keep ending up out here. I've tried to shape up, all kinds of ways. But just like one of them walking pink catfish, I'm always looking for the right stream."

"How poetic."

At that moment, a burly man stuck his head into our boxcar. He wore a maroon cutoff sweatshirt bearing the visage of a bulldog. "Yup," the stranger began, "nothing's been through here since the morning local." He noticed Kit for the first time, then made an adjustment in manner. "Where you headed?" he asked all of us.

"The Coast," Kit replied.

"Is that right?" he smiled. A glint in his eye, a boyish demeanor. "You might want to think about changing trains. I got it from the brakeman this one's breakin' up." Kit looked triumphantly at Rodney, awaiting his response.

"I guess we were steered wrong," Rodney said in his laziest, most cloying drawl. "Don't surprise me none."

"I got my eyes on one a couple tracks over," the stranger continued. "Don't look like it's got much to ride on, but I'll betcha it's a screamer. Westbound, too."

"Maybe we should mosey on over," Rodney answered. "If you don't mind some company, that is?"

"I don't mind. Only thing I got so far is a lumber flatcar, with a bit of space on the end. Everything else is locked up."

"Any piggybacks?" Rodney asked, slowly rising to his feet.

"Didn't see none. But we can check again."

We gathered up our belongings and jumped down to the gravel bed. We followed along behind our rotund guide. Our new leader had a huge, canoe-like pack on his shoulders, stuffed and rattling. He was breathing heavily from its weight; beads of sweat were dripping from his nose. He had three separate pairs of sneakers tied to the frame by their laces. They flopped around with each stride he took. "Name's Ray," he said, stopping to rest for a moment. Rodney introduced us in turn, then asked him what he was carrying inside his massive pack. "Only what I need," answered Ray. "I got my hardware in there, you see. Pots, pans, casserole dish. I like to cook." He exhaled with difficulty, winded from our short trek. "Used to do it professionally."

"How about them shoes?" questioned Rodney. "Why you got so many?"

"Feet stink. Got to keep the rotation going."

We'd just about reached the flatcar Ray had staked out when the train started to move. The creaking diesel push, the catch-it-now signal. We started to run. The lumber car was moving slowly some twenty yards distant. Rodney was in the lead, with Ray a puffing second. Kit gave me a questioning look, but there was little time for explanation. Rodney hesitated, gauging the angle of approach. There was a gap of about thirty feet between where the lumber was strapped to the flatcar and the vertical steel lip, which could serve both as windshield and backrest. We formed a loose file behind Rodney. The train was getting louder as it moved faster. I shouted to Kit that she should do what we do. Rodney ran alongside the car for several steps, then threw his luggage on first. He followed, knee up and on. Ray was close behind, grunting as he heaved his lead-weight pack onto the flatcar. Then he slipped, but caught himself with his forearms. Kit and I and Timothy each scrambled up and on in turn.

"Whew!" sighed Ray, visibly exhausted, leaning his massive backside against the rectangular steel lip. "I need some whiskey." My hands were sweaty and shaking. Kit seemed dazed. I sat next to her and began massaging her neck. "Sure beats waitin' for the next one," Ray added.

"Lucky it wasn't going any faster," Rodney shouted. "Sure hope this load don't shift." He motioned to the stack of pine board, fresh from the sawmill, that towered above where we lay. Ray plumbed the depths of his canoe pack and produced a pint of whiskey. He shivered in recognition, then sniffed the contents.

"Have to prepare myself for this," he shouted—a prerequisite for successful communication now. Ray sucked in his barrel chest, then blew out. "Here goes." He raised the pint to his lips, then took three substantial gulps. "Goll-eee!" he shivered. "That's a great way to wake up."

"I thought we was gonna lose you back there," Rodney shouted.

"Might have, if I didn't keep in shape like I do. Push-ups, sit-ups every day. Like the way we did 'em in the service. I always make sure I got a clear head if I'm catching it on the run. Ever since I saw a buddy of mine go under. I didn't know him that good, but I seen it happen. He was drunk."

"Personally," Rodney answered, "I don't think it's worth it. Running for trains. What's the point? If you in such a big hurry, what're you doing out here to begin with?" He looked over at Kit. "You did good." She made no reply. Ray offered his bottle around, but there were no takers. He took a couple more swallows. The countryside was speeding past us; occasional sawdust in the eye, but not too bad.

"Wanna see me throw my axe?" Ray suddenly shouted.

"Depends on what you're figuring on using for a target," answered Rodney.

"That woodpile there oughta do."

"Go ahead."

Ray stood up. "Watch this." He reached down to his belt and unsheathed what looked to me like a hammer. He took aim on an imaginary point within the crease of the wood stack, squinted his eyes, then let his axe fly. "Bingo!" he exclaimed, as it found a resting place in the open grain.

"Hey," Rodney laughed, "you a bad hobo, ain't you?"

"I've picked up some things." Ray shrugged modestly as he dislodged his weapon. "Here and there. I got time to refine it now."

"Yeah, we got plenty of time out here."

"Didn't use to be that way. For me, I mean." Ray grew pensive. "Yup, all those years chasin' that dollar. Never had the time to enjoy the fruits of my labor. I was making good bucks, but so what? I couldn't relax enough to feel good." Ray chuckled. "Now I got all the time in the world. I'm enjoying myself. Get my stamps at the first of each month. Live thrifty, stretch it out. Read, build things. Cook. You sure you don't want a swallow?" Rodney shook his head. "Well, I'm gonna do one more."

"You deserve it," Rodney said. "That was close back there."

"I had it all right."

"If you say so."

"Yup," Ray continued, preparing himself for another swig. "I'm a fortunate man. I've had a lot of jobs, been down all kinds of roads. But what good is it if a man don't know himself?" He went through his ritual again, then stashed the bottle back in his pack.

"What kind of work you had?" Rodney asked.

"Oh, about everything you can think of. I was in the service. When I got out, I worked with heavy machinery for a while. Then I went to cooking school and got my certificate."

"Yeah, you mentioned you like to cook."

"Used to make a living at it. Usually end up getting fired, though. Cooks are some temperamental bastards. And I'm a cook. Thing is, when I get mad, I get *mad*. Don't mess around. End up scaring folks, I guess."

"You're a big fella."

"Yeah, but I never killed no one. Hell, I like people. Most the time, anyway."

"They aren't perfect, I suppose," Rodney answered.

"I've been lucky," Ray continued. "One step this way, or that? That's why I say there is a God."

"Well," answered Rodney, "that seems beyond gainsay to me. What do you think, Kit?"

"Oh yes," she answered sarcastically. "Beyond dispute."

Ray remained engrossed in his thought. "It's just a matter of a few inches."

"This God of yours," Kit continued, "does He have a special place for transients? In *His* heart, that is?"

"I don't know about that," answered Ray. "Maybe. I've sure felt His presence out here from time to time."

"Am I closer to God just by being on this train?"

"I don't know about that either, little lady."

"But you do imply that there is some kind of Railroad Deity?"

Ray laughed. "Shoot, I'm not gonna try to sell you anything. Besides, you're too smart for me anyway. All I'm saying is that I've come close to death several times. But something, or someone, intervened to save ol' Ray."

"And the world is so much richer for it, eh, folks?" Rodney joked. "Why would Ray here have survived these various perils? Unless there was some kind of divine power involved."

"I find it hard to believe that it could be as simple as all that," Kit replied. "It's a convenient, easy solution to think like that."

The train sped up again, which meant the end of this round of conversation. Ray took a snooze, after telling us about his shack in the jungle of his adopted railroad yard. "I'll be going there soon to get my stamps," he said. "It comin' up on the first of the month and all. What I got, it's not too fancy. But it keeps me dry, and I got the river right next to it." Ray extended an open invitation to *us kids,* and within minutes he was fast asleep. His snoring was drowned out by the roar of the train; I envied his or anyone else's ability to sleep so easily on a freight train. Soon Rodney and Timothy would be veering south to the city, leaving Kit and me to each other. Of course, we could tag along with them if we wanted.

What I'm used to, making decisions that affect only me. Apart from having to defend Kit from I don't know what, I'm afraid of further issues in the emotional realm. In the same way it'd be easier to stick with Rodney, it'd also be easier not to make the effort with Kit. Spare myself a bit of trust in the future. No more blunt reminders. I should tell Kit that I'm beyond my limits with her.

My God, I had problems. I suppose that's the difference between twenty-six and thirty-three, or at least that's been the case for me. Being estranged from my family didn't make it any easier, though I think it had to be that way. The loss of my parents has had an impact. I've been released from my prodigal role, at this point who's watching? Who am I rebelling against? And yet the momentum of my life choices continues unabated, framed as they've always been by my contrary nature, a deep rebellion that I've always felt. Oppositional Defiant Disorder—I read that in a magazine article. Their judgment is still with me, especially my father's. He could never comprehend why I made the choices I did.

How can I forget his grief at my mother's funeral? I had to go home for that. The whole town seemingly assembled in the brick fortress of St. Ignatius Catholic Church, him crying out my mother's name as her casket was ceremonially wheeled down the aisle, tossing his beloved baseball cap onto its flowered shell as an intimate farewell to his partner of forty years—a gesture that only the two of them could fully understand. The bells ringing at the conclusion of Mass, the timeless feeling of abandonment overwhelming me as she was lifted into the hearse, gone to the wooded green cemetery of our small town. Tears.

I've left the Hope House workaday scenarios behind. Still, I worry about the long-term fate of the program. How will our fragile residential facility sustain itself? I carry our donor list in my head. I was never good with professional paperwork; so too with our incarcerated applicants, so much blank space on our Hope House intake forms—I'd essentially make my decision within three minutes of an interview. Not exactly professional. The grants I think will be okay, since they're all in a file somewhere. Inertia had become the constant with the passing days and months, especially toward the end. I'd practiced my letter of resignation. There was another last push against the municipal codes, and being *non-compliant* became a final reminder of how difficult these programs are, not only to start, but to sustain. Halfway houses in every neighborhood, I say. There I was in his office, the zoning commissioner, my new friend, and I was talkative, evasive, and honestly fatigued by the end of our meeting, trying to read what his final decision would be.

My beloved program *could* give way to disrepair if I wasn't there. No longer the colorful premises of healing. This could happen. Sweat into dust, manic yet crafty explanations at critical times—the undoing of an enterprise like this so easy. Problems when newer neighbors arrive—there's a *what* down the street? Operations like ours always on the defensive, and the municipal codes don't help. I reached a personal benchmark when rules were an open question.

Others were eyeing the door as well—Board members. Conflict can take down a nonprofit, which is not exactly conducive for volunteers. This is among the reasons that societal change is the dumbest possible idea ever. Volunteers will save the day? Right? I couldn't continue my pitchman's role in good conscience, seeing little evidence, the why-fore of it all? And with my Board President and her alliance gunning for me.

One thing I'm noticing this time around on the freights. I have no desire to meet or engage anyone out here. Unlike last time, when I was wary but still curious as to what drove others to the hobo life. Back then it was as if a random encounter might yield answers for me. I grew up in a family where there was no such thing as a wrong question, a testimony to the parenting skills of my mother and father. Now I just can't be bothered, less innocent, sort of world-weary I suppose.

July 17, 1987

> Much has happened since I last spoke to you, my patient and *Dear Diary*. Kit and I are alone now. Rodney and Timothy caught another train west to Seattle. We considered joining them, but that would have meant plugging back into another manifestation of what we were trying to avoid. I'm using my flashlight pen as a kind of magic wand, trying to figure out what comes next.
>
> It started when Kit and I decided to take Ray up on his invitation. This stemmed mainly from our indecision over where to go next. It was an immediate and obvious solution to the problem. Turn around and get off at the next major yard, Ray's yard, three hundred miles back the other way, east, not west. We had nothing better to do, and Ray had gone on and on about its attributes. Plenty of jobs available if we were so inclined, the proximity of a river, the contemplative rhythm of life in the hobo jungle. Rodney cautioned us that the yard was surrounded by a hard town, an unusually hard town. Lyon, Montana was throwback to earlier days: pistols, poker, cowboys, Indians. Factions were open and unrestrained, their anger noticed only by outsiders. Territory not an empty word.
>
> But Ray had such a child's face, with his animated blue eyes, and Kit and I decided to make his shack our next destination. It did serve to lessen the burden I'd expected with the departure of Rodney. That issue was settled. Now we could move on to the more challenging ones. Such as where she and I stood with each other. Two hours after we lucked into a slowly chugging eastbound, we were intimate again. She

initiated it, kissing my neck and blowing in my ear. The assumptions bobbing on top. We'd been drinking, so I for one was very relaxed. I answered with the predictable moves. Her tight jeans were pleasing. The beat of the train enveloped us in its tornado roar. She went straight for my essence, *down there*, and her perfect mouth took over. I liked it (*what's not to like?*), especially when I realized that I was merging with her, not just physically, but feeling sensations overwhelm my very being, and complications fade away.

There was triumph in our emerging touch, the deepening of it, and she looked pleased with our romantic ride. Nice, yes, but a voice returned, as it always does, its import clear and unmistakable. A temporary advance, but the balance will turn. You can be with her for a while, but *can it last?* You'll be back where you started. Further back, because each failure steals.

"Are you okay?" Kit asked me gently, finding my hand inside my sleeping bag.

"Definitely," I replied. "I'm fine. More than fine."

"You sure?"

"Definitely."

"I like how you touch me," she continued. "You're very sensitive. I like that."

"Ditto."

"We have a lot in common. I realized that the first night, in the bar."

"And yet we're so different."

"In a good way," I said. "And I'm very attracted to you, in case you haven't noticed."

"I've noticed."

"I just don't want to hear about your crazy times. If you don't mind."

"There haven't been that many. It's kind of a front I put on."

"It's *my* issue," I clarified, apologetically. "You have nothing to answer for. We're the sum of our experiences and all of that."

"Listen, we're early into this, you and I," Kit interjected, but softly. "We have much to learn from each other, I can tell."

"And to *explore?*" I added suggestively.

"Yes," she answered. "Very much so. I feel you … in a way that I haven't with other men." She caught herself. "Not that there have been so many."

"That's okay," I sort of laughed. "Just be patient with me?"

"Chapman Murphy," she answered softly, "you have no idea …"

It's so weird that I am out here like this, with all of my issues. But that guy, that father of mine, he just doesn't get me. How could he? Especially when I set off in this direction. I kind of found this on my own—off-site, so to speak—and this wasn't supposed to have been the trajectory of my still-to-be-realized life. Not after college, Dean's List, my Ivy League career as a punt returner, the campus honorary societies. For all that he (and my mother) knows, I went off into this confusing netherworld they find difficult to comprehend.

He's rough on me. He has this glare, which I've probably inherited, and he's certainly entitled to it, as he took the time to father me and all. Everything is money to him—you are what you earn. Restaurant jobs and seasonal apple picking just don't compute in my family. Nor does this Western landscape of pure space and sky, how it welcomes you each morning in the open air, even if I'm greasy and dusty from miles in the wind. He never hit me. But he didn't have to when we clashed, which was often—despite my bringing home the grades and the friends and the all-conference honors in pick your sport. He made his point with that look of his, "Hear my words, mister," he'd begin. "Can you talk without moving your arms like that, waving your hands like a girl? You need a haircut. If I say be in by ten, I mean be in by ten … and don't be a wise guy."

I guess I've always felt his disapproval on some level, even if things were relatively peaceful in our affluent household. He'd lose himself nightly with the glasses of bourbon, as I have mentioned, and the office was always his top priority, so I had plenty of room to do what I wanted, despite his opinions.

But back to my current rolling saga. After winding our way through miles of parched hills—following the course of a torpid, algae-encrusted river—our train pulled into the sprawling yard of Ray's adopted hometown, Lyon. The midafternoon, midsummer sun was out in full force; as the train slowed, I could feel the heat. A couple of switch-offs had landed our boxcar at the back of the train. That meant a long walk into town, this tough town Rodney had warned us about. I jumped first, then helped Kit step down. Rodney had also mentioned the railroad detective in the Lyon yard. Friends had spent time in jail on account of him. I surveyed the immediate landscape, looking for a place to stow our packs. A pair of tramps lounged under the shade of a lone willow tree stranded between adjacent parking lots. They nodded to us, taking more interest when it dawned on them that my partner was female.

"Fuck it," I said to Kit. "I don't see any hiding places. Let's just carry these things into town with us. I'm hungry."

"I'll buy."

"That's okay. I got money," I replied.

"I can't wait to use the ladies room."

"You don't look too bad, considering. We haven't been out that long." We were walking across a vast expanse of deserted parking lot.

"I don't know about that. Say, this is Thursday, right?"

"I think so."

"Well, where is everybody?" she asked, regarding the absence of cars in the shopping center lot.

"I guess people aren't in the buying mood today."

"Yeah, but all those stores are open. Strange." We crossed the highway, our destination a combination gas station and grocery store. The cashier, a middle-aged man, watched us closely. When we emerged from the store, a double-barreled truck crept past, its driver staring at us. "Uh, Chapman," Kit whispered. "Are we doing anything wrong?"

"We should've stashed our packs. They're like little red arrows." Another car, a similar response. "See what I mean?"

"Why do they care?"

"I don't know. They must get a lot of transients through here."

"Yeah, but aren't these supposed to be people of the earth, busy with other things?" Kit replied with a surprising lack of irony. "Yeoman farmers."

"Maybe you're not as cynical as I thought."

"What's that supposed to mean?"

"You're the resident expert on humanity's darker side, aren't you?"

"Yes. But I do have stereotypes in my head. These people aren't supposed to be like this."

"We just got here. Maybe it'll change."

"But what can a girl believe in anymore?" The irony was back.

"I don't know. Maybe Ray will know. Let's get something to eat before we find out."

We decided on a restaurant that gave every indication of being open, despite the absence of customers inside. It took several minutes for us to get our menus. When our young waitress appeared, I dismissed the idea that it'd been intentional. She smiled brightly, then ran down the list of daily specials. She didn't ask us to leave our packs outside—and for that, I was grateful. She also seemed willing to believe that we were capable of paying.

"One time," I said, after our waitress left the table, "I was much cleaner than this, and this restaurant wouldn't serve me. The waitress like … insisted on seeing the money first. Before she'd take my order. And all I was having was a cup of tea."

"I'd walk out."

"I'm sure you would. But some of us don't think that fast."

"Thinking fast has nothing to do with it. She was insulting you."

"Yeah, I know."

"What's that in there?" she asked, pointing to an adjacent room from which we could hear a television blaring.

"There's a bus line insignia over the front door. The place seems to double as a hotel."

"You know, Chapman, I don't know how to tell you this, but I feel like I should. You take too much shit from people." Pause. "I don't mean it as a put-down or anything. It just upsets me to see you giving up territory. Other people, they don't know squat."

"You think I get pushed around?"

"Not *that* so much. What I mean is, since I met you, there've been several times where you just kind of … disassociated. Like when there's somebody in your face. Or when someone disagrees with you. You sort of just let them have their way."

"I'm not so sure about that."

"Well, you know yourself better than I do. All I'm saying is that people, if given the chance, will take advantage."

"Thanks for the tip."

"I don't mean it like the way you're taking it," Kit said, taking my hand. "It's just something I've noticed. And when I see it happen, I keep thinking you deserve better."

"Well, so does everyone."

"Skip it, then," she said, withdrawing her hand. "You're not hearing what I'm saying."

"It just hits a nerve, that's all. It's like, if you don't push people around, they resent you for it."

"Okay, I'll admit it, it doesn't make sense. It's unfair. But that's the way people *are.*"

"You sound like Rodney."

"What choice do you have but to acknowledge the rules? Or lack of rules."

"You always have a choice."

"If you say so. It sure is hot outside."

"Sure is." Pause. "Kit, what do you think of this living on the move?"

"What do you mean?"

"Like, how far do you want to go with it?"

"I'm still not sure what you mean."

'The reason I ask is because, well, it might be a good idea to stick around this town for a while. As bleak as it seems."

"*This* town?"

"Why not? I'm sure it can grow on you. And remember what Ray said about there being work? Out in the fields? It's harvest time, I think."

"You've got to be joking."

"Well, you probably ought to decide how far you want to go with this … with me. Like, I need money now."

"I can lend you some."

"That's not the point. That's no solution."

"Why not? I got plenty of it." She caressed my thigh. "And I like how you touch me. You're very talented, you know."

I cringed, doing my best to follow her lead. I was fairly certain that she wasn't mocking me, that she meant what she said. Still, I wanted to go on about the requirements of this road stuff. I thought about the right words to say. "Kit, this isn't a game. Not for me at least."

She bristled. "Don't tell me that."

"Wait a second. What I mean is, well, if you're going to do this … it's like bad karma to do it in the spirit of a picnic. Even if that's what it is."

"You mean to prove myself I have to work as some kind of fruit-picker?"

"Actually, it's planting trees. The Forest Service will be hiring."

"And what am I supposed to do with what I got tucked away in the bank? Pretend like it's not there? Why *should* I work if I don't *have* to work?"

"It'll be good for you. You know. Hard work. Sunshine."

"Sounds peachy."

"You said you were desperate for a change."

"When did I say that?"

"That night."

"You're reading too much into things."

"I am?"

"You are. I like money. Why shouldn't I? Everybody else does."

"Great. That's fine. So maybe you ought to go back to that precious town of yours." I was surprised at the tone of my voice.

"But," she said with a smile, "I have an obligation to follow my man. That's what a woman does. I read that somewhere. No matter what kind of mole hole he's digging for himself."

"Not you too."

"What do you mean, *me too?*"

"You think I'm in a hole? Is *that* how you see me?"

"No, not entirely."

"Partially?"

"Everybody's in some kind of hole. I'm not saying you're any more lost than anyone else I know."

"Well, if I'm in a hole … what are you in?"

"Can we change the subject?"

"I'm trying to be serious."

"So am I," she replied. "But you're making it difficult." The waitress appeared with our food. Kit looked at her omelet, touched it, then shoved it away. "I can't eat this. It's not even fucking warm!" Our young waitress was visibly embarrassed. She apologized to Kit and asked if she would like to see the menu again. "Fuck no! Just give me a hamburger. Your cook ought to be able to handle that." The young woman reddened as she returned to the kitchen.

"Did you have to do all that?" I said.

"It pisses me off, that's all. The food was cold. Cold!"

"It's not *her* fault."

"I'm sorry. I get carried away, that's all. It goes back to my family."

"That girl's just trying to do her job. Have you ever waited tables?"

"I'm sorry already. What do you want me to do, *whip* myself?"

"No. But it's embarrassing."

"What am I supposed to do? Smile and say, 'Gee, thanks for the cold omelet that tastes like a sponge-board?'" To change the subject, I asked her what a sponge-board was. She replied that it was what it sounded like. After her hamburger arrived, we finished our meal in silence. "I'm sorry," she said in a sincerely contrite voice. "I don't like the way I am. But I want to change. That's part of why I'm here with you."

"That's okay," I replied, unsure if I wanted to be in this role. I searched for something wise to say, but could only manage, "Well, we are who we are." Kit was especially bothered by being unwashed. Apparently the restaurant ladies' room was not up to the task. When she discovered that there was a college in town, she suggested that we visit the campus, in the hope that their gym was open. Then we could venture down to the hobo jungle and find our friend Ray. I was agreeable, hesitating only at the prospect of lugging our packs that much farther.

CHAPTER 12

We need miraculous situations—for people to be better than they are—for places like Hope House to flourish. As with anything, self-interest can be your ally.

There could also be the miracle of a reformed criminal coming back to actually run the household (*that* would bring me back, just to witness it). Maybe someone like Maestas. He's so young, but smart, wicked smile, tattoos, wire rims. And for the duration we'd be able to convert the surrounding drug-addicted folks as he'd transformed himself. This was (is?) a necessary belief, that this *could* happen, though not with Maestas, who's probably dead by now. Hell, maybe they're all dead. Except, of course, the memory of them—*all* of them, even beyond that initial bunch—though their names might escape me. *That* endures. Meanwhile, this freight jolts wildly through the high mesa; we're off the siding now (still California bound?). But I'm stable here, underneath the truck chassis, leaning back against the tires, worrying about our program.

Of course there are plenty of other bad scenarios to consider. The wind through the Hope House compound, no reassuring presence of barely functional cars. The reality wasn't what was rumored about my leadership, or what some on the Board thought. Smoking cocaine was not permitted on the porch at night. Sexual contact wasn't permitted between our residents.

Parole officers were never denied access to our facility. We were a household flirting with chaos perhaps, but none of those accusations was true.

Loyalty has always meant something different for me, something extreme and not always warranted. Our household, though, *they* understood loyalty—ex-cons—the beautiful logic of having another person's back, the alternative representing a very dark night.

I needed the miracles more than anyone. The problem of faith can be vexing. The uncertainty of Kit's health, the fact that there was no one but me to take care of her—having been left alone, the two of us, the rejection of our respective families, who were in distant states. Hope House had always been a escape from difficulty on my relational front. The stunning example of lives remade, and the challenge presented to make these transformations lasting. Witnessing their level of effort made it worthwhile, at least on a good day. It's a long trek for those of us who have difficulty retaining faith.

In the land of the real, there were enduring, uplifting examples of what was possible—maybe not in our original household, though they had a fine resilient spirit. Ernestine, perhaps the best wager for the miracle situation with her grim deviant's fate. She had the anger to carry it through toward something more positive. Ernestine's skepticism and its polar opposite, that one successful afternoon when it carried her through the department store without succumbing. "I didn't boost *anything,*" she told me in amazement that night she called me. "Seriously, Chief."

"All right, then," I replied, always learning.

Why should I have been driven away from my own unconventional household like this, our programmatic attempt at Heaven? These bitter struggles between the well-intentioned Board, the paid staff (just me at the beginning), as a priori hatred shows up one day from some distant Eastern state. No one there to back me up, except for my distracted residents. And a Board member or two. The resulting silence, the uncomfortable gazing at the door. Once the conflict is joined, the calculations and opinions are set—alliances; I have to be finely tuned yet coarse enough to maneuver with the best in these adult games.

Suddenly I couldn't linger at my own program anymore—what had once been so natural—the new hire didn't want me around. She was from New Hampshire. And of course she had an instant ally in my Board President. I represented the opposite of the change that needed to happen, she maintained. She brought in her own hires, of course—sometimes their warm voices would stop with the sound of my footsteps on the gravel and then give way to overly animated pleasantries. We'd pretend to get along. I'd time my exits and entrances, and resume my labor off site.

My work thing was, strangely, *enough,* for years. How else to live a life but commit to that kind of deprivation? Sacrifice bestowed meaning, and I'm freakish in that way. It was enough to fulfill my dinner duties nightly, welcoming the latest group of errant residents and pleasing the church volunteers. Handshakes all around, sincere prayers, and the newer residents picking up immediately on my acquired but genuine street manner. I'd preside over the dinner table, Wednesday master of the house, and all could feel comfortable. This particular routine probably grew tiresome for my new colleague, but she had to discharge it also, as we were in this together. I, on the other hand, enjoyed it, at least in the moment. Did she resent me for it?

That was when the tactical began to take over, that temptation to anticipate how everything would be received. Or not received. This was a lesson already known by those at our table who'd used their very beings as barter, our random colorful residents who excelled in their roles, everything ultimately being excused by the church presence at our dinner table each weeknight.

I was successful in securing the funding—no one could deny that—and with each passing year I learned new tricks. It became a kind of slow descent into the truth discovered in any workplace am sure. I can see now that these strategies had their consequence, and here I am on this truck trailer bed. The earnest impulse can triumph, universally, more than is acknowledged. Or at least this has been true in my case. So too when we would visit the churches and supermarkets, selling our tickets. The A Crew that I keep getting back to. Ernestine conspicuously absent, her surly manner *not* an asset in these sales, and Samuel likewise with his moods. Those early days were *so* in the virgin light, everyone at their best—congregants, felons, me—deep, lasting, and healing change *everywhere* in the promising Sunday morning.

"Chief," Mary Lou said, suddenly at my table. "I need more tickets."

"Don't take any of this money," I teased.

"Chief."

"Or you'll die in shame."

"You're not making much," Maestas interrupted, looking at Mary Lou. "This fellow here has the touch."

"They come to our table because I give the speech," I shrugged. "That's the only reason. I'm the white guy in the tie."

"No matter," Maestas countered. "You're my hero."

"If you look at it proportionately, Mary Lou is doing the best."

"What about Lewis?" Mary Lou asked, new tickets in hand.

"He's the one stealing," Maestas answered. "Crack cocaine'll fry your brain." Pause. "I should know."

"He's not stealing," I said with emphasis. "Maestas, we're all in this together. In case you didn't realize it."

"That's right, Chief," Mary Lou echoed, walking swiftly back to her station. "We're a family."

"Yeah, right," Maestas laughed. "Like the Bradys."

I should be more cautious guessing about their current status. But by the time we see them they haven't exactly had a promising trajectory. The shady world is fairly dependable overall. Overdose, in Maestas's case, a real threat. He almost died twice under our watch. I feel bad. We had the understanding that one day we'd drive my British sports car north, to Montana, after

Cortez was finished. Maestas mentioned the television show he used to watch in the juvenile home, black and white—the kind of road adventure reserved for college graduates—sunglasses, girls, the selection on the car stereo, promise of a new town. "Montana," he'd say in awe, out of nowhere, pronouncing it with the wonder of a new language. "Cowboys up there?"

"There have to be," I'd reply, it being our fourth such conversation. "It being Montana."

"They won't like me."

"Yes they will."

Now he's gone and so is my sports convertible—dismembered somewhere, probably in Mexico, and I'm without compensation other than the evidence of my own naïveté. Maestas walking down the weekend avenue to his dishwashing job, Easter basket and giant stuffed animal in hand, the little gangster. His outrageous hope for a do-able, normal life. That quick smile of his and his unpredictable, swift mind. No attention span, but his random phrases like gems I'll never forget. A black 60s Lincoln glides by, and *Kennedy* he says.

How is being carried away on this freight train any different from submitting to an uncertain choice in love, or vocation, for seven years? The sense is the same — momentum, the purposeful direction. At least now it's elemental and in the present tense, no illusion of anything except flight.

Not that any choice has been so bad. Lucky grace carried me through on all fronts, made certain that I returned to my uneasy home and, of course, my criminally impulsive household. The winnable battles in both realms, especially in the spirit of erasing history and inventing a future. The ideal characterizing everything, never having been fully initiated into either darkness or light. Everything must work out because I have no idea what the alternative is. I just don't know any better.

The lead engines are warm up there. The promise of those deafening engines. The remembrances of our good days at the facility envelop me—warmer than these engines or this puffy red sleeping bag. Briana was difficult to look at, I acknowledge that, but her remaining eye had its own beauty. Green. A kind of calming effect. She was petite and at one time coveted by the boys. Surely her face could have been re-sewn with a little more attention to detail A horrific traffic crash and an under-staffed hospital. We were worried about the impact she'd have on our stream of dinner guests—she was a shock, at first glance. Selfishly, we didn't want to be seen as some back-lot carnival. Everyone adjusted, including the volunteers, and several minutes into conversation her one eye began to captivate. It was green, as I mentioned.

"Do you think I could be excused from dinner this evening?" she'd ask me, always with her disoriented rhythm. "My parole officer recommended a special anger management class. But it's not required."

"Sure," I replied, always struck by the strangeness of my authority role. "It's not your dish night, correct?"

"No, sir."

"You don't have to call me that. Do you have transportation?"

"Yes, sir. I mean … what do I call you, anyway?"

"Mr. Murphy is fine."

She'd had an even stretch, the usual six weeks. And then it began to deteriorate, her glowing recommendations washing away, the ink of her sincerity. It wasn't just her; the darker energies reemerged in the household, frequently. The corrupting influences were in play, constantly, this time in the form of her two roommates, Cruzita and Tammy. The opportunity in a borrowed car, liberating money to be made, the three of them cruising with Briana, the lamb. In they went to the state authority office. Briana was high—so very high—with ice cream running down her face. The normally sober officers couldn't keep from laughing. They even discussed giving her a break, but the policies and procedures, along with possible repercussions, mandated that handcuffs be produced. Her two roommates escaped a similar fate, anticipating the situation with their quick, child-like protestations of innocence, "It was *her* car. She was driving."

Briana went back, which was often the case with residents, only to resurface months later in my office. By then my office was off-site. Her parole finally over, she was released, a free woman in an uncertain world, falling back on the remnants of her beauty, seductive in my office and wanting money. My response was the predictable motivational speech and wishing her the best, as I led her back to what awaited her on the street. We could track her progress in the following months with the warrants that arrived in a steady stream along with our utility bills. As with so many of the others, Briana's challenge was to withstand her own freedom.

But in our household there was always the surprise of a resilient spirit, as in how the diminutive Eppie made his comeback as an ice-cream-truck driver after his time with us. The bells tolling his childhood dreams as he struggled to make change with the coins. Those of us who knew him were incredulous. Who would give this individual the keys? He'd visit my office, long after he finaled his parole. My office became a kind of satellite for our precarious Hope House alumni. "Mr. Murphy!" he shouted. "I need your help. Please, please, just this one time?"

"It's okay, Eppie. Just tell me what's going on," I replied, putting my hand on his shoulder.

"I did a bad thing. I'm sorry. You know the money you lent me for the rent? I spent it all. I owed this person money."

"Eppie," I scolded, "I can't help you this time. Seriously. I don't have it."

"I know," Eppie replied, crestfallen and guilty, growing pensive. "I'm in trouble."

"Have you met with your caseworker, like we talked about?"

"I got the date all wrong. But I will, I promise. Can't you help me just this one last time?" His voice had become even more agitated, in his stylish beret and scarf, his version of a nautical outfit. Here in the high desert. Eppie, our mascot.

"All right, here's twenty dollars." Others on the sidewalk were looking at us; we were a strange pair. "That's the best I can do."

"Can't you make it forty?" Eppie replied, desperately apologetic. "I *promise* not to ask you again."

"I *can't,* guy. I'm sorry."

"Okay," he answered, clearly worried. "Thank you, Mr. Murphy. God bless you."

This off-site function was more pervasive than I realized at the time. Boris would come by too. After his shining eight months, establishing a personal best, sober and incident-free. But the inevitable tailing off happened once the novelty wore off. "Kola," he'd say with his Lakota accent. "What's my horoscope?"

"What have you been up to?" I replied, letting him interrupt my office routine once again. "The guys at the gym have been asking about you."

"What, your team?" Boris asked.

"No, you know … the guys we'd run with. We should play again."

"Oh, I don't know," he said, looking down at his feet. "I don't have shoes."

"Yes, you do. I still have them at the house."

"No, Kola," he replied, embarrassed. "I've been on the street, you know?"

"You do look terrible," I said. He did. "How'd you get that black eye?"

"Oh, that?" he answered, using my office window as a mirror. "That's not anything."

"Why don't you come back to the house? You're not on parole anymore, right?"

"I have a girlfriend now."

"You did so well, Boris … just to get back on track for a while? I can arrange it with Annette."

"Who's at the house now?"

"I don't think anyone you'd know. That was a great Christmas, right? Remember?"

"I still have those shirts."

"You're such a cowboy."

"Western style, Kola," he laughed. "You hitting your shot?"

"Sort of. Come on, we could do the fast-break thing. You run that lane like you must've done in high school."

"Rez ball, up tempo."

"I believe it," I replied.

"Do they ask about me?"

"I'm serious. You're the best basketball player we've ever had in the household."

"Nobody could run with us back in the day. We won state."

"That's your game. Like I said, they ask about you."

"You mean those professional people?"

"Yes."

"Well, maybe when I work out these other things. So what's my horoscope?"

"Nothing but positive things," I answered. "Here's ten bucks. Stay out of trouble. Jerk."

"That's not why I came by, you know."

"I know."

The thing about being out here now is the relentless wind and booming sound—which I suppose is part of the charm. How can you not lose yourself? Of course there's the magnificent scenery. I still remember seeing the Columbia River Gorge for the first time, or coming upon that glacial lake in Idaho, like a small ocean, up near Crystal Point. You have full view into backyards, getting that sense of daily life, whizzing past the cars as they wait for the rail arm to go back up. Expressions of impatience, checking their phones. Being out in the open air on a freight train has an effect on your hair and skin, and the notion of a shower has increasing appeal as the days go by.

I don't know what Annette had been told about me before she arrived at Hope House from back East, but I don't think it was very positive. Her mandate was to run a more traditional operation—less freelancing, less enabling in the eyes of the Board—and I was to get back on my original and best task of bringing in the money, working the community. I wasn't good as a keeper of the rules, I'll readily admit. But my leadership wasn't so bad, in fairness to me. I knew the house might have a raucous energy once I left after dinner each night, but such tales could be exaggerated. Our residents were talented at manipulating a certain incident to their advantage—for the benefit of a visiting church volunteer or a Board member. It isn't like any of the residents wanted me axed. It was just their way of navigating the moment.

Their information proved irresistible to both Annette and her instant ally, my Board President. I think the rest of the Board was generally okay with how things were being run, and the last thing a volunteer wants to deal with is conflict.

And I had problems at home, with Kit. Her puzzling health issues didn't help matters, and my overall absence—very late hours, as if I ever clocked out from my troubled charges. It did *not* feel right leaving Kit, vanishing in this ceremonial fashion, but she seemed to understand. Though I would die for her, such devotion couldn't necessarily carry the day in a real relationship. Or so it seemed, especially as she began to decline, which was real enough, and this emerging answer called chronic fatigue, vague and misunderstood, but very real, I'm sure. There was always some degree of nostalgia about returning to our previous time together—in Montana, after Seattle—in my adopted town of Luxor. But our task was to join the world, both individually and as a duo (I had coaxed her out of Crystal Point), and we were definitely *in* the world. Our respective pride had always been a problem. She drove me away even more when she was facing her fate. I think about her constantly.

July 17, 1987

> "Can you believe that this is a *college* town?" she exclaimed, after walking up the street a distance.
>
> "Maybe it's more of a … technical school."
>
> "Who cares? School-for-fool anyway."
>
> The wind kicked up and blew dust in my face. "I suppose it does rain here. On occasion," I muttered.
>
> "Rain? Fuck no. It just blows."
>
> We were walking past a cemetery when a pickup slowed down beside us. A group of young girls rode in back, decked out in softball uniforms. "Hey!" one giggled and said. "Are you two lost or something?"
>
> "What's it to you?" Kit fired back.
>
> "Only screwheads would be wandering around lost. On a day as hot as this!"
>
> "Well, what is it you suggest we do?" flared Kit, investing each syllable with fierce precision.
>
> "You probably ain't got much alternative," laughed another one. "It takes a lot of money to travel like that."
>
> "Yeah," piped another, "you two must be pretty well off!" More laughter. "Do you got your bankbook on ya?"
>
> "Fuck off, girlies," answered Kit. "Go play softball." There was a moment of silence. Then, the unseen driver punched

the pedal, and the truck lurched away, exhaust pipes firing. Kit and I looked at each other. "Porkers," Kit sighed. "Taking their frustration out on a ball."

"I keep thinking about what Rodney said," I said. "Maybe we shouldn't stick around here. We could move on."

"I thought you wanted to get work"

"Yeah, but I don't like the vibe here."

"How're we going to get out? I mean, if you think I'm going to hitchhike around here, you're nuts. No offense, Chapman, but I wouldn't feel safe."

"That's okay. I wasn't thinking of that anyway. We could turn around right now … go back to the yard. Then catch the first train out. Either way, it doesn't matter."

"What about the cinder dick, or whatever you call him? I heard what Rodney said about him."

"We'd just take our chances, that's all. The yard seems safe to me. I bet we'd be okay."

"I think we should stay. At least until I can get cleaned up. My hair is beyond belief." She cringed as she touched it. "And what about the whole reason we're here? What about Ray?"

"He'll never know the difference," I said.

"What about his teachings on God? And Natural Law? We'll be the losers in the long run."

"I suppose you're right. It was just a thought."

"Much more than that, dear, it was *your* thought." Again, I couldn't tell if she was kidding.

We continued toward where we thought a college might exist. Eventually we did reach a couple of institutional-style buildings, but there was no gym in sight. We abandoned our designs on a shower and agreed we should seek out the promised safe spot instead. We could bathe in the river.

We were beginning to feel the weight of our packs. The rest breaks came more frequently. As we approached downtown once again, I felt dazed, slightly unreal. There was no wind, no humidity—just heat. We appeared to be the only people out and moving around. We were crossing Main Street, to the shady side, when I noticed two youths staring at us. I overheard the shorter one say something about my pack. He seemed to be waiting for us to arrive on their shoreline of sidewalk. "Hey, you!" he said in what I concluded was my direction. "I want that pack." His large friend moved behind him, as if in support. We kept moving, pretending to ignore them. "Hey! Did you hear me, bud? I said I want that fancy backpack of yours." The pair had fallen into step behind us.

"Ho, wait," the short one said. "This guy has a *chick* with him." Kit and I didn't look at each other, though I was acutely aware of her response. "She's pretty, too. Real pretty." He tried to caress her neck.

"Hey!" I interceded.

"Take your slimy hands off me, shitface," Kit said, throwing his hand aside.

"Ho!" he laughed. "She's one of them headstrong bitches. But she's pretty. Is she pretty enough for you, Josh?" The large one grinned shyly, then nodded his head. "She is, eh? I'll tell you what. You can handle her. I'll settle for the guy's pack. Is that okay, Josh?" We were walking fast. I was searching frantically for a shop or restaurant into which we could escape. They both had been drinking.

"Hey, bud," the shorter one continued, his chin almost in my ear. "Where you from? What stink-place do you call home?"

"Why do you care," I hissed, without turning around. "Why don't you just leave us alone?"

"Because me and my friend here are in a bad mood. We don't like bums coming into our town. Even if they bring their slut women with 'em."

"Go fuck yourself, buster," I said evenly.

"Hey now, the guy is getting mad! You don't wanna fight with that pack on, do you?"

"Buzz off," Kit flared, "you dragon-breathed jerk."

He laughed, then motioned to his friend.

I saw our opportunity. "Hey, Kit, in here. Quick!" It was the restaurant where we had eaten earlier. They didn't follow us inside. I could hear the short one's verbal barrage as they continued down the sidewalk.

"Assholes," Kit said bitterly. There was no sign of our young waitress or anyone else in the restaurant.

"Let's go into the lobby over there. And settle down." My hands were shaking. I tried to calmly assess what our next move should be. Would they be out there, waiting for us? This was a foreign situation. The television was blaring in the lobby. Two old men were sitting on a beaten couch. I glanced furtively out the lobby window. They were not in sight. The desk clerk wasn't exactly thrilled by our presence. I gave it five minutes before he would ask us to leave. I shuttled Kit into the corner for a less obtrusive strategy session. "What do you think we should do?" I whispered.

"I need a drink," she replied.

"Great. It's not five o'clock yet."

"That guy behind the desk keeps looking at us."

"Fuck him," I said." This is a bus station, too, isn't it? An all-purpose, um, place."

"I think I want to go home. Take a bath. Play some albums."

"I figure we should just chance it. And head for the river."

"But what if they're out there?"

"I don't know," I shrugged. "Let's just hope they're not."

"Wonderful."

"Well, it doesn't look like they're still around. And we'll be all right once we get to Ray's."

"You mind if I have a cigarette first?"

"Sure. We should give them time to get bored anyway."

"Assholes."

It's hard to believe that Kit is the same person that I've come to know and love. Hopefully I've changed as well, for the better. Mirroring each other toward a more positive incarnation of who we are, deep down, is the whole point of a relationship, correct? The way she insulted that waitress, her overall provocative manner—she rarely does that anymore. Maybe she channels that anger into her artwork. I wouldn't know either way, because she's always been very protective of what goes on in her studio out back, and I don't mess with her sacred space. I would hope that I'm less sensitive to the past she had before I entered her life. As if she should have to explain or rationalize anything! The present tense is so healing.

Of course, a big reason why we were drawn to each other has to do with our respective family money, to put it bluntly. I think she came to realize that my whole attitude toward escaping its presence had some degree of wisdom to it. She understood at some point that she could use her good fortune to commit entirely to her art—trading in her skis for paints and canvas. She even maintained a part-time job at a local gallery; she wasn't the same Kit that I fell in love with seven years ago.

Becoming a nonprofit professional softened my own ambivalence about what my brother Frederick managed in his distant Seattle suburb—or at least I could easily ignore its existence as I dove into the lives of my mercurial facility residents. I had this fierce desire to *make my own way*, to join the surrounding world on my own terms.

We're still on this siding. Time has its own logic out here.

July 18, 1987

> We hightailed it across the railroad overpass. Our antagonists had apparently moved on. We made it to the river and to the bridge. We scanned the undergrowth for a path and found one that led underneath the bridge, to a slope of mud and trash where a man sat staring into an empty char pit. "Howdy!" I ventured. He didn't reply. "Do you know a guy with thick glasses, and uh …" I wanted to say bad teeth. "Wavy hair?"
>
> "Nope," he said without looking up.
>
> "Well, he told us it would be okay to leave our packs here." No response. "He said no one would mess with them."
>
> "I ain't gonna steal 'em," he said testily.
>
> "I didn't mean it that way."
>
> "Hey, Chapman," Kit interjected. "You want to go swimming?"
>
> "Here?" I said, surveying the broken glass and empty cans that extended beyond the muddy bank.

"What's wrong?" said a voice from the direction of the char pit. "The water too dirty for ya?"

"It's not that," I found myself answering.

"Why don't we head up there some," Kit suggested. "It looks like the trail goes that way." I wanted to ask the fellow if the hobo jungle was up that way, but I was fairly certain it could be nowhere else. The yard was in that direction, and I thought I could detect the smell of campfire smoke. We lingered in the shade of the bridge for a couple of moments, then reharnessed our packs. "Nice guy," Kit said when we were out of earshot.

"Not an amiable hobo."

"That river looks inviting. Even if the shore looks funky. It's still hot out today."

"It moves kind of slowly, too, doesn't it?" The trail made its circuitous way through briars, tall grass, and willow trees. Mosquitoes were out in full force. I kept being bitten in places I couldn't reach without taking off my pack.

"Fucking horseflies!" Kit exclaimed, slapping her arm.

"I think it's not too much longer."

"I'm hot."

"I can see the smoke up ahead."

"These burrs are sticking to my socks. Do you think there's poison ivy around here?"

"Nah."

"Whose idea was this, anyhow? Did I consent to this?"

"You look old enough."

"I want to go home. Back to my life."

"Are you serious?"

"I'm never serious, honey. Mother took care of that. You should realize these things."

"Well, I'm not trying to sell you anything. If you want out, you should say so. Go back to your skiing or whatever."

"You're so serious all the time. Where's your sense of humor?"

"There. Somewhere."

"Didn't you ever play one of my grandfather's games?"

"Probably."

"Well? Didn't any of it sink in?"

"I guess not."

"*I guess not*, he says. You're strange."

"We're almost there."

We came upon the first campsite of the jungle: a plastic lean-to, a radio assembled from broken parts, the ubiquitous trash. A striking, silver-haired man eyed us with curiosity. "Do you," I began, "know a guy named Ray?"

"Ray? Mmm … Ray, huh? Can't say that I do," the man replied. "What does this Ray look like?"

"He's a barrel-chested guy. And he's got a beard. Short hair."

"Blue eyes," Kit added.

"Yeah. And he, um, carries an axe around."

"Sorry. I don't know him." A smile began to form. "But there's more than one tramp up that path."

"Is this a big camp?" I asked stupidly.

"It is. It's an extensive one. Oh!" the man suddenly exclaimed. "Why didn't I think of that earlier. I should ask my partner if he knows this Ray guy. He's sleeping, but I'll wake him."

"Oh, you don't have to do that," I said. "We can find him okay."

"He won't mind. He can go back to sleep after you leave." The man seemed intrigued by our presence. My attention was scattered, or, rather, funneled into the many variations of the same question. What should we do *next?* The added weight of another party, with its readout on my own masculine value. The man disappeared behind the plastic lean-to, then reemerged, saying, "Ozark'll be out in a sec." He carried with him what at one time must have been a lawn chair. "Have a seat. Don't worry, chair won't tip." He lifted a nearby pot by its handle. "You want some coffee? Tea?"

"I'm okay," I said, easing the pack off my shoulders.

"How about you, young lady?"

"No thanks. I'm fine."

"Well, I'm gonna have some." There was a pause. I felt an obligation to keep the conversation going, so I asked him how long he'd been living here. "Long as it's taken to establish residency. It's necessary for the stamps."

"Is this the only place you can get them or something?" Kit asked.

"No. But you gotta choose a permanent home. In order to be eligible. And with the first of each month, they're kind enough to dispense 'em." Irony. Behind him, Ozark was approaching.

"Like Griffin here says," Ozark began, "this camp ain't too bad. You got your water over there. Wood too. Only thing wrong is the skeeters."

"Ozark," Griffin said, "this is …"

"Chapman's my name. And her name's Kit."

"Chapman, Kit—this is Ozark Range."

"Mighty pleased to meet ya'll," he replied, extending his hand. He was especially gracious with Kit, studying her with interest and surprise. He looked like a wizened old prophet—a gray-haired black man in faded denim overalls.

"Then you must be Griffin."

"I am that man. So, tell me, what's a pair like you … doing in a place like this?"

"We want to visit Ray," Kit chimed in. "He's very outspoken on the nature of the universe."

"Really?"

"Plus," I added, "we just ran into some trouble. In town. It seems to reason we would be safer down by the river."

"They's in your face?" Ozark wore a knowing expression on his furrowed face.

"Literally," Kit replied. "Does it happen often around here?"

"Sure enough. But it don't do no good to get yourself riled. Don't make sense. Just gotta turn the other cheek, like The Almighty says."

"Yes, but," I found myself answering, "doesn't that get hard? After a certain point?"

Griffin chuckled. "You do this long 'nough, ya grow accustomed to it."

"Yassirree," added Ozark. "Just turn the other cheek. Let them be the ones to burn in the fiery furnace."

"Well said, Ozark."

"In my family," Kit said, "the motto was fuck with others before they fuck with you."

"We're all products of our environment."

"That's what I mean. It's alien to me, this idea of letting lowlife assholes get away with this shit."

"By the common definition," Griffin continued, "we're the lowlife assholes."

"You're just talking semantics now," Kit replied.

"Am I? Aren't we bound by what society thinks? Who can exist without its influence? Unless you remove yourself entirely."

"This," I said, motioning to the surrounding camp, "seems kind of far."

"Yep, I guess it is."

There was another awkward silence. I felt no desire to leave, which could be unsettling if I cared to think about it. The hobo jungle was where we belonged. Men like Ozark and Griffin were our allies. Outside this sanctuary we were regarded with contempt. I wasn't sure whether we'd revealed too much in the way of our naïveté, though it must've been obvious we weren't exactly hobos. I didn't think that these two were the type to take advantage. We excused ourselves and continued up the trail in search of Ray. We passed several more sites, from one of which emanated a particularly offensive smell. The fruity, sour odor of these hobo camps was the most difficult thing to get used to. We were nearing the end of the path when we spotted him—his tubby, hairy chest drooping over his cutoffs.

"Hey, Ray!" Kit shouted. "How's it going?"

He didn't recognize us at first, but then he lit up. "Hey there, kids! This's a surprise. I thought you were goin' to the city."

"Nah," Kit answered. "We decided to visit you instead."

"Where your two friends?"

"Oh, they went on ahead," I said. "To Seattle."

"Well, you make yourselves right at home. You been swimmin' yet?" We shook our heads. "No? Well, you two gotta go swimmin', that's all there is to it. Smart person beats the heat by using that river there. Shoot, I just spent the last couple hours floating down from the bridge." Indeed, Ray was dripping like a cocker spaniel ready to shake. "See this empty milk jug? I just put the cap on like so ... and bingo! There's my raft. How about that?"

"Looks like fun," Kit replied without irony.

"Tell you what. Put your packs over there by that tree, and I'll show you the best place to get in. Be back in a minute." Ray's shack had a plywood roof less than four feet off the ground. It was kept upright by crates and branches and whatever else he could find. There were twenty-five-pound sacks of rice and kidney beans propped up against one tree, and a plethora of canned goods. He had a collection of makeshift cooking utensils arranged neatly on a tree stump. Compared to the other neighboring campsites, his was a paragon of order and cleanliness. A hardcover edition of *The Peloponnesian War* by Thucydides lay open on a nearby rock.

Our friend reappeared from the shrubby undergrowth. "You kids ready?" he asked. "Just had to fix some stuff with my neighbor before we went."

"Sure, we're ready," answered Kit.

"Lead the way."

Ray showed us his shortcut to the river, then left us alone. We stripped down and hung our clothes on the bushes. A tree snagged on the riverbank functioned as a dock. I waded out to the river's midpoint, while Kit soaped down and brushed her teeth. The river was almost as warm as the air. Its muddy bottom squished between my toes. Kit and I dried in the sun, exchanging backrubs. Refreshed, we regained the path back toward Ray's camp.

"So," Ray said upon our arrival, "how was the water?"

"Sublime," Kit answered.

"Real nice."

"You two gonna hang around for a while?"

"Maybe," I said. "You mentioned they might be hiring, Forest Service even."

"Darn right they are. I've been turning down jobs. Got me one as a cook, I'm pretty sure. On a ranch outside of town. Like my haircut?" Ray turned his head in profile.

"Looks sharp," Kit said.

"Yup," he sighed. "I do believe my luck is changin'. There's tons of work round here. You two oughta stick around."

"Possibly," I said. "But I don't know about this town."

"Lyon is a tough place, I'll admit. But they're hiring. Like crazy. Why, I got another interview tonight." He stopped to search for his bottle of whiskey. "You mind?"

"Not at all," Kit said.

"Go ahead."

"Don't mind if I do." Ray handled the bottle as a priest would a chalice. He sniffed its contents, then took a deep breath, "Gotta get ready for this," he said, then quickly gulped the contents. "Weeee yowww!" He shivered. "Tastes good."

"So, you have another interview tonight?" I queried.

"That's right. First Harry and I are gonna go dumpster diving. He's the guy lives over at the next camp. I've been having luck over by that supermarket." He took another swig. "No locks." Ray stood up and walked over to the clothesline. "See this here?" he asked, pulling an oversized coat down from the line. "Found this in a trash can. All it needed was some cleanin'. Washed it in the river, and bingo! Like new." He put it on for our benefit. "Fits pretty good, don't it?"

"Yeah. You look sharp, Ray," Kit said.

Ray seemed quite pleased with himself. He replaced the coat on the line, then went over to see if Harry was ready. "Okay, kids," he said upon returning, "Gonna hit the dumpsters now. Then I got that interview. Don't know what time I'll be back, but you're welcome to stay here for as long as you like. You help yourself. There's some coffee in that tin, and you can see that bag of beans over there. They take some time to cook right, so you might not wanna deal with them tonight. There's drinking water in that jug there." He paused for a moment. “All I ask,” he added, “is that you don’t rip me off.”

“All right,” Kit replied. “We won’t, then.”

CHAPTER 13

It's not as if everyone out here on the trains is a boozer. Take this conversation that I just had, silent on a siding again, a break from the relentless thundering, as the engineer waits for the green signal to go again. I'd noticed him for the past several hours. He was already established in one corner of the boxcar when I leapt in, after my trusty duffel bag and the plastic gallon of water. We ignored each other for the first hundred miles or so. Then, an invitation, a question, from his corner of the boxcar.

"You have a light? By any chance?"

"Sorry," I replied. "I don't smoke."

"No problem," he answered. "Should probably follow suit. But you know how it goes with an acquired habit."

"Where are you heading to?" I asked. He sat up on his bedroll, pulled his coat around his shoulders.

"Mind if I join you over there?"

"No problem," I answered.

"I'm not sure," he continued. "Think this train will change crews in Flagstaff, though. I'll make my decision then."

"What's that yard like?" I asked.

"You new at this?" he asked, looking directly at me.

"Down here I am. I know the Spokane yard well, from my days up North."

"So where you headed?" he said. "If you don't mind me asking."

"Flagstaff, I guess." We both laughed.

"Name's Samson."

"How biblical," I teased. "Where are your golden locks?"

He laughed. "I get that a lot. I used to have them when I was young like you. Easier out here without your hair blowing all over the place. But then time took care of that."

"My name's Chapman." We shook hands. He looked to be in his mid-forties, sunburnt, couple of tattoos on his forearm, a pleasant demeanor. "And I'm not that young," I continued.

"If you don't mind me asking, what're you doing out here? Despite what you say, you seem young to me."

"You go first," I replied.

He laughed. "Let's skip it, then. Sure, we both have our reasons."

The train started up, but we continued our conversation over the noise. Turns out Samson wasn't exactly a seasoned hobo. He'd served ten years in the Army. "Didn't know any better," he laughed. "It was what you did after high school in my town." He could afford a bus ticket if he wanted, but preferred the freights, though he acknowledged that it was increasingly uncertain who else you'd encounter out here. More violent than it used to be, he said. I didn't press him on the specifics of why he was out here, but I guessed it had something to do with disappointments in his life.

This particular train must have been one of their priority ones. It didn't stop again for hours, and kept a fairly swift clip. When we reached the outskirts of Flagstaff, or what we both guessed was Flagstaff, the train finally slowed to a pace slow enough to disembark relatively easily. I'd decided not to risk the open question of how best to go about a large urban yard, so Samson and I went our separate ways. "Good luck!" he shouted to me as made my exit, jumping down from the still-moving boxcar. "You too, guy!" I shouted back, now safely on land.

Looking back, I realize I've had some talent for maneuvering out of situations or circumstances when something inside commanded me to do so. But with the household, I'd become a prisoner of my role, a visible citizen of my animated city. It was important work, and it existed well outside the vagaries of any personal moral code. The novelty of being salaried had carried me forward successfully, as this was, in fact, my life. I could do the pitch in my sleep after the first couple of years, and whether it was a church or a civic group, it went something like this.

"Look, over ninety percent of people in prison will be coming out someday. Do you want them living, unsupervised, in some cheap hotel, alone, in the part of town we all try to avoid? Or, say, in your own neighborhood, down the street? Or would you rather have them in a supportive, drug- and alcohol-free residential community, where they're monitored, as they genuinely try to live a crime-free life? If someone doesn't re-offend, that's one less prisoner the taxpayer has to support. At well over fifty thousand dollars a year. Our community is safer if a person can actually live a law-abiding existence, and Hope House is there to facilitate these positive transformations. Over seventy percent of our residents do not re-offend, which is in stark contrast to the usual recidivism statistic. As a private charity, we rely upon individual donations to sustain our vital enterprise, as well as volunteers who cook dinner at our house on many evenings. Such a hands-on involvement from these volunteers sends a clear message to our ex-felon residents that society will accept them, give them that second chance, if they in turn are willing to change their lives. In this way we become a community of reconciliation, and truly serve a larger agenda of public safety in the process."

And so forth. Okay, so this is *not* what fellow graduates from my college chose to do with their respective lives, but we all have our challenges, right? Plus, something deep within has always pushed me toward the more unusual choices. Just trying to find the right life. I did enjoy a given day's chosen finery and the amnesia of a late morning, which sometimes led to an afternoon of good deeds; this vocation created out of thin air, a blend of self-interest and caring.

It was a low bar perhaps, but I flinched when Callahan appeared in my father's donated khaki suit on Sunday morning, ready to sell tickets; there he was with his cigarettes and card deck and thin frame, alert after sleeping it off in the woods again, we suspected. Watching me from a distance, his countenance impossible to read—that's what twenty-five years in prison will do. "You forgot your coat," he said softly, with that Southern drawl, handing it to me. "And your keys." His years of observing, silently, in the various institutional yards The high art of not being deciphered.

Callahan. He was always there, making sure things in the house didn't get crazy. We deputized him almost immediately—his wiry presence and continual cigarette. I couldn't bring myself to read his file, but at some point there was no need, as I was in charge of simply getting the funding. I got the gist from the others. In many states he'd have warranted the electric chair, but he was released to us under geriatric parole. Suffice it to say that in his youth he was a jealous Irishman just released from his service in Korea, and his rage extended beyond the object of his affection to her immediate family. The Callahan that I came to know was not the Callahan of his crime. Come Sundays he was with me—always—though he'd never actually go inside the church, as I went about the task of explaining Hope House to the assembled. "I'm not big on religion," he'd tell me with that South Carolina twang. "But you go on ahead. I'll make sure the tables are in the right place, and we'll be waitin' for the folks when they come out."

We had some very financially rewarding weekends together (*all* of the services, including Saturdays), and I considered him staff, as he slowly counted the money and arranged the raffle stubs ever so neatly.

It's not easy being outside like this when it rains—and it does rain—my favored piggyback again—but the truck undercarriage only goes so far in the way of shelter (the water's seeping into my sleeping bag). Samson notwithstanding, most of the folks I encounter out here want to be left alone. My look might be puzzling to some, as it was to Samson, but they have more important things to concern themselves with. I'm polite, and if someone wants to talk, that's fine. It's kind of hard *not* to, given the absurdity of the circumstance. The only danger is when you discover yourself to be outnumbered—groups can be problematic. There was that time up North I had to jump off the train just outside Sheridan, before it made the yard. I don't like to invoke stereotypes, but that particular group was intoxicated and angry and didn't care for my presence in their vicinity.

It's *different* down here. I know the routes in the Northwest well—the best yards to catch out from, where there's a security presence—but down here is a different matter. I know that this train is headed to California, I can figure out we're going west. But I have no idea where the crews change or what town comes after

Flagstaff. What might await me there in the yard? I've been told repeatedly that they arrest you on the spot, unlike up North where it's understood that hobos built the West. And as a rule, the urban yards are somewhat menacing, in vivid contrast to the sleepy, rural yards in Montana.

There was always that strange unity that I felt with the Hope House residents. We gathered during the dinner hour, at the table, and their stories were made starker by those of their tattoos that were visible, even with some residents wearing our recommended long-sleeved shirts. On a good day we could take on anyone or anything—the uncertain energies vanquished. On a good day there was the sense of an unlimited ability to assemble a life. I would dare anyone to accompany me to the bus station, where we'd pick up our innocents in their prison blues. I received nourishment from not only their sincerity but also their uneven efforts. How was I supposed to go back unchanged into my former world?

It was never my intention to become so unusual. But I could lose myself in our shared triumphs of won jobs and perfect attendance at the parole office. And yet, in their lives of lost connections, when things went wrong, they went wrong.

But *not* on a good day,

"Eee, no," Ernestine sighed, with her lunch pail and new boots. "It's hard work," as she got into my idling car. "*Damn.*"

"But the job is working out, right?"

"Yeah," she replied distantly. "They're good people. My bosses."

"That's a snappy uniform you have on."

"You mean this shirt?" she said, pointing. "It's red, isn't it?"

"Yes it is."

"Seriously red." She laughed, which, for Ernestine was rare.

"It looks nice," I replied.

"I guess it's all right. What kind of crazy can we expect when I come home tonight?"

"You just have to give Maestas a chance," I answered, pausing. "He's younger than you. And with his issues—"

"We all got issues," she said impatiently. "We're convicts. No offense."

"None taken."

"I just need to relax when I get home. Don't need to deal with a lot of crazy. That kid's got no respect."

"Can't you at least look at him? You two make for tension in the house."

"Eee, no," she protested. "I just need to be left alone. Is that unreasonable? To not want anybody in my face?"

"That's fine. Just remember we're a community, you know? Like we talked about in your interview inside. Remember?"

"That must have been a trip for you, eh?" she answered, smiling. "Coming into our world with your questions. Most people wouldn't bother."

"It's my job."

"But you could be doing something else. Smart people gave up on us a long time ago. Have you read my file?" She looked at me with curiosity.

"Of course I did. It's part of my job. Obviously."

"Well, it's not so bad. I just needed money. And I get mad."

"You have issues."

"That's right," Ernestine laughed. "I have *issues.*"

"I've noticed."

"You should've seen me a couple of years back. Sheeit."

"You're doing well right now, Ernestine. That's what matters."

"It's nice of you to pick me up and drive me back from work. I told my girlfriend back inside. She'd like to meet you."

"That would be fine. When does she get out?"

"Not for a long time."

"Are you going to a meeting tonight?"

"I probably should. I'm just tired."

We pulled into the driveway. Home. Maestas emerged from the house and didn't acknowledge us.

"Little punk," Ernestine said between her teeth.

"It's okay. Just don't let it get to you."

"You know, it shouldn't be so hard … to stay sober in a program like this."

"You mean it's on that level?" I tried not to show my hurt.

"Stuff goes on here you don't know about."

"Maybe I know more than you think," I replied, trying not to be defensive.

"Whatever. I know you do your best. Not bad, coming into our world like you do."

"Come on. I know *some* things. I got arrested once as a kid. Fourteen and intoxicated, after curfew—"

"Yeah," she said teasingly. "I could see you doing that. You remind me of somebody I knew, this white kid—"

"Back in Dulce?"

"No, later than that."

"Anyway, just try to make this work, okay?"

She was silent for a moment. "All right."

The fact that Hilda, my Board President, was a minister didn't exactly help my situation. She probably gave me a chance in those initial few months, but any good feeling between us seemed to evaporate as my management style became increasingly apparent to her. Rules existed for a reason, and, especially with this population, needed to be enforced. It wasn't as if I gave our residents secret second chances all of the time—hardly—but all it takes is one confidence betrayed, and the perception settles in. I can't deal with being patronized, or the way she'd talk to her doctor husband as if he were a child man. It was probably a generational thing—roles understood and unquestioned early in life—but don't come my way with nonsense Kit and I would never allow in *our* relationship. Kit and I were equals, always. I was not a child man, at least in that way, and I'd never be condescending toward her. I probably shouldn't have rolled my eyes at the Board meetings. "Why didn't you send *me* an invitation to our annual fund-raising dinner?" the Reverend Hilda wanted to know. "Gee," I replied, trying to restrain my sarcasm, "we've only been working on it, talking about it, planning it, as an organization, for the past *four months*. You've been a part of all of those meetings. I didn't realize that you also needed to be sent an actual invite."

The rest of the Board seemed to be fine with my leadership (they should have been, seeing as how I recruited most of them). And of course when my basketball buddy Salazar was elevated to Vice President, that should've been enough to protect me from intrigue. But when Annette arrived as the new hire from back East, her alliance with Hilda was immediate, and my fate was sealed.

Back then I traveled the parties, some of them memorable, for pay. On behalf of Hope House. Back then, when donors at their banquet tables stretched their giving range and were open to possibility, despite the lifeless monotone of the annual United Way breakfast. But always for a good cause, especially ours, and me trying to be positive in the face of the assorted cheesy donated items; securing those donations, projecting gratitude, sometimes being surprised by authentic generosity. And on the basketball court, hitting up my jock friends:."Why do you bother with those people?" was a response that I remember. "Can't they fend for themselves?"

All of this activity, for *years,* trying to remember the names of our nightly volunteers. For what? To end up sleepless and muttering on a now eastbound freight train? (California no longer). To be overt with my backpack, walking down the avenue of a strange town? There's a statement, I suppose, in this vanishing, my absence.

I should mention just how deep my connection with Kit is. I take it for granted. We had good times in our small-town Montana existence, which I recruited her to from her lakeside Idaho ski mecca. I remember her walking the dogs along the Yellowstone, excited after a successful morning in her studio. She was always my fun companion. We'd cruise the thrift shops, make fast friends of interesting strangers, even host Thanksgiving dinners in our adopted town of Luxor. We were a pair, and it was safe to tell *anything* to her—that was our understanding—hopefully I lived up to my end of the bargain. But we were so young and so lost, trying to find our respective adult lives. We rejected so much—that too was our bond—and I loved the defiance in her clear brown eyes. She's still so beautiful, with her thick, curly auburn hair and self-effacing manner—*not* what she presented when we'd first met—and her quick humor. That is what I see instead of her illness, whatever it ultimately proves to be, suspicious as she is of her diagnosis. It's not as if I am abandoning her by leaving—she told me as much, that she has to handle the future on her own—but clearly I'm not exactly a noble helper by being out here. Plus, our relationship has always been defined by contradictions. How we'd split up, get back together, never split up, and so on. I love her *so* much. And miss her when she's gone, like now.

What will they say about me in the elegant foundation office? Will they continue to support Hope House? Their urbane foundation director who adopted me like a wayward boy, the subtext of our worldly understanding—he knows the complexity outside his office's polished floors. It'll probably not surprise him. Foster had seen so much in his law practice. If he *was* waiting for me to outgrow the annual chore of philanthropy, what I'd signed up for, then there you have it. He probably observed signs toward the end—late as I was with the reports and deadlines, showing up characteristically distracted and at the last minute.

Foster had my back, as Cortez and the many others had, over these seven years. Periodically we had our charged needs when the funding stream stopped, and then there were the inevitable emergency Board meetings. But he responded—representing the family foundation—timely, sensing trouble on our end, yet always with the formality of the monied. In the middle of our nonprofit drama, some of my well-meaning Board members resigned, invoking reasons such as a sudden desire to travel, or to learn a foreign language; perhaps it was *not* the emerging tension between Hilda and Annette and me that sent them away, having to witness it at every monthly Board meeting. Their letters of resignation were careful, magnanimous, and always submitted before the actual meeting, so that they didn't have to attend.

All Kit wanted from her quiet life was a hint of sanctuary and what we maybe couldn't have together. This direction showed promise despite the thievery in our neighborhood—yet another burglary of our house, which was ironic, given my line of work. Meanwhile, I was so consumed with the adrenaline rush of working at Hope House that I was certainly not much of a partner. No wonder she had doubts about me, or at least difficulty in visualizing our future together. Then the halfway house drama began to take over her life as well. She'd have to answer the phone, or the front door sometimes, and handle the pathology of addiction. Was it Cortez who'd sat in our front yard howling that one night? And the *cars* that would pull up, speakers blaring. Kit looking at me like, did she sign up for this?

I still couldn't pull myself away from Hope House. It's something deep inside me—this need to work, to occupy myself in the consuming light of activity—and why wouldn't it have an effect on my personal life? Back at college, I sometimes passed on returning home to Iowa for the family holidays. My idea of a restorative break was to be virtually all alone in the campus library, catching up, their abbreviated hours getting on my nerves.

And yet here I am in this sprawling yard—big for a smallish city like Gallup—heading East now indisputably; I had no burning desire to go to California anyway. The tracks stretch in either direction, and that's the closest I can be to the concept of infinity, or so it seems. In the other world—the salaried one—there was always some urgency, some resident conflict or problem with meeting payroll or a neighbor concerned about what was happening across the street. Kit deserved something better, and with her illness, why couldn't I get my priorities straight? Especially when Hope House was less able to provide the escape that I seemed to need, as I was suddenly not welcome on the colorful premises I helped to create.

Still these images come, well beyond my fabulous five, the remembered world of Hope House alumni. Like Taneequa. Where do I begin there? What a good singer she was, though other residents would roll their eyes as she treated the house to her version of "Amazing Grace." Overweight, yes, and liking crack, which seemed to be a contradiction. I met her mom one day as I waited for Taneequa to get dressed for Sunday church. The house was well kept and in a decent neighborhood, just across from an unusually green park, close to the airport. Her mom told me Taneequa had been homecoming queen her senior year in high school, that others had ridiculed her prospects—given her weight—but that her daughter had insisted that she could win that crown, and win it she did. It was a great moment for their family, watching her at halftime with the tiara and the robe in school colors, her attendants following in procession. Better days.

And there was Charlie. A solid fellow who anchored his offensive line in high school. I can't remember exactly what his crime was—I was always bad that way—and from the rural part of our state. I don't think he was ever in trouble before, so he stood out when I interviewed him at minimum restrict. As with Callahan, we elevated him to house manager almost immediately. If nothing else, he was *normal*—and an imposing physical presence, a man of few words. The other residents respected him. He was also a skilled mechanic, so finding gainful employment for him proved to be no big deal, unlike with many of the others. He became one of our success stories, He'd just wanted to put the whole episode of incarceration behind him. After he finaled and was off paper, I remember him asking me if there was any way that he could get his gun license restored. He missed his autumn hunting trips. I told him that I would look into it, but a felony is a felony, so he shouldn't get his hopes up.

Of course I can't forget Randi—a smart girl who should've been in graduate school somewhere, very proud of her newfound sexual orientation. She looked like a wood nymph, with sort of elfin features and a quick way of moving. On one of our many car rides, Randi insisted that I change the radio station. In the process I discovered techno and then upgraded my car speakers accordingly. I also remember when she ran into trouble—I think she was trying to steal someone's identity. There was something in the way she immediately put her hands behind her back when the parole officer asked her to turn around, just how *familiar* she was with that specific movement, that told me all I needed to know.

I'm continuing to give free rein to the memory of these Hope House alums. I wonder where it will end? I clearly stayed at the job too long, which is a common occurrence no doubt in the workaday world. That much is clear. My mom always told us that anything worth doing is worth doing well. I can't escape her legacy. Or my dad's.

CHAPTER 14

"What're you doing in here?" The ray of a flashlight on my red marshmallow bag.

"Just waiting for this train to get moving."

"Don't you know that you're on railroad property?" the man continued. "You're trespassing."

"I'm not bothering anybody."

"You're bothering *me,* and that's enough. Now gather up your things and get out of here. Or I'll call the police."

"So you are not the police?"

"Railroad security."

"Give me a minute," I replied, quickly taking inventory—flashlight pen, my journal, water jug, my special boots. "It's all right as long as I'm off railroad property, correct?"

"I wouldn't advise running for any train. Some guy lost his leg doing that last month."

"I'm just saying."

“If you're crazy enough to try. But they'll get you at the next yard. I guarantee it.” He paused. “I'd make a point of alerting them to your arrival.”

“Okay, I understand,” I answered, continuing to gather up my things from the rain-soaked rusting-steel surface. “But for extra credit, can you tell me where this particular train is going?”

He hesitated. “Well, as you can tell, it is on the eastbound track. That should give you a hint. “

“Fine. But I mean, Gallup? Or Durango?”

“Don't you have anything better to do with your life? Now get the hell out of here.”

I jumped down, duffel first, the sound of the rocks under my feet serving as my soundtrack as I found the edge of the yard, just over the strands of barbed wire fence. I'd been watching the movement of the other engines, and I thought I had the main track confirmed. I'd been in bigger yards, so it wasn’t that hard to figure out. But my antagonist, ready to follow through on his threat, made sure that I saw his headlights. It helped having done it before, knowing when to start running, the leap up easier with the piggyback cars that I preferred because they ride lower to the rail-bed. Spokane kept coming back to me—that one time.

I made it, though, having jumped on just before the train gathered momentum. Because I was in the open air, I had to glide past the waiting railroad detective. I probably could have waved, but I didn’t want to be disrespectful. I knew I'd have trouble up ahead, wherever that might be.

July 20, 1987

My name's Chapman. I have to remind myself of that sometimes. I'm writing this journal under the assumption that I can figure it all out—the source of my conflict. Right now I'm with a woman named Kit Jones. We're huddled together before Ray's campfire, waiting for him to return from his latest job interview. We're his guests. This is the hobo jungle.

I'm anxious most of the time. When I do get distance, that's the conclusion that comes filtering through. I have these dreams. Dreams overflowing with portent, full of episodes of failure, the planes crashing, the fumble at Dartmouth in front of thousands, Father and I duking it out on various cliffs of the world.

My family embraced routine. Tradition. That's a better word. Now my life spreads before me as a lie. Or, at the very least, a blatant misreading of what I was taught. I can't help but look backwards. I know it isn't healthy, but in many ways it seems preferable to my present surroundings. Not that I find it insulting to break bread with hobos; it's simply different from what I'm used to. I'll admit it. It was a brighter world back then. Meaning was not an issue. Give me back those playing fields, those gymnasiums. The classes. And the friends—we were the cool kids.

I am thankful for my immediate surroundings. Little is asked of me here. The transient camps, old hotels, and freight yards. And me, with all my advantages.

Maybe there was a downside to my athletic past—the inescapable conversations of the locker rooms, impossible to tune out or forget. As if the others were guardians of some dark truth that always mocked my sensitive ears. It seemed wrong to me—a misreading that went against my experience in these matters—but undeniably I was being initiated into what the people around me believed it meant to be a man, just because I was there.

This is how it went with Kit, in our recent conversation:

"What now?" she'd asked, riffling through Ray's shelves in search of something.

"Um … I don't know."

"Shit! I can't believe he doesn't have any cigarettes."

"If we stay here, we could get jobs. Like Ray said."

"*Jobs?* We've been through this."

"It was just a suggestion."

"What are some others? It's too late for pretending I'm just like everybody else."

"Well, we could get back on the trains."

"What would you do if I wasn't around?" she asked.

"I'm not sure. Maybe stay here with Ray. Learn about dumpster diving."

"Oh, come on. Don't give me that hobo crap."

"I guess I'd probably head to Seattle, after spending some time here. See what Rodney and Timothy were up to. I have a feeling Rodney nixed his cannery plans."

"You like that jerk, don't you?"

"I don't know. Nobody's perfect."

"That's for sure." Pause. "What do you do for money, anyway?"

"Odd jobs now and then."

"How are you going to support yourself in the city?"

"I got some money. At least enough for the time being."

"Well, let's go to the city, then," she said, waving her hand. "What are we waiting for?"

"We could be back in that town of yours with the next westbound—"

"Fuck that town. I should have left Crystal Point a long time ago. And besides," she cooed, drawing up next to me. "You're my dear."

"Dear?"

"Just kidding," she said, withdrawing her hand. "You're so cute. And sincere. I don't think I've ever known anyone like you."

"Um," I squirmed, "are you sure you don't want to hang around here? I mean, we at least ought to stay here until Ray gets back."

"Why?"

"Oh, I don't know. Wouldn't it be rude? Just to leave?"

"See what I mean? You're so *nice*."

The ten o'clock sunset's coming on, July on the Hi Line. Mountains in the distance, like tiny forgotten colonies. My flashlight pen. What I have not told her looms in the mountains' red silhouette—what is, what has been, and what shall be. What am I doing here, in this situation?

What I haven't told her is that my brother lives in a suburban community not far from Seattle. I've resolved to meet with him at some point. I intend to clear up my financial status once and for all, to cease this charade. Either I give it all away, or I swim in it happily, without ambivalence. It's come to that. But the mere act of reconnecting with my family's attention ought to be significant enough. There's always the chance of a head-to-head with Father himself.

I haven't told Kit about this, my real situation. She might sense it, as evidenced by her sardonic comments about my being a hobo. But she must realize that un-ambivalent (is that a word?) identity is for other people. I am this. I belong here. Not in the standard world. What is my deal?

July 21, 1987

"How are we going to locate these friends of ours?" Kit said, sleepily rubbing her eyes. "That is, if we decide to go to Seattle?"

"There are a couple of places."

"Hotels?"

"You could call them that."

"How long do you want to stay there?"

"In Seattle? Well, it depends on … how things go."

"What things?"

"Oh, just things."

"You know what I like about you? You're so direct."

"All right, I'm going to tell you some stuff. I've waited this long only because I wasn't sure how you'd take it."

"Don't tell me … you're wanted for some crime? You're on parole?"

"Nope."

"So you're not on parole?"

"I'm serious."

"It's always serious with you."

"If we go to Seattle, I plan on visiting my brother." She waited for me to continue. "I mean, this is a big thing. For me at least. I'm not on the best terms with my family."

"So? Who is?"

"It relates to money. You see … I have this inheritance."

"I *knew* it!"

"Oh, come on. It's not that much."

"Bullshit!"

"I mean, compared to what *you* have."

"You don't know what I have.'

"Well, it doesn't matter. I've decided that it's time for a resolution. Of some sort."

Kit laughed. "You're too much. Here you are, giving me a hard time about the way I live. And meanwhile, you're out here playing hobo."

"I haven't touched that money in years. If that's the way you see me, then we probably should go our separate ways."

"Oh, get off it. Can't we be honest about this?"

"I'm trying to be. I'm just sensitive to certain assumptions—"

"You're the one who's assuming things."

"Look. I've supported myself. Largely."

"What do you want, a trophy?"

"I don't mean it like that. All I am saying is that for some reason, it's been important to do that. I'm aware of the contradiction. It's been eating away at me."

"So why don't you just give it away? To charity or something. Otherwise, you might end up like me."

"I've thought about that. Not about ending up like you, I mean. But it's a legitimate question."

"I don't understand how your brother fits into this."

"Well, he's my money manager. All of my dividends go straight to him. He kind of lords over it, under the assumption that I'll come to my senses. One day."

"And has that day arrived?"

"I don't know. It might be fast approaching. All I know is that something has got to give. I can't continue living like this."

"So change things then. You worry too much."

"I can't help it."

"Take it one step at a time. Talk with your brother. Then see how you feel."

"Well, it's a little more complicated than that. If I show up there, the word gets out. Then I might have to face the whole family. Specifically, my dad."

"Do they live around there too?"

"Not at all. But they're always having these *gatherings*, you know? Reunions. And they expect you to follow their impulse. Catch a flight. Money being no object, of course."

"Of course."

"So, if word gets out, he might come himself."

"I see. I don't know what to tell you."

"Well, for starters, would you be interested in meeting them? Or my brother, at least?"

"I guess. I don't see why not. But your family's different than mine, I can tell. My folks don't want me around. I don't get your red-carpet treatment."

"How about the money stuff? We're similar in that respect. Do you have any ideas?"

"We're different there too. You have these problems, or whatever."

We found Ozark and Griffin playing cards. They were surprised to see us. "Did you locate that individual, Ray?" asked Griffin. We nodded, and he said, "Ah, good!" They were engrossed in a game of blackjack. "Should we choose another game?" he suggested to Ozark. "For the benefit of these two?"

"Maybe so," answered Ozark, peering at his face-down card. "But we gots to finish what we got goin' now."

"Okay. At the moment, I am in a very precarious situation."

"Man, you only down four stamps. Quit that cryin' and deal."

"Yes, but we got *company*, Ozark."

Ozark looked at us, then shrugged his shoulders. "The one thing we all got out here is time," he began. "Time and skeeters."

Kit suggested we go into town for a drink. Neither Ozark nor Griffin was keen on the idea. "Hey," she persisted. "I'll buy."

"That's not the point," answered Griffin.

"Then what's the problem?"

"This town. You said yourself you had a taste of their hospitality."

"Oh, *those* guys. I'm sure they're gone by now."

"You sure of that?"

"Hey, we survived. Thanks to Chapman here. You should have seen him."

"Now, Kit," I said, squirming. "Don't exaggerate."

"I'm not exaggerating. You did some fast thinking. Like Ray said, why be intimidated by a bunch of punks?"

"Because," Ozark replied, "I value my safety."

"Not only that," added Griffin wearily, "it's not like I got anything clean to wear."

"Oh, come on. You think the people around here will actually notice something like that?"

"You don't get what he's saying," Ozark interjected. "The clothes say a lot. Once they get to sniffin' you as a tramp, you in trouble. They like a pack of slobbering dogs. Cowboys, Indians—it don't matter."

"We ain't exactly popular 'round here," added Griffin.

"They'd just as soon kick our ass," echoed Ozark.

"But I'm *thirsty*," Kit protested. "Come on. guys, let's have some fun!" They said nothing. "Don't you get bored around here? Just sitting around the campfire? Moaning about life?"

"I like it," Griffin replied.

Ozark nodded in agreement. "That ain't our world, see?"

"What do you mean, it's not your world? You're here, aren't you?"

"She doesn't give up," Griffin said in my direction. I nodded. "I guess it would break up the routine. It's not like I don't enjoy a drink now and then. And a free one too."

"Now you're talking."

"Give me a minute to change my shirt. You got any place in mind?"

"We'll find one."

"I guess we will. What about you, Ozark? You coming?"

"Hell no."

"You sure?"

"I'm black. Case you ain't noticed. Plus, I got my bottle cooling in the river. You go on ahead."

The name of the bar was Cowgirl Corral. Heads turned as we entered. Kit sauntered up to the bar like one entirely at home. Griffin and I were a little more tentative. We looked at each other, a silent understanding passing between us, *An unobtrusive corner, and pop the bottlecap with caution?*

"Come over here, fellows," Kit entreated. "Tell this big-guy bartender what you want."

"A beer's okay for me," I said.

"You have any wines on special?" Griffin asked. "By the glass, I mean?"

"Of course he doesn't," Kit snapped. "Remember where you are."

"I forget these things, you know. How about a glass of cognac, then? I don't need the glass heated." The bartender hesitated for a moment, then disappeared into the back room.

"Why can't you have a shot of whiskey? Or a beer, or something simple like that?"

"You embarrassed?"

Kit reddened. "Not at all."

"Good."

"Why on earth would I be embarrassed?" she said with emphasis.

The bartender returned with our drinks. "Amazing," Griffin remarked quietly, after sniffing his drink. "The real thing."

"We don't get many requests for that," the bartender replied. "Only reason we got it at all is 'cause the owner's wife likes to drink it."

"Well, then," Griffin replied. "Here's to the owner's wife."

"The way I see it, I got mine," said a voice in the distance. "And if anybody's gonna take it, they gotta get through my line of defense." The man grinned, his gold-capped tooth on display. "And I been known to kick some ass."

"Is that necessary? Does it have to come to that?" Griffin asked the stranger, who'd suddenly invited himself to our table.

"I think it will," the man replied.

"You mean, you *hope* it will," Kit added caustically. The man laughed, his laugh full-bodied, guttural, knowing.

"I'll say this. If it does, I'm ready."

"Yeah, but," I began, "if everybody took your attitude, then it probably would come to that."

"I don't give a fuck one way or the other. That's my right. Big Joe's the name."

"Nobody's saying it isn't," Griffin said. "But when everybody's thinking in the negative, then it comes true."

"Let me ask you something," the man replied. "If you was in a tribe, or village, how you gonna choose your leader? The chief, I mean?"

"Well," Griffin began, "I guess our *tribe* would elect one."

"That's right. And what man'd you choose? The man who could do what for his people?"

"You've got women where they belong in this movie, don't you?" Kit interrupted. "I don't like men like you."

"Maybe so," he answered, grinning. "But least you know what I am."

"Oh … Gawd!" Kit said.

"What you're saying …" Griffin continued. "I think it'd be the man, or *woman*, who had the most integrity, foresight, and good judgment to lead the tribe."

"That's where you got it all wrong," the man replied. "It'd be the man who could provide for his people. Put meat on the table!"

"Of course," Kit sighed. "Meat."

"I don't see your point," Griffin replied.

"What I'm saying is when the shit starts flying—and it's comin', someday soon—only thing that'll mean a goddamned thing is a man's ability to provide for himself."

"Or his community?" Griffin added.

"That's right."

"Do I have to listen to this?" Kit sighed.

"I'm still not clear on where that community fits in" said Griffin.

"Think of it like what you'll be needin' when the time comes."

"Who knows?" Griffin shrugged. "Maybe your theory'll be borne out."

"Either way, it don't matter to me."

"You're such a *man*, Big Joe."

"That's right, baby. And if you ever wanna find out just how much, you feel free. I live just outside of town a ways."

I'd been growing increasingly uncomfortable ever since Big Joe intruded on our world. From the first time he leered at Kit across the adjoining table, I knew that a challenge might be in the air. That secret masculine code. I sat there in my chair, hoping that Big Joe would stop short of where I sensed he was going.

"Why don't we go?" I asked, finishing my beer.

"Sounds good to me," Kit added. "I don't like effeminate men."

"You'll find out one day, honey," Big Joe continued, smiling. "There're still men in this world. You just ain't looking in the right places."

"Come on," Griffin said, anger supplanting his usual serenity. "Have some class."

"See what I mean, baby?"

"We're having a sincere conversation. And you go on and debase us all," Griffin continued.

"Is that how ya'll talk down there by the river? You bums, in your jungle?"

"Come on, Griffin," I said, grabbing his arm. "This guy's an asshole."

"What'd you call me?" He was out of his chair.

"Don't mind him, Chapman," Kit said nervously, trying to whisk me away.

I hit him. I don't know where it came from, but I landed what I suppose could pass for a right hook. He laughed, staring down at me with a mixture of disbelief and anticipation. Before I knew what had happened, he lifted me off the ground, gripping me by the shoulders. "I didn't think you had it in ya," he began. "Squirrelly guy like you. Not too smart to mess with Big Joe. Guess it's time for me to show you why." He sent me flying into the table next to the wall. What happened after that I don't remember, though Kit later told me there was a big scene. The sight of someone actually taking on Big Joe had struck some responsive chord in the bar's inhabitants. Pathos apparently moved one burly farmer to rise from his stool and say, "Big Joe, you shouldn't be picking on young sprouts like that. I think you're a pansy." What ensued was a blur of flying bodies, airborne chairs, glasses breaking. My friends picked me up and whisked me out a side entrance, leaving the locals to release their pent-up emotions.

It got out of hand toward the end. The accusations against me were outrageous—surely Annette and Reverend Hilda could have done better. That night I kept my hands touching the stucco wall and followed the abandoned brick stairway to the city yard, where the freight cars slowly rolled past in chaste invitation. I needed to think.

So where *are* we without refusal? Otherwise the hair's dyed, the various psychotropic medications are slurped down, the boozy lunches are endless, artificial turf replaces the lawns, and life is measured by the hour. And so, what is it that I'm holding out for? What dimly recalled, seductive promise? Did I always have to wait for my cue from the priest, smiling his introduction? Searching the faces of the congregation for clues to my own sincerity—my intended humorous anecdotes sometimes falling flat. Back outside again, assuming our carnival tables, I'm an interloper among these good people, a stranger who doesn't hesitate to ask for their money.

Work became problematic under these conditions, though if it mattered there existed sweet esteem in the fives and tens. Always *that,* especially back when it mattered—me and my A Crew. And later on with Callahan. Those brilliant Sunday mornings when we had all of the doors covered, an announcement at the end, and everything seemed funny, even my anecdotes. No rival charitable groups in sight, no *sharing* of the proceeds, just the question and our unusual family at all the doors. Toward the end there was that Sunday in the small rail town, which doubled as a prison town, the historic blue walls and comforting Catholic iconography in contrast to the grain train in full silence outside. I wanted to catch it at that moment—it was beckoning me—as we waited in the silence at our tables, waiting for the parishioners to be released. It was hard to concentrate that day, as the trains kept rolling by. But I had my crew with me, and we were in our hustling mode. I wasn't ready to leave. Not yet.

CHAPTER 15

And now, booming activity all around—this empty automobile carrier, an expansive living room with sunlight pouring through. I have no idea where I am, but I should jump off before we reach the next yard—I'm sure that guy followed through with his threatened phone call.

No one can say that I wasn't involved daily—waiting for the donor prospect to produce his or her checkbook, the awkward silence after asking for the money, and to what end, ultimately? An endless river of clients who were sincere in their opportunity, but up against so much. Cortez's cursed life mirrored in his goatee, that severe expression of his when he worked on my vehicle. Then the handshakes, the hopeful banter of our program—dignity there, the larger picture—and perhaps it did make a difference. We'll all remember the cool autumn nights.

Enveloped as we were in the warm, earnest work, other things would be neglected. But what other deeds were there to do? The gracious, thankful felon and his new landlord—still unconvinced. We do prove ourselves, those of us who try.

Even these elevated moments couldn't prevent the onset of my own building doubt. I became weak against the darker forces—dark, like a living room full of wealth. I had a longing for a better world. Such faith.

There are so many beautiful reasons to be out here again, if I stop to think about it. Is this not in fact a celebration of life? The world we created together, Kit and I, paced off by her icy walk to the freezing studio in Luxor, and the wild river snaking past its outskirts. Heady exploration and the importance of animals, elemental cold, clarity distilled. The warmth of our youth, back when she could walk as far as anyone without getting tired. The pretend holidays with our family of dogs. The excitement of new dishes and the wind like a bad ocean.

Before that, in my real childhood, back in the green days framed by my small Iowa college town, coming home exhausted from practice, the sweet relaxation of order, the rotating seasonal games, the masculine smoke of the coaches' room. Wind sprints until the purity could be soaked out of us, August early-evening humidity. Lines of cruel boys in a Midwestern eagle dance, suffering understood. The relentless need to comply and the welcoming top ring on the depth chart. The hopeless, complex world out there, removed, waiting in all its futurity. The sadness of the ex-athlete.

Or Briscoe's left-handed shot during my workaday pickup games, arching so high. Briscoe the smallest and quickest one in the gym, in the late-morning games of the business professionals, of whom I was one, would set me up on the wing, encourage me to shoot. I've never been able to fully absorb the beauty of these games—personalities at war, joking accusations, the symmetry of success. Playing out like a ghost dance sometimes, what Boris would talk about—the trance attained, nervous and ecstatic, *heightened*—then back into the work afternoon. Followed by the pressure of Reverend Hilda waiting, and a kind of dazed clarity that would extend into the evening. Afterwards, over the seared tuna, I'd muscle toward Kit with fleeting empathy, trying to ignore the old voices. The sense of *everything* being one extended tease: victory, meaning, lost years, the wild moon. It should've been enough that she wanted to be with me, and I with her, our hands under the table, not desperate. But some hesitation, always, a loyalty to a past sadness that kept everything in place. Alone is what I know; I've always kept my best from everyone.

There are a few things that I am vigilant about, however—the horn of a distant train, morning concoctions, and who's in the room at any given time.

In those first few months of my position, I'd wait in the cold steel corridors for the locks to open. Lewis had come in with his folder, wearing those big glasses, and the guard took his leave politely, following decorum. We shook hands and the door closed.

"Well, Lewis, we received your application, as you can see. How're you doing today?"

"Fine, sir. The guards have been *so* nice to me."

"So tell me about your offense."

"Well," he laughed. "I can say I made some terrible decisions."

"What's with this late-in-life stuff?" I asked, having thought about his file during my drive to the penitentiary. "I mean, from what I can tell, you have no offenses in here until age forty."

"Yes, indeed." He laughed again, apologetically. "You see, I was going through some things, and I got caught up in this other lifestyle. I'm terribly disappointed in myself."

"You have a family too? A wife and two kids?"

"Yes sir."

"And you can't parole out to them?"

"Well, you see …" He hesitated. "I have some damage to repair. Things've happened to make them look askance. I want to make it right. Your program would allow me to do that, so that I could ease back carefully on the other front."

"Makes sense. Can I ask you something?"

"Of course." He met my gaze.

"What are you doing in here?" He laughed. "I mean, you just don't seem like you belong. Honestly, you remind me of my roommate in college."

"Well, sir, I think of that very fact often. Daily." He paused. "As good as people have been to me in here. It's a deep mystery. And the Lord will make His will known—"

"You know that we're not a religious program."

"That's fine. Beliefs shouldn't be pushed onto others. Rather, we believers aspire to lead by example."

"Well, then," I continued, "is it crack cocaine for you?"

"Yes," he laughed, "yes it is."

"So how will you stay clean on the outside?"

"I am confident that I will, as I have availed myself of the resources in this facility to examine my problem."

"Will you go to meetings?"

"Meetings? Yes."

"Well, I think you'd be good in our program," I said, with the finality my position afforded me. "Any questions about the rules and so forth?"

"No, sir."

"You do not have to call me sir."

"Okay," he chuckled again. "You just pick up certain things in here."

"I just have to clear it with my Admissions Committee."

"Bless you—" He caught himself.

"It's all right. This is what we do."

The interviews tended to go like this, the prospects presenting themselves in an understandably sincere light. It was probably too easy for me to cut the formality short and say, "You're in." I was lousy with the required paperwork, as I have mentioned. It was much harder, of course, when the answer was no. I'd lie about there not being enough beds. Or I could conveniently invoke the Admissions Committee, which didn't exist. I missed a lot in these interviews, it being a fairly random prediction on my part as to whether a prospective resident would work out, no matter how strong the intake might feel. It wasn't like assembling a city league basketball team, but no one could accuse anyone involved of lacking sincerity. The mistakes were easily absorbed, learned from—translated, stay away from younger inmates and beware of heroin. Early on, there was that fellow who pretended not to know me at the bus station, waiting there, ignoring our warm greeting. He kept on walking, no hesitation, to the Barcelona Tavern directly across the street. The two women who were of course lovers, but I didn't realize that until we'd assigned the pair to the same room in Hope House. Do you like living here? *Of course we do.* There was the psych ward, not necessarily the best recruiting ground for potential Hope House residents, as sympathetic and convincing as these individuals could be. They were always so attentive in the afternoon, after their therapeutic encouragement.

The doors would open to these prospects and they'd venture outside to try again. There was that guy with the scalded neck and my father's eyes—plucked from the psychiatric pod—and how he'd twitch. A nervous veteran. But I liked him. We read about him in the paper, weeks after he left us. No one was hurt, and he didn't have a bomb strapped to himself there in the bank lobby. Still, he was my intake, my mistake. He was just so sincere in his interview, with those soulful green eyes, which actually weren't exactly like my father's. I do feel bad about Maestas. We were going to journey North along with Cortez. I can understand now how unnerving it was for Board members to see Cortez and Maestas driving down the street in the executive director's British sports car—they were working on it, engine and body, as a house project. Taking turns with their version of resurrection. First my car, which was beat up, and then themselves.

Why should they *not* have a road trip? The innocent kind—nothing involving convenience stores or dark parking lots. Up North, where I assured them that they'd be well treated, although probably more conspicuous than they were used to being. They could take photographs, document the week like that celebrated week-long mountain adventure in reform school that I'd heard so much about from Maestas. It would represent a kind of high point in their quest for normalcy. Now where are they? Gone? I mean *gone*. That was the word on Maestas, and Cortez hadn't tried to contact me for months, which was kind of a relief. The indications were there for both of them: euphoric correspondence from prison after the inevitable parole violation, apology, intimations of a religious awakening, and no more threatening phone calls. Like the ones I'd received from Cortez. Still, there's always the possibility of a surprise encounter with either of them in the parking lots of the world.

The way Kit waved goodbye, cheerful, as I remember she could be, walking into her uncertain future, our shared secret fate still a question mark. Her brown eyes alert as they always were, and the delightful sway of her humor, even if it was cutting most of the time. She couldn't help it, coming from the family that she came from. We were determined, both of us, to live with or without the other, and in our off-and-on stretches of separation we were never truly apart. Kit and I confused everyone, including ourselves. Determined to reject each other, yet avid for each other's company. I can't even keep track of when I occasionally moved out—always into some temporary hotel—and when I moved back in. Our bond was problematic.

The memory of Kit waving is with me, suddenly hopeful as she turned and strode down the public concourse, evoking a better remembrance of our life together. It stays out here. Goodbyes can be final. Is this what I wanted?

At Hope House, our residents were always my steadier teachers. Starting with how the darkness within us was at least acknowledged by them and proceeding from there. Cortez in particular had my soul, which was most unfortunate. He got in there somehow. And his lying wasn't meant as *lying*; it became code for the truth of a situation, whatever that situation was, and our bond was one of faith in something better. Healthier, better, if he'd gone to the meetings, if I'd been clearer with him on my boundaries, et cetera. Problem was, I didn't understand where all of this was leading. He understood it as something else. The price of a life measured out in the weekly one hundred and forty dollars, which I couldn't afford but gave to him anyway. Crazy, this dynamic. No wonder he wrote me those letters from prison in his surprisingly feminine handwriting. Or his violent friends in the car, waiting for me to come out, my obvious concern for Kit inside the house, all of them knowing that there's no such thing as innocence. I was always amazed at his ability to track me down. When Cortez is arrested again, as surely he will be, maybe I'll visit him inside. Safer that way.

"This's my apartment and shit," Cortez motioned to what represented his latest hopeful plan. "What do you think?"

"Looks great," I replied. "What's the rent?"

"Three hundred and seventy-five dollars."

"You can't beat that."

"Charisse and I can make that between us." He laughed apologetically. "If I can do better with my problem, that is. I'm down to twenty-five dollars a day with the methadone. You know that shit eats your bones?"

"Yes, we have established that fact. But at least you can hold a job now."

"It's nasty. I've seen what it does to people," Cortez continued. "They'll be holding themselves, aching."

"Yeah, like I've seen you do."

"Boy, that last time, I thought it would never break."

"The key is to build on that, right? Once it *breaks*?"

"Do you want to buy my truck?"

"No. We've been through this," I sighed.

"I'll make it up to you someday, I promise," Cortez said. "I'll fix up that old Chevy back home. It's worth some money—I bet seven thousand dollars. I've had offers."

"Get your life together, that's all. Then we're even."

"You're a strange one, Murphy." His tone was teasing, affectionate. "Where you from, Eye-o-wa?" he asked, in his best version of Midwestern speech.

"Yes. And you're from this godforsaken place."

"You liked that menudo that night, didn't you?" he smiled. "I was watching you."

"You put a lot of effort into that, remember? I think everyone in the household appreciated it."

"I'm sorry I messed up and shit." His shoulders sagged.

"Look, it's a long road."

"You know, I didn't use to have this problem. I mean, I had *other* problems … but not this one."

"Did you pick it up in prison?"

"I know, man, it's fucked up. I swear I never tried it before. I'd look down on those kind of people, you know? The junkies."

"Why didn't you tell me that in the interview?"

"You wouldn't have let me in."

"Good point."

"Besides, you should know. The signs were there."

"I can recognize them now."

"Good. You're learning."

"That's right. Everything I never wanted to know."

Looking back on it, I truly can't believe I put myself in these situations—the limits of sincerity. These lessons I could absorb, but the other kind was another matter. The Board. Reverend Hilda. Her new ally, Annette. Bitterness seemed to come my way in this operation. The nerve of me, to be who I am. My sense of entitlement.

But out here, on the freights, I can soar, that's for sure. As long as no one messes with me. I can resurrect, perhaps, in a solitary way, brighter notions of human praise. Cortez was right about me being odd. Any number of reasons could bring me back, though, to Kit and Hope House. The camaraderie of the groups, and my limits when it comes to being alone. I do have them.

CHAPTER 16

Two hours of late-morning, masculine grace several times a week—that was almost enough reason for me to stay in my job. It reached a point where the longing for another world became too much to absorb on a daily basis. Teammates looked in my direction quizzically, wondering about my hesitation to shoot. I have a good shot. The younger ones were especially puzzled—implications of trouble, of complexity awaiting *them* in future years? This empty gondola car makes perfect sense, the idea of being carried off—of being truly unavailable—in some random direction, my conventional ambitions exposed.

To those who are *for reals* different—having the mark, born to be crushed, born to fill the graveyards—this should be no mystery. Stamina, absolutely essential, reasons to soften and slow down. Memories of family tragedy held in our Hope House gravel. People knew me around town for numerous reasons. Not that I can see a better way of being known, if it comes to that. Once released from the standards, and trying hard not to *confuse activity for accomplishment,* as my father used to say, we marched forward into our expansive clearing of promise—setting up a determined camp of reclamation—a program that may or may not survive the next year without my presence.

I was able to dodge my railroad detective by leaping off the train at the city's outskirts. I'm not exactly sure where I am right now, except that I was able to walk clear to the other side of the yard, off its premises, and climb aboard this stationary empty automobile carrier. Darkness definitely helps, I see no advancing and threatening headlights.

My favorite Board member wouldn't even talk to me. Harold was his name, one of the originals I'd recruited—he was in *their* camp now—eighty-something and staring straight ahead at the stop sign, ignoring me. For a reason. What I would've sacrificed for him, if he only knew, gray hair and hard of hearing and stooped over, but still driving that vintage Volvo coupe. He, along with some others on the Board, truly didn't understand the *larger picture*, my side of the story, which made for a somewhat depressing place for me to work. The Board. Our tangible phenomenon of shared history and simple loyalty gone at the stop sign. He was told things. By Annette. By Hilda. Predictable, how these alliances unfolded, spreading. A simple wave at the stop sign could have softened the reality for me a bit. There, at the stop sign, the two of us, as it was originally, before other personalities triumphed.

July 25, 1987

> They took me to the hospital. I came to as they were wheeling me into the emergency room. The throbbing in my neck and head was intense, but there was also a strange euphoria—the standard litany of worries gone, a cathartic fuzziness as I tried to hear what Kit was saying. Broken,

nonsensical thoughts orbiting in circles outside my body. Is she having a good time? Why do nurses wear white? What was my batting average that summer?

"What's your name?" someone was asking.

"Huh …"

"Your name. Who are you?"

Something inside made me laugh. That was a mistake. Something like lightning in my skull. "Oooh, man!"

"Is it bad?"

"Ooh …"

"Who are you?"

"Uh … who am I?"

"Yes, who are you?"

"Who *am* I?"

"Who are you?"

"*Who am I?*"

"Yes. Who are you?"

"Who am I? You mean, who I am?"

Walking the wall and captivated by my own shadow. On the grounds of the chalet lodge, now turned country club. The distant echo of forehands from the higher fields, and the musty, spider-ridden greenhouse. The pool is a section of cake unearthed and frozen in cement. Inside the lodge, ominous, labyrinthine hallways—irresistible, and so much like a life. When I fell that day, my head went crack. Like now. Freezing the parents where they stood, as the tennis balls rolled unheeded to the back fence. I awoke dazed, queasy, and wondering at the serious faces—the hijacked attention of grownups. I learned then that the course of destiny is often determined by crisis. Our goofy universe.

Who am I?

And the vacations. Right around this time of year, a station wagon instead of a vacant boxcar, a cache of candy off-limits but very visible, the rotten-egg smell of a brand-new air conditioner. Word games—animal, mineral, or vegetable? Down the highway with our motel guide, a four-star family. With two invited friends, Father absent, back home building a town. We're rich and getting richer. I crave a motel with a pool. A spaniel's bedtime—after reveling in the water, a grateful boy. Two more days of sugar-coated routine, the candy tin hidden underneath the front seat. Two more days and we make the ranch, bed down in the bunkhouse.

A stellar vacation, flapjacks molded by a grizzled cook named Blackie—I recognize him from TV. My very own horse for a week in a real corral. Horseshoes before dinner, square dancing after. A five-day backpacking trip into the real mountains, beyond evidence of civilization. I climb onto my wheezing, sure-footed horse named Smokey, and look-Ma-no-hands, but my cowboy hat is fastened tight. The rhythm is set, our slow line forward. Wrangler Sam stops dramatically to point out bear tracks—probably a grizzly's—in the mud. I'm Sam's favorite. I get to fly cast from his horse, behind his saddle, learning. At night, the smell of canvas and into my long johns I go—a warm child. For days the trout glide along beside us, a bent rod proof that we're guided. This was my favorite home movie. When it was time to leave, they had to drag me away.

Who am I?

Nostalgia. The longing for home, those vacations when the family would bend itself around a single promise. We're the family whose attention grabs the room. Every summer a celebration of that fact. Two weeks of open-ended sunsets; pickoff on the dunes, a baseball green with use. Sand and leather. A lone cottage, the knots of the varnished pine. Town boys, their crewcuts bristling, purity and forward motion. As the next-to-youngest, I would tag along. The daily rentals—go-carts and surfboards. Buffeting my brothers' reluctance, Mother is my champion. Still, I prove myself in the improvised games. Slow-motion boxing. Pickoff. Rock/paper/scissors. We're healthy boys— a jockish breeze blows through our family. Sweat drying in the cool wind. Healthy boys, lorded over by the absent executive father. Bourbon and profit, an unbeatable combination.

But for two weeks each year, he is actually *with* us. Father, possibly the most difficult word in any language. Silent, immovable, the lone rock I'll always wash up against. We boys, satiated with attention—surprising how it's suddenly enough. Two weeks spent in the weathered clapboard cottage. No phone. Cape Cod shortbread, a rumor of rusted chains under the sea, happily grappling with my tie. Even at that age, the mirrors were there. Mother explaining the reason for a widow's walk, the universe made comprehensible.

My world then, framed by hasty pudding in the morning. And bedtime stories. Games, improvised and traditional. Good-hearted competition. Excitedly nursing my jack of diamonds, my hand an open telegram. It's Father's turn to deal. The game is rendered special by his presence, an intimation of what a family could be. Bedtime and my special prayer. *Dear God, please keep us going like this.*

The other fifty weeks. Take, say, autumn. Father returning from work—fedora, black mustache, black cashmere coat. We boys in the den, guessing his mood. Usually severe, absorbed, weary. We'd watch him through the picture window. Father too intent to notice, taking inventory of the demands of the self-made. The crew at the office, a group in tomorrow from Burlington. The office. Today at the office, tomorrow at the office. His swiveling, long-backed leather chair, steady in its authority. We can be found within the picture frame on his mahogany desk. His staff deferential when we visit—secretaries, architects, all alert to our wants. The boss's kids. He rarely wanted us to visit, liking to keep this other side to himself.

Cleansed each Sunday, he never missed a day's work. Yet gone each evening by his third glass. Tall-glassed relief. His planned ascent into the propertied class, coming as he did from nothing. He finds himself a *boss,* with grown men under him, eager to please. His hard-ass reputation. Nightly we'd observe the transformation: from his car to the front door, the metal slivers in his wingtips click click on the slate walk. Perhaps he's anxious to begin his walk, sighing at the coat closet, sighing on the bed as he changes into his walking shoes. Whistling for the dogs and ruffling their fur as he sets out toward the woods. The woods, his escape, his domain. Our woods that he made happen through his hard work.

Through an open meadow and a clearing within sight of the house, then toward the distant back acreage. Our very long driveway, concealed from the highway. Dogs weaving and yapping to his determined pace, as his wife cooks soufflé and lamb chops and the kids trade baseball cards. Early-evening sunlight and a life cozy with routine. Routine softened somewhat after dinner by candlelight, drinks, and boys being boys. The evening paper on his couch, by the fire the boys built.

Father had his reasons, and they need to be respected. He's nobody's business partner, or the type who prevails in the end. The smell of leather in the back seat and the inky blueprints we hoped would reveal him to us. On Mother's cue, we blink at what should not be seen. I held my breath for the first seventeen years and learned to let the fundamentals wash past me. He grew accustomed to his influence, took it under his tongue like a communion wafer.

The woods—rusted barbed wire, oaks, and the echo of a woodpecker. A magnificent tract substantial enough for an echo, and no roads except an old farm lane. A trickling spring and a walk with my girl to the hidden, back acreage. Phoebe's fingers dutifully exploring, and my first requests lost among the sounds of the forest. In the meadow with her, a late November night after curfew but parents asleep. Pickup idling, the heated, wide-seated cab. My first pawings—uncertain, innocent, compelled. The tufted meadow luminous silver, Phoebe doesn't trust me *completely*. Initial clue to my complicated heart.

The woods, it all returns to the *woods*. "He's on his walk in the woods." Or, "We're going to pick blackberries in the woods." Or, "Mom, can we camp out tonight in the woods?"

Or, “Let’s go look for arrowheads.” Or, “Let’s find this family’s soul once and for all. I’ll bet it’s in the woods.”

Who am I?

The Fourth of July, parades, carnival booths, Tilt-a-Whirl. I file past with my teammates and wave my glove toward a flag as big as my grandmother’s door. The grownups gathered on her pillared front porch, toasting the passing horses. Visiting carnies, with their easy grins and foreign odor. Big-Hearted Bill From Over the Hill and his air guns with crooked sights. We gravitated toward *his* booth—manhood in a pack of cigarettes and the glib click of a lighter. “All you have to do is knock the pack off the shelf, and it’s yours.” The Ferris wheel gets boring. The Roundup, good for tricking a girl, to see what it does to her dress. But the Salt and Pepper Shakers, now that's a *ride.* Change from your pocket pinned against the cockpit as you kamikaze toward the pavement. Then reverse. Always a line for this one, the four-at-a-time thrill.

We'd count the days, our summer stamped official at the sighting of the first giant flatbed truck. We’d spy on their camp at the edge of town, take open delight in their coarse language. The way they pumped life into our town. Someone mentioned a cousin who'd run away with them. It stirred our hearts as they fitted the various sockets together. Cotter pins, scaffolding, and the smell of axle grease. It lasted for three days. Turns on the dunking-machine, ring the bottle and win the bottle. Too basic. Let’s hit Big-Hearted Bill’s again. At night, music and the tractor pull. Square dancing on the sawdust-sprinkled pavement. Let’s go sneak a cigarette instead, Big-Hearted Bill slipping us a pack like that, winking.

The parade, floats, jets buzzing Main Street, and cotton candy sticking to your fingers. No one's anonymous; even the Rotarians take their bows. It's easy; all you have to do is keep formation. Others eat snow cones, dress their children in plastic shoes. *Our* teams win. Later that day, I went three for four, including a bunt down the third-base line.

My *brightest* summer. Sweeping the boards, shoelaces in line, our tent the honor tent of the entire summer camp. In the afternoon, wind off the lake puffing the canvas flaps, and the mountain opposite. My initiation into privilege; these kids were different. I wondered about their diets, their teams back home, if they had any. They could neither hit, field, nor run. They cried a lot, threw tantrums. Among the counselors I became a magical boy, though my teammates back home could have seen through that in a second. I was chosen quickly. What were their lives like beyond this L.L. Bean world? Safe in their strongholds, yet denied ownership of their little native bodies, hesitant even at the sight of their own bare feet. Unversed in freeze tag and war ball and other games—what I knew in my rural bones—and how fearful they were on the low diving board.

I couldn't make sense of it. Even when we did what I didn't know at all—archery—I'd find myself in the winner's circle. In the lodge smelling of wood smoke, before the two hundred campers assembled, they awarded me the Camp Spirit Cup. I was embarrassed. Prodded for a speech, I stammered something about home, which I missed terribly.

My brightest summer. The Fort. Spigots. And preppie counselors who'd rather sun themselves than pay attention to us. Camp war games—naval and land—the Reds against the

Blacks. I'm a fleet-footed corporal. I dart past two sentries, running toward their camouflaged goal. While circling the senior aide entrusted with its defense, I'm tagged. Meanwhile, I long for Iowa. For the cracked infields of my home county. Parents' weekend especially rough—tears welling up—but given permission to at least call home. Growing weary of these clammy-handed boys with their myriad complaints.

Who am I?

Eagle Junior High, smokehouse brick, the barn-door gym, grasshoppers buzzing. The first intimations of pairing, like reluctant dragonflies. Mr. Lovejoy, with his bulging veins and short-circuited tranquility. We found the pills in his desk, his secret revealed. He baited his history lessons: palpitating hearts, the gavotte, the iron dragon with its razor tongue. The scent of *girl* everywhere; love as a leather bracelet with knots. Messengers were necessary, intermediaries, the baptism in being a diplomat. Our archaic school building by the railroad grade, aging, like the rusty county road signs. Our devotion was to our older brothers and sisters, to quarterbacks and cheerleaders. Our backfield mirrored theirs, a face mask like your brother's. After practice, the love knots around your wrist. Phoebe wore mine, along with leather boots and a pleated skirt. She displays, with the authority of rehearsal. *Two-bits, four-bits, six-bits a dollar / all for the Cougars stand up and holler ...* school as schedule, school as order. The darkened cave of the cloakroom, and a girl named Becky who wore gartered stockings and short skirts. (Instructions on the darkened wall.)

Other girls nicknamed by us swaggering boys: Snow White, Onion-Breath Beth, Four Eyes. Tentative laughter, as if confronting God head-on. A laundry bag full of gear—the jock badge—and savoring the bus trip each morning. No threat of a traffic jam as they take us to the boondocks and our 1919 building. Courtship, fledgling, daring, confused. In search of sheltered, warm places. The post office after dark. Or the boathouse, even though there was no lake. Cinema as pretext, plotting kisses and more, the back rows less conspicuous. Flocks of bandy-legged girls surrounded by packs of yapping boys.

Who am I?

Golf, long summer evenings, my terraced thirst, and a tin cup of water drawn from a pump. French-fried etiquette, the etiquette of brothers. We keep score because we are brothers. There we are, behind a foursome of grown-up fathers. A stocky man hurls his club into the woods, cursing the whiteness of his spikes. As for ourselves, we're brothers and therefore want the best for everyone—in all of its annoying simplicity. I, the younger brother, triumphant as my tee shot splits the fairway. Older brother mutters as he shanks right. Middle brother nudges younger brother, winks at his own decay. Two practice swings and the seconds before impact; hilarity and last night's date. What awaits this threesome after this round? An icebox full of cream pies. Steaks, deviled eggs, strawberries. Summer and Mother reign. Lightning bugs too, right outside the screened porch, where Father quietly sips his bourbon. Three brothers, their lives like whipped cream. Knowing nothing else except at night in the dreams they don't remember. We fit like the woolen sleeves over our drivers.

Who am I?

Sweating in the humid August morning, my summer job with Randy on the asphalt crew, after his mid-morning snack of donuts and cola. We covered the territory, only the two of us, on special assignment for driveways and seldom-used county roads. He teased me about college, called me "Slick," and we compared stories of our high-school feats. Randy was tanned, stocky, big shoulders, and he did not drink. Which I noticed for the first time when we cashed our paychecks, the union-scale road crew assembled, at the Summit Bar slightly after four in the afternoon on Friday, as we were paving professionals who built up a thirst as we met the demands of our chosen craft. We would take turn buying rounds, it still being daylight, and I became giddy with the taste of adulthood within the green bottles of Rolling Rock.

Who am I?

My own first vacation. Off to the Smoky Mountains and a healthy start with Phoebe. Her high-top leather lace-up boots, understood as parody, and her irresistible defiance. Senior year spent on her living-room couch, her mom asleep upstairs. She's bold, and I'm persistent. Surprise everywhere in that darkened room; I riot in the discovery of the feminine. We sneak away for two weeks in my pickup truck with camper, heading south. We pretend honeymoon, swimming naked in the mountain stream, young and gift-strong. Bedtime becomes my obsession, the vacation a mere pretext. She's willing, or wants to be, but has problems. I find one of her letters and discover the wisdom in boundaries (never read a woman's journal). I stomp off, making deep tracks in the sand, plotting my next move. The darkening motives with each decision. How does it square with bedtime? A stumbled-upon, hardcore solution. The motel room upsets our delicate passage. And for me, the first hint of a difficult masculinity. What it means to be a man; a life reduced to maneuver.

And then college, the Green Room, wind off the ocean, practice. Warm with books, threading past the thick-backed library chairs, all of them taken. Except my special one. Outside, the chilly wind tosses the leaves. A time when the assignment book reigned supreme. Late-night hours alone in the stacks, intent upon making up ground on the others. The others were spoon-fed Greek. My rural legacy and the irony of *that.* Girls in the hallways and my carefully planned visits to the water fountain. And practice, always practice. A red metal-grilled cage, pads mildewing inside, turf shoes and chin straps. The beery weekends and girls who would go only so far. You squeezed what you could out of bagels and ice cream. Muscles relaxed, you carefully polished off another book, a rigorous workout for the mind. In pursuit of the loaded résumé, my door-to-door campaign, to the dorms I went. I was elected. Senator Murphy. Dirty-nailed truth lay elsewhere. We all understood the concept of résumé.

Culminating in a Rhodes Scholarship attempt and my essay on how to make the world a better place. Ambushed by eight professors, the shock of being taken seriously. A long oak table. Glasses of water. Manila folders. A life according to the rules and certain revered, unquestioned paths. These men around the long oak table, sweating all over my innocent essay, using their well-trained minds to dissect the statement of an adolescent. “It reads like a letter,” one says. “This won’t do at all.” But … but … *I* wrote it. Eight pages of what I‘ll give back. And I will, too, if I gain admittance to this elect bunch. Afterwards, I await their verdict. They didn’t *like* me. They were not impressed with my answers. Whirling, I make for the sanctuary of a phone booth. Dialing the number for home, I’m not sure what to say. Strange tears. Mother answers.

All in the way of a self-definition. *Dear Diary*, you remain so patient with me, so forgiving, so understanding. In that spirit, the way Kit and Griffin and even Ozark have been coming around, checking on my status—Kit comfortably solo in her hobo jungle sanctuary. I'm feeling better, should get out of here soon. I hate to put others out like this.

July 28, 1987

“Well,” Griffin said with parental concern, “at least you’re on your feet. Might be a good idea for you to remain here in the hospital for a few days. Don’t suppose you could afford it, though.” I laughed. It hurt almost as bad.

“That’s okay,” Kit said. “I’ll pick it up.”

“My name's Chapman,” I heard myself saying, with more conviction than usual.

“Good, good,” answered Kit, visibly relieved. “Now tell me how old you are.”

"Uh … then? Or now?" They both looked puzzled. "Fifteen before. Twenty-six after." I was being tickled inside, though I dared not laugh.

"I think he's trying to make a joke," Griffin said.

"Oh, come on. Chapman?" Kit said. "He has no sense of humor."

"Well, a touch of irony, then."

"What I mean by that is, um … I was in a fight?"

"Yes, honey, you were magnificent. But maybe you better lie back down."

"Seriously?"

I checked out yesterday evening, with various pain medications, courtesy of the Lyon General Hospital. The shift in Kit's manner has been noticeable. She's been veritably fawning over me since the incident. I'm not sure how to take it. Not used to receiving all this nurturing. But it makes sense. I still can't walk for an extended period of time without getting dizzy. Kit improvised a heating pad made from a pair of Ray's flannel pajamas. She's been intent on success in this role, and some noteworthy side effects have begun to emerge. Like the appearance of the word *please* in her vocabulary. Or the way she suddenly bites her lip. It's been interesting to see this transformation unfold, though the implications have made me slightly uneasy.

If I weren't a floater, like I've become, then perhaps I wouldn't present myself as something other than an emotional diplomat-ambassador from the soft heaven of somewhere. Then the conversion would be one of appetite and muscle. No dimly vague notion of a better world to chase down, no last-minute heroics. Only an unhesitating brutality of benevolence as the world is truly joined. No more conspicuous moments. Explain to me how *this* isn't a valid choice, inhabiting a cold gondola car—wind through the vents—finally moving and gathering speed. Make an argument for me not to succumb to the vagrant path, with its benefits of anonymity and open-air nights. Perhaps for me it's a simple culmination of what I figured out early, instinctually, so why not give it a try?

The only possible vocational resting point for me involved an evangelistic gig, as if there was some big prize to be won. The prisoners, multiple in their ghostly visitations, and grateful even after their inevitable unraveling, which they always claimed as *their* fault, not the program's. Surely I could've been a better guide for them.

With some of us, all is won and forgiven in the immediate present—apprehension, brooding, sorrow—like addicts in a meeting. The ghosts who have the likelihood of death or relapse about them—Maestas, Cortez, Boris, Mary Lou—are like a parade of sincere, wildly unsuccessful phantoms. Their collective voice is one that needs work but shows promise. Yes, the healing in our shared agenda had proven extensive and transformative, a complicating shift negotiated as the surrounding world became more of a home—more than it ever was before, at least. My parents, and especially my dad, never understood that—why I cared so much about them.

Yet here I am, outside in the cold in the throat of my chosen deprivation. My prisoner ghosts are an understanding lot, being familiar themselves with barren circumstance, to say the least. Perhaps I'll run into someone like Boris out here on the freights. We used to joke about it.

CHAPTER 17

In the history of Hope House, the craziness started early on, in the form of a hefty Board Chairman who liked to talk big—this was before we even opened, when we were in our start-up phase. Dallas had become Chairman of the Board, maybe by default, and his meetings were colorful and full of references to imported steaks. I was new in my suit, charitable dollars starting to materialize as deposits were made. Our meetings increased, as a group we visited possible locations for our program, and we were euphoric when that one grant was doubled. Surprise awaited us, however, at the bank. Bad tidings. With urgency I dialed his familiar number.

"So Dallas," I said, "there seems to be some discrepancy between our books and the bank's. Would you know anything about that?"

"What's the problem?" he replied, voicing surprise.

"Well, they're saying that we have considerably less than we thought we had. The bank, that is."

"How much less?" More sincere concern on his part.

"Eighty thousand dollars."

"You're kidding!" More silence.

"You and I are the only signatories on the account."

"Are they sure? The bank?"

"Yes."

"That's fucked up."

"Yeah, it is." Silence. "Where's the fucking money, asshole?" I continued.

"I don't know, Chapman," he replied evenly. "Why don't *you* tell *me* where the money is?"

"You big fuck."

"As far as I know, you were the one making the deposits."

"Don't go there! Where's the money, guy?" Silence. "Come on, where is it?"

"I wish I knew," he said with a new plaintive tone. "I wish I knew." More than a hint of confession.

"I thought we were friends." I don't know why I said that at that point.

"We are."

"Bullshit."

"I'm sorry you feel that way."

"You fucker. Why'd you do it?"

"I think I should see a lawyer."

What followed was a turbulent summer, full of meetings, with our nascent effort hanging in the balance. The Board was ripped in two—the inevitable heated discussions about what to do and what not to do. Embezzlement. Doctor, lawyer, businessman, priest, our original Board all looking for the door. The messiness of a charity. Duped by one of their own, subject to unwanted scrutiny, reputations jeapardized, our nascent creation stillborn. Funders, law enforcement, zoning. The press. We somehow managed a legally binding confession from Dallas, in tandem with law enforcement, and no media coverage. But we never saw that eighty thousand dollars again.

Still, we survived. But not before I was warned by our newly elected Board Chair, Hilda, never to cry again at these meetings, that it wasn't becoming in a man. We absorbed the loss, miraculously, and one of our Board members produced an anonymous donation of fifty thousand dollars. Incredibly, we found a house—two adjoining houses, actually, with a large parking lot—and a neighborhood that didn't mount heated opposition to our presence. Papers were signed, our neighbors uneasy but agreeable, and off to the women's correctional facility I went for the first intake interviews. Then, the following month, to the minimum restrict corrections facility, so much like a summer camp in the distant mountains. I was the enthusiastic agent for all who'd listen—individually, collectively—to the prospect of a new life. Odell and the others were ready to be sprung, and none of their crimes were too severe. Mountain lions and the strange innocence of grim institutions.

My distant supervisor, Jerry, was a good model for me, streetwise in his middle age, caffeinated and thin, talking smack with our new residents. But he lived in another state where we had other houses, so he was of limited help to me when things grew problematic; he only came out occasionally to check on things, not to tread on internal divisions. He did, however, teach me the nuances of freeway driving in his hyperactive way, and he'd insist upon certain songs as we drove deep into the night on our way to Kentucky, anticipating the lanes and talking about the importance of our work. He was a wise man, dismissed by virtually everyone. He understood the gift of a large family, freakishly assembled around the dinner table, which was the model for Hope House. I trained in Lexington and was impressed, though he himself was ultimately exiled, representing a hint of what was in store for my own boyish reign.

And there was my other supervisor, resisting Jerry's teachings on all fronts, her scolding and relentless march toward propriety a throwback to the New England Puritans. New Hampshire. Her name was Brenda. Allied with Hilda and Annette, I was in trouble. The two of us—my distant misunderstood Kentucky supervisor and I—were to be converted by Brenda somewhere down the line, scolded into obeying the rules; hair up, Brenda's flowing dresses and humorless manner, a force to contend with by any definition. I was a problem for her—it seemed to be a pattern here. All of this was so new to me, I did my best. Or, at the very least, I learned to be tactical.

We'd have these good days, though, when everything seemed possible. Not just confined to our original five resident beds, we gradually expanded to seven or eight at a time. There was one rather odd grouping consisting of Raphael, Chunk, Doretta, and a couple of others whose names I can't remember. Jobs for everyone, I would say, and off we'd go together in my car, employment opportunities to provide a cornerstone for the much-sought-after positive, law-abiding life. Raphael, recounting his days as the locally notorious Living-Room Burglar to me, in between our targeted stops. The light through my sunroof, my black foreign car, which fit so well with the suit and tie. Chunk as solid as her name indicated, and her overall truculent demeanor. She had a kind of disturbing grin, and she seemed dazed by this new straight life of hers, or at least the attempt to attain one with us. I asked the restaurant manager when she was out of earshot, laboring over her application, "Can you hire her? She's sincere and doing well in our program." He looked in her direction uneasily. "Even dishwashing? She wouldn't have to deal with people," I said.

"What was she in for?" he asked.

"Oh, I don't know. It was drug-related. She's clean now. And under supervision."

"Well, let me review her application. Can I call you at this number?" he asked, pointing to my business card. Outside, Raphael had leisurely reclined in my front seat, awaiting his turn at gainful employment. His chances were much better than Chunk's, since he had an amiable manner and at least two marketable skills. But there was always the looming shadow of their inescapable history—the word *criminal*—that could be glossed over only in limited ways.

For lessons in loss, regard your brilliant Hope House residents and listen accordingly. This is a group experiencing lowered expectation and genuine trauma. Eppie could relay his imprisonment, what it was like for a young boy in the midst of incarcerated masculine brutality. Or Mary Lou's parental desertion. The way Ernestine was fed gin at age two. Cortez killing his own father.

I didn't have the training of clinical distance—I didn't know what that was. I learned what I needed to know daily. Then there was the phone call, through an intermediary, a fugitive coming your way with his crew, any personal affection lost in his cold eyes. Cortez was out again, high on meth and an early-morning six-pack, coming our way. Whatever transpired in that Army town at 1:00 a.m., the family brawl that led to his father's death, he'll live with that forever. But now he's crazed and scared and looking for you, the only one he believes can help him. He's in a white nondescript sedan with anonymous plates, doing what criminals do.

I did the best I could with these situations, obsessed with trying to convey upbeat assistance while protecting Kit. When he inevitably came around, flaring, talking about how he would turn my world upside down—I calmly replied that I wasn't afraid of him and that I didn't have any money. He showed me the serrated knife, the intensity of his threat increasing—implying possible harm to Kit, who happily this time was in her studio, away from the house—and I continued to remind him of the imaginary childhood that we could've spent together, referencing the sports that tended to calm. However, my gift for disassociation was hitting its limit.

Ultimately Cortez started crying, right there in front of me, knife still in hand, his friends waiting for him in the white car. The erotic tattoos, the muscles of a mid-heavyweight, and guilt that would not relent. He returned to his companions, who were stereotypically all wearing sunglasses, and the variations of relapse that defined their existence. The following day, there were long messages of apology on my phone, Cortez sincere in his wild terror of what's not right.

I'm certain that Annette and others might have experienced similar situations, though I'm also sure that they had better boundaries than I did. The next day I tried to ignore my shakiness in the gym, surrounded by all of their innocence on the hardwood, my other life. And I didn't mention any of it to Kit.

My commitment was for the duration. How was I supposed to go back into my previous world after inhabiting this one? There was a sense of something having vanished with the wind. Donations were exposed for what they were. Not enough. Never enough.

The word was that Cortez was on a spree and rumored to have killed again. Yet another reason to be out here, I guess, for my own safety. He didn't scare me that way, and it was probably just a rumor. Still, in the Board's eyes, we were linked by association—Cortez and I, plus the others. At this point our road trip North was just one big fantasy. I did get into this work with the best intentions.

The dutiful, conventional world will continue on as it has, regardless of what I decide. And why wouldn't I have believed what we could accomplish at Hope House? That fountain at the elegant foundation office and the urbane executive director, Foster—the disbursement of healing monies. Minimal explanation, his instinctive understanding of our ragged need, charitable banter, a welcoming within which everyone could flourish, a utopian breeze. There, in his well-manicured courtyard, calibrated humor, and the locks open. Foster, the foundation, had our back—*thank God*—after his years back East in the finest schools. His assistant, with her love of Mozart, acting as our instant advocate. Joking, both of them, about the actuality of our work, but in a respectful way. The check was signed for Hope House and the program was rescued. Again.

With Annette, substantial feats within the workday—one would think that in itself would keep us allied—a complementary duo at least some of the time. We could be good together on certain days, until she appeared before the stunned Board asking for my resignation, saying that she couldn't work with me any longer. She was poisoned toward me by New Hampshire Brenda before she even arrived in New Mexico. Hilda trying to conceal a knowing smile. And in that moment, our previous months of noontime triumphs—the hours in the car, gallows humor after our unnerving prison visitations—our past history was gone in that moment of betrayal, though I should've seen it coming. It should've been clear to me, if for no other reason than the high doses of psychotropic medication coursing through Annette's veins.

August 23, 1987

We're in Seattle. The Monroe Hotel, to be exact, complete with elevators and lobby. There are plenty of old people here, and the place has its charm. A reminder of a bygone era, destined, no doubt, for conversion into something more upscale. But at the moment it remains the dwelling place for both the very old and the very young. The middle is elsewhere, flourishing as it should. We stick to ourselves, and so do they, the hotel residents.

By we I mean Rodney, Kit, Timothy, and myself. I had a feeling Rodney would still be here, under the pretext of helping Timothy get settled. As much as he purports to loathe cities, there's much about him that's tailored for urban life. His thirst for new experience, new faces, new tales. The original plan of riding north to the cannery could be delayed easily enough. Besides, Rodney has an obligation to make certain Timothy doesn't hurt himself.

Kit and I ran into the others quickly enough; there are only a handful of hotels like the Monroe remaining in this city. Timothy found employment as a busboy at a nearby French café. And Rodney is now an actor. A *method* actor. Having gotten their room number at the desk, Kit and I knocked— only to find that we were interrupting rehearsal. "Oh … hey … uh, good to see you," Rodney muttered distractedly as a dark-eyed girl peered up from the table. "Hey, I'll talk with you later, okay? I'm in character right now, and Lois is tryin' to find her objective."

"My *action*," the girl corrected him with surprising intensity. "I already know my objective."

"Yeah, as you two can see, I'm busy right now." Rodney closed the door. Kit and I looked at each other in amazement.

"Well," Kit said with a laugh, "what do you make of that?"

"You got me."

"Maybe he's in love."

"He's always in love. I don't think it's that."

"He seems to have undergone a change."

"Seems that way."

"I remember him saying he wouldn't be caught dead in a city."

"It's been over a month."

"People change."

"I guess they do."

Right then, Timothy rounded the hallway corner. He hesitated, then said in his characteristic monotone, "I do recognize these people."

"Hey there!" Kit exclaimed. "How's your art work?"

"On hold," he replied.

"Timothy," I began, "what's with your partner?"

Timothy looked surprised. "Is he in there now?"

"Yeah," Kit replied. "But he's a busy guy. You better not disturb him."

"His rehearsal must be running over. I came back for my apron. I keep forgetting it."

"Do you have a job or something?" Kit asked.

"Up the street. Cleaning off tables. It pays."

"What's up with Rodney?" I asked. "He's like a serious guy now."

"Is he? I should pay more attention. He's been studying acting since we got here."

"I thought he was going to head up to the cannery."

"He was," Timothy said. "But he met this woman. I think it was at the Dragon Club. Up the street."

"Yes, but *acting*?" I asked again.

"The woman, what's her name … I forget. Or I never knew. She's involved in theater. Teaches, I think."

"Oh," Kit said.

"Yes," Timothy said. "She gave him encouragement. I must return to work now. I'll borrow an apron."

Kit and I are sharing a room on the eleventh floor of the Monroe. Rodney and Timothy are a couple of floors below. Kit's job in Lyon was short-lived, but we did celebrate her first (and only) paycheck in an appropriate fashion. We're do well as a couple—especially after that night on the train. That was a night. I haven't had the opportunity to savor it, given my preoccupation with my impending meeting with Frederick. Will he secretly summon my father, as is the way in Murphy Land? And exactly where is Pleasant Lake, Washington? Kit's getting sick of hearing about it. I should get it over with, she says repeatedly.

Besides that night on the train, we had a remarkable afternoon interlude several days ago, after we upgraded to this higher floor in the Monroe. It's stayed with me, so I might as well write it down:

"Did something happen to you as a boy?" Kit asked me out of the blue, as we were resting together in our new, comfortable room.

"What do you mean?" I replied, immediately on the alert.

"Things happen to us as kids, of a sexual nature. It's quite common."

"Why would you think that something happened to me?"

"You don't seem to fathom how special you are. You know, in the way we are together."

"I don't know," I replied, understanding her intent. "I don't remember a whole lot from my childhood. I think something might have … I get glimpses. Like in my dreams sometimes."

"Just hold me, okay?" Kit wrapped her arms around me. Increasingly, we've been doing just that—holding each other, with some selected music in the background (courtesy of Kit's recent purchase of a stereo cassette player). Her songs are different from mine. But we're both committed to this silent processing of our respective pasts through music. And silence.

"It's okay, sweetie," I said that afternoon, running my fingers through her thick short hair. She was crying.

"Stuff happened to me," she said quietly. "I had this uncle. On my mom's side …"

"I'm sorry." I didn't know what to say.

"I have this veneer. Like when you first met me. Just to protect—"

"I understand." I love it when she's soft like this, unguarded, no wisecracks. The world we're creating together is becoming a sanctuary. We're opening to each other as the outer world recedes. Touch is the important thing, the safety it brings, its warmth. "You're *so* beautiful," I said, meaning it to my very core, drinking in her soft pale skin, her brown eyes that held such deep mystery. Her voice—inviting, reassuring, gentle—except when she's caustic, which is often.

"I like you, Mr. Murphy," she whispered to me. Between our musical selections, you could hear the traffic on Ballard Avenue. There was a great used record and tape store a couple blocks away from the hotel.

"Kit," I began, my own tears beginning to well up, "I think we're similar here as well. There was something that I don't like to think about … when I was a teenager. Not good."

"It's okay, handsome," she said in her softest voice.

"I grew up in a small town. It had its dark side." Emotion was coming now.

"It's okay."

"Older boys—"

"We don't have to talk." She held me closer. We had our clothes on, which made it even better. I felt something rising from deep within, a kind of euphoric comfort.

I'm crazy about this girl.

The evidence of our collective possibility was clear that Sunday morning when the boy clung to Alonzo in the small inner-city church. *Brother Murphy has brought his guests today. From the home that helps people.* It was the point in the service, second hour, when the children were summoned to some other room, and Marcellus wouldn't relinquish his grip on his dad. Alonzo had always been gone, leaving behind the rumors of his major dealing. He was raised in this very neighborhood. A muscular guy with a bright smile, , a natural leader of men, unfortunately often lost in the trade. We're all swaying as one by the third hour—testimonials and fine singing, the hope in any Sunday morning, especially in *this* gathering. Finally Marcellus was convinced that he could release his dad and actually see him again. Taneequa, who'd earlier in the summer patiently endured what she called my *white church* helping with our raffle, and who had also grown up in this neighborhood, kept nudging me and smiling. Alonzo had done well in our household and was soon elevated to house manager. Months later I saw Marcellus riding his bicycle along the drug avenue, a Sting Ray like the one I had at his age, his father missing in the familiar manner, the parole officers having led him away.

Alonzo's girlfriend, Charlayne, also a resident, spoke of many things at our dinner table. There was a halfway house in California where they, no lie, had hot tubs and massages after dinner. Or the tales of her supervisor at the pancake house and the inappropriate things that he'd say to her, knowing her past. How the customers were, in fact, *great,* always respectful and surprisingly generous. She was the leader of our women's wing; Alonzo, the men's. Our queen and king respectively, reigns short-lived, but that's to be expected in our turbulent household. Inevitably the parole officers arrived, relayed to us the relevant accusations. No, they hadn't been home today or yesterday, but their stuff was still here. Annette and I were characteristically surprised, though less so as her months and my years progressed. Our dinnertime attendance would fluctuate as our normal visitors arrived. We had our own unique sense of decorum. The table had a few conspicuous empty chairs, but our remaining residents always brought their best ironed selves to our table, and we loved them for it.

This was about the time of Solomon's incident with the neighbor—the faces and durations run together with a tidal recurrence of potential and failure. My sense was that Solomon might ultimately turn it around. It was bad leaving him out on the avenue like that, his version of events completely obscured by our own expediency. After all, it was an assault by our neighbor. *Solomon* was the one pulled through the window and hit with a shovel. I was still inexperienced and alone, facing down the aggrieved man and the unassailable monotone of parole officers with their inside knowledge. Solomon seemed to understand my limitations in this situation. He tried to be upbeat leaving my car, released to his own need in that part of town.

August 31, 1987

> It was a quiet Sunday afternoon. I had little difficulty finding the community of Pleasant Lake, though I did have some problem locating the house—the basketball hoop over the garage should've tipped me off. I took the bus, so my quest had to be continued on foot. I stood nervously at the door. When I heard footsteps approaching from within the house, it was too late to salvage the initiative. Frederick emerged alone.
>
> "Hi there," I managed quickly. "Remember me?"
>
> "I don't believe it."
>
> "I could have called, but ..."
>
> "How did you get here?"
>
> "The bus goes right by your house."
>
> "The bus?"

"I've been staying in Seattle for several weeks."

"We could've come in and picked you up."

"I thought I'd surprise you."

"Well, this is a surprise."

"So how's Gretchen?"

"Fine. She's out with the kids. I was on my way to the gym."

"Do you work out much?"

"Not as much as I should." Frederick laughed. "I've been putting on some weight. Too much lasagna."

"Ah, you don't look so bad."

"You don't either. At least you're not fat like me."

"You're not fat."

"That's not what Gretchen says. But it's her fault. And those lunches I have to take with my clients."

"How's business been?"

"Pretty good. I've been losing on some accounts, but not yours, not to worry."

"As if I care."

"The market's been acting strange. Your portfolio is looking strong, though. All those blue chips. My associates at the office kid me about it. They call it the Ghost Account."

"Are Mom and Dad around?"

"No. Why would they be around? They live in Iowa, remember?"

"I just figured they might be visiting. You know, them being grandparents and all."

"What's bringing you around today? Checking up on the bourgeoisie?"

"Oh, I just figured it was time. To come around, I mean."

"I'd ask what you've been up to for the past couple of years, but I'm not sure I want to know."

"Oh, come on. You did some offbeat things in your day."

"I damn sure didn't jump freight trains. I assume you're still doing that."

"What about the time you spent in Texas? Driving trucks? Before you got thrown in jail that one night?"

"That was a phase. Not a … life, the way it is with you apparently."

"It was a pretty long phase, don't you think? What was it, close to two years?"

"So I learned I'm not geared to be a truck driver."

"I always thought it was pretty interesting."

"Look, I'm not giving you a hard time. It's great to see you, goddamn it! Want to play some ball? I got some extra gear in my closet somewhere."

"Your feet are bigger than mine. I'd need some sneakers."

"Those you're wearing look okay."

"Yeah, but there's no tread."

"Then it'll even things up. Assuming you haven't lost that much in the way of speed."

"All right," I said, patting him on the back. "Let's go."

We ducked inside for a moment, as Fred gathered his gym attire. It was a nice house, tastefully furnished, with a big yard out back. Children's toys were strewn everywhere. Gretchen and Fred have two already, with one more on the way. "Isn't it something?" Fred said, addressing the condition of the living room. "You'll understand some day."

The health club was actually a high-powered YMCA. "Kind of impressive, huh?" said Frederick, as he produced his ID. He signed me in as his guest. He was amiable and easygoing, and it seemed as if the entire locker room knew him. The familiar male conversation, with references to sporting events upcoming and past. And the athletic confidence in the way we move. In the steam room, I noticed that he *had* put on a few pounds. He divined what I was thinking, then grinned. "The domestic life. Like I told you."

Out on the court, however, he was as smooth and agile as I remembered. He could go to his left as easily as his right (a skill he learned during his college days), and when he drove the lane, he was always under control. His passes were crisp, his shooting accurate as always. We were on the same team—presumably we were the guards—and the ease with which we dispatched our opponents rekindled memories of past triumphs. Like that time at Candy Cane playground in D.C., the one with the striped poles and racial tension. Or back home in Alliance, during my college summers. I was feeling my lack of practice, especially in the breathing department. And my shoes were most definitely not up to the task. Still, a surprising number of moves came back to me. When I cleanly swiped the ball from my opponent and then hit Fred streaking toward our basket for the winning layup, it was like old times.

"Good job, bro!" Fred said as he gave me a high five. "You damn sure haven't lost much."

"You neither," I answered, doubled over in an attempt to find oxygen.

"You been practicing with them hobos?"

We both laughed, the old easiness returning.

"Not exactly," I replied. "Though I do know this guy who played at college. For that coach, I forget his name—"

"Neary. When did he play?"

"You wouldn't have played against him. It was a long time ago."

"This guy's a hobo?"

"No. An attorney."

"I bet you meet some interesting people out there. On the freight trains."

"It's not like I've spent the past few years *entirely* on freight trains. You have to get off sometimes, you know."

"I imagine you do. We get plenty of transients through here. In Seattle, that is. I check them out sometimes to see if I recognize my kid brother."

"Oh, come on."

"Seriously. Do you sleep on benches and stuff like that?"

"Hell no."

"That's what I told Gretchen. We had an argument about it one night. I told her no brother of mine would be passed out on some park bench."

We both laughed again. "Why? Did she think she saw me down at Pioneer Square?"

"Nah. It was strictly hypothetical."

"Does she think I'm weird?"

"You *are* weird. But that's okay. You're family. I wish you'd stay in touch more. I worry about you. We all do."

"Could you do me a favor, Fred?"

"Maybe."

"If Mom and Dad call, could you not tell them I'm around?"

"Sure thing. But they'd love to talk with you."

"I know. But I'd rather not, all right?"

"Sure. You want to play another one?"

"Why not?"

That evening Fred gave me a ride back to the Monroe. He handled it okay—the contrast, I mean. He even joked about it. "Most people," he said, "aspire to improve themselves. If you aspire to do the opposite, I say fine. It's weird, that's all." And with that, he put his expensive foreign car into gear. "Call me," he said, then revved off into the urban evening.

I'm thinking these crazy thoughts. That I could maybe go home now, for instance—to Iowa—and have it be okay. It certainly went well with Fred and Gretchen. Any awkwardness they felt had more to do with lack of information than a kind of judgmental trip. Sure, we inhabit different worlds, but we share the same past, the same family. It's almost enough. Heck, maybe it *is* enough. They seem to respect me, the choices I've made. That they can find humor in the situation is a good sign. (Gretchen has dubbed me Hobo Murphy.) I don't know how to act around their kids—my nieces—but that could come in time. It's not like I'm entertaining notions of sticking around. What I am thinking of doing is fairly challenging, though.

Why not go home? Seize the initiative, surprise Mom and Dad. Declare myself once and for all. Establish an honest connection; clue them in as to who their son is. Maybe even bring Kit along, if she's willing. The point here is resolution. That's the point to *all* of this.

CHAPTER 18

Unraveling should be *celebrated*, I think, at least some of the time. As the well-intentioned voices recede and the limitless track frames my horizon—the legacy of travel—the healing is familiar. The problem is that less-than-kind energies can too easily overrun and assume control—as we witnessed daily with our residents—and there are always consequences. I guess I did become effective at some point, in service to the program, or at least many on the Board seemed to be happy with my performance.

I also made them nervous—certain members more so than others—especially the ones brought on by Hilda and, later, Annette. No one seemed to dispute that my qualities would be welcome and appropriate in other workplaces. I didn't know where those were. I truly didn't know any better and couldn't see what's obvious to me now. Situations would find me for a reason, I guess. Cortez in the rearview mirror, gunning his latest car immediately on my tail, wanting both money and guidance. Or shopping with Lewis for the most effective detox teas. Driving Ernestine to work every morning—she was extremely appreciative in her naturally gruff way. There honestly seemed to be no other alternative. And these jobs were critical for our residents.

I was relentlessly odd in my interpretation of assistance—going against rules that I dimly understood or cared about—all in my fierce determination to bring about positive results. The Board meetings were usually amiable and worthwhile enough—as who wants to insert conflict into a room full of volunteers? And of course charitable involvement was an afterthought at best. Ultimately concerns did emerge, legitimate ones, I suppose, and not only about my style of leadership. My eyes would roll in response to certain Board members, (well, just Hilda), and mischief would ensue, especially if I wasn't in attendance. Never miss a Board meeting was one of my first lessons. This was before I became limited in my influence, my authority taken off-site, politely, and for my own benefit.

How about that time we galloped up to the state legislature, in session, in my black car? Marble rotunda, the revered inlaid state seal, travel passes for everyone. We took advantage, silencing the gallery and the distracted legislators with voices rarely heard. I can't remember her name now, but she had a knot on her forehead and knew intimately the wages of living in harder towns. She apologized for her nervousness and began to speak in a modest yet firm voice:

"People like me," she began, "we don't usually come to these kinds of places. But I wanted you to know how important our Hope House is. I had nowhere to go, and they took me in. I want to get my children back." The tears started and the room fell silent. "I know I've done bad things," she continued, "but I *have* to believe that it can be better. Mr. Murphy," she said, looking in my direction, "and the others, they care about us. I have a job not far from the house. We all support each other, because we're dealing with the same kind of things. The volunteers too, they come for dinner. Bring dinner even." She paused, wiping her eyes. "It's going to be different this time for me, because of Hope House. I know it. Thank you very much." Our legislator sponsor gave me a thumbs up from the dais, and there was spontaneous applause.

We talked excitedly all the way back home about our triumph, the moment, and the prospect of state funding. We alternated who'd pick the radio stations, jovial conflict between hip-hop and country, sunlight streaming into my car, nothing but possibility on a very good day.

We *always* made an impression, often positive, though how quickly it could revert to petty grievance was another matter. Our residents had a raw hunger, or most of them seemed to, and the consequences of their actions were often flagrant. On the way back from the rotunda we spoke euphorically over the loud music, all of my speakers working. Heads turned. We made cashiers in department stores and club members at my fancy gym nervous. In the circular concourse of our State Capitol, however, where the populace was entitled to its five minutes, we had that and then some.

Could I have been more effective? "*Those people* can fend for themselves," Decker had said, speaking about my program in between games. "Right?" Progress could be made, inspiring individual breakthroughs—undeniably—but we'll see what happens in the long run. When the pivotal, visible moment came when a difference could be made, the uncertain energies would all too often return and the moment would slip away, ensuring that everything would remain broken, as it had always been. Not on a good day, though, like the one at the Rotunda.

I could leave this yard right now and resume my duties. I think the Board would take me back now that Salazar is Board President—and I'd do so if it would help residents like Maestas, Boris, Mary Lou, or any of the others with their respective transformations. Champion for hire, ready to assist the process if people would only trust my methods.

Being out here isn't punishment for any withering vision of mine, or a cagey grab for sympathy. I tried to do something about this resistant world, in the spirit of idealism, and the endeavor itself turned me upside down. Ill-prepared for how little my efforts mattered, ultimately, and at the same time riveted by the sincerity of our residents, with their looming problems, I could be an advocate, a leader, or just a white guy in a suit. Should they not be allowed a legitimate chance? I chose to remain there, with them, for seven years, in the clothing store or in the T'ai Chi Studio or in the parole office until *someone* apologized for the botched world outside. Of course, it was an impossible role, and what was the value of it? If, among other things, it ultimately propelled me into this familiar routine?

Retrospect from my immediate home, this empty gondola car, my recent transient friend now gone, avoiding his sadness. My God, a person gets dirty out here; my hair feels like a matted rug. Subsisting on sporadic dashes for fast food within reasonable distance of the train yards probably isn't an ideal nutritional regimen. Then there are the *looks* I get once inside such establishments. But, more than anything, these relentless visitations, softening my time with the intimation that we were all better for it, that *I* was better for it—that gap between effort and reality. Even those recovery slogans were welcome, *anything* hinting of change, *Live and Let God.* On a good day, we could overcome the uncertain energies, enlivened, not beaten down, by the promise of another life. Even Cortez, who'd chase me down with his wild need, could have graceful stretches. Others—many—could ride for a smooth six weeks.

This was the lesson. The intrusion on their intention to live straight, and whether or not, at that precise delicate moment, while it could still be salvaged. The household was a sensitive place. Weekly problems wouldn't go away, and they always seemed substantially more complicated than what my previous definition of trouble had been. For instance, the time when Carmelita returned from her lumberyard job with a half-severed finger. She was upset, her anger flashing, as we all commented on the beauty of her remaining digits. Whatever my troubles had been before she came through the door for dinner, bandana around her jet-black hair, they were instantly gone, exposed for what they were—trivial. In this way the household would pull me out of myself. Carmelita didn't relapse, as we suspected she would. Instead, she joked about her lost finger and doubled her meetings.

Some episodes ran past us weekly. Callahan suspiciously gone again, on the mesa meditating, or the woods, the cigarette smell of his empty room in our non-smoking house. Maestas shivering in obvious withdrawal—I can see that now—sweating and pale, as our kindly volunteer cooks ask after him. Ernesto and Boris full-on fighting in the kitchen,shortly before dinner, both with history around the knives that they held. Ricardo, the young writer—lucid dark eyes and his willingness to attend university lectures with me if maybe I'd look into that. The gang siren eventually proved too strong, and back he went—two days before Christmas, but not before he caught my gaze in between servings one evening and said, "Bro, you're like a *hustler*. But for a good cause. You're all street." How could I not take that as a compliment? There was the night we went searching for the childlike Cristella, one of seventeen children with inappropriate fathering and a soft, medicated gaze. We never found her, the truck stop being notorious and within walking distance of our facility. The women we loved had a history that way.

Our ongoing household—what an engaging refuge it proved to be for me, how *gone* I was from Kit and other aspects of my life, starting with our first intake interviews, shadowed by the slamming metal doors and bored guards. First day in the women's facility, wearing khakis and a tie, ready for class. Encountering the themes that would frame my next years, each family story topping the previous one. My father who burned me, or worse, injecting heroin at age twelve, my mother who sold me on the street, my boyfriend who botched the drug deal, my brothers who are with one exception likewise incarcerated, my seven children. And so on. By the ninth interview, I was asking myself what *is* this world and how can I account for it? People like these had been largely invisible to me—gone before I hit high school, banished to those special schools that normal kids feared. We partied back then, broke plenty of rules, but never on *this* level. And off to college I went. Had I been so sheltered? What else had I completely missed?

The men's facilities were equally challenging. One inmate's comment, "I had to put the body *somewhere*," which made sense to me, phrased like that, the logic of it all. Or the fellow with my father's eyes and his own occasional twitching, there in the mental health unit. Not a good intake, as within weeks he threatened to blow up the bank down the street. Cortez's grief-stricken tale of a Super Bowl party gone awry, cases of beer, and a dead father on the kitchen floor. Not the best intake either, as I would *personally* discover. He didn't mention the heroin, and it wasn't in his file.

We were a group of like-minded people, many volunteers genuinely trying to do something about our troubled world. The men and women in jumpsuits would listen to us, all of us, for obvious reasons, then reply with their own plans to attack the awaiting, skeptical world. During our intake interviews, some of us would be stunned at their focused attention, their intense listening, despite the noise. (I would bring Board members along on occasion.)

The interview would unfold, with me addressing my clipboard and the problem of saying *no*. I'd invoke our limited beds, the waiting list, or our ongoing zoning problem with the local authorities. I was bad with my follow-up too, I admit—terrible. My files weren't entirely nonexistent, but their sparseness certainly gave ammo to Annette and Hilda. It's hard to explain, but these people meant more to me than what could be captured in a file. Selections would be made to the best of my ability on the basis of house chemistry and measurements of attitude. Acceptance letters would arrive like prized April letters for college admissions, but delivered by case workers instead. I was that functional at least. We were the Cadillac of halfway houses.

Early on, Annette had made the mistake of surrendering to her negative feelings toward me and bringing them before the Board. She shared her conclusions secretly with residents who were more loyal to me, and she did the same thing with the Board, where I did have allies. Most of her comments came back to me, and I would go off stunned and insulted. So began my scanning the household parking lot for Annette's car. Trying for the high road, I made conciliatory gestures in her direction—Saturday morning walks, references to our shared Irish heritage, voicing cheerful comments about her fashion choices. Whatever her grievance toward me was, it wouldn't go away. "I have information," she said before the Board, this time with me in attendance, "about Chapman that is damaging to our program's reputation."

Jarring, the way it comes back to me. "I intend to salvage our reputation," she had continued, "and turn this enterprise around." She didn't look in my direction, where I sat in a daze. I hadn't been prepared for this kind of battle, and was searching inside for which of the many possible transgressions she could have been referring to. The money for Lewis's blue car? My help in shopping for his teas? The numerous off-the-record warnings to Maestas? Samuel, clearly inebriated on sweet vodka at our nightly dinner table? In short, I had my own private brand of second chances. Am I in trouble now? Am I going to be arrested?

There was an awkward silence when she finally concluded. And then you had a group of several volunteer board members looking for the door. "I take issue with your comments," one of them began, his voice embarrassing to me. Salazar, my hero. "The notion that Chapman here is anything but devoted and competent is absurd." I'm far away at this point—report cards, punt returns, heated first dates. "He's the reason that we even exist, and *everyone* speaks highly of him." What other transgressions was she talking about? I couldn't help but wonder. "Supreme Court Justice Ramirez," Salazar continued, "last week was telling me how remarkable Chapman is." By then, I was wondering about her distant training in New Hampshire and whatever she was told about me before she arrived. "And the Mayor. The Marino family, our biggest donors. I could go on. So," he then turned to her with a stare, "I want to know what in *hell* you are talking about?"

"I have information," she replied, nonplussed.

"What information?"

"It's confidential. But I've shared it with the national staff."

"So are we going to deal with this in executive session?"

"I don't know."

"I have real doubts about *your* leadership at this point."

Her face reddened, and surely in retrospect I should've left then.

"I am trying to provide leadership," she replied.

I should have departed. Fled. Right then.

"We need to set up a mediation," another member interjected. "I've spoken with national about this." If I had left I could've dodged what was to come. "We set up a meeting for next week." Could have reclaimed my life, made amends to Kit, headed back into something softer, less conspicuous, and away from this.

"Well," another member began, "perhaps we should move along, take this up later? What's the next item on the agenda?"

The mediation day was set and her empty chair said it all. The Board was giddy with their secret knowledge, and wanted me to share in that euphoria. The part of me that was in the room that day would have liked to comply, or at least participate, but nothing in my upbringing was of any use at this point. Instead I was characteristically polite and appreciative and secretly very discouraged. I found my car and sat for a long time, then made it to the gym earlier than usual. I'd won.

Enthusiastic and hungry, we hit church that Sunday with our tickets and our stories, and the congregations responded—it was the day for remembering the people who're broken, especially the thieves of the world. Then with the unscreened public at the entrance of the supermarket the following week. We always had the makings of an all-star crew in the household, or certain roles that were clearly possible. Odell auctioning himself off that hot Saturday afternoon, jokingly, promising a good time, confidence and charm as customers tried to place our unusual group. "A week with me," Odell said, "on an island with you and such. I'll be modest in my companionship." I could never reconcile his file with the dreadlocked leaper that we all came to know in the gym. The files were always a mystery to me. About Odell, my friends at the club would say, "If he had a shot to go with that vertical, he could play somewhere." The files were always there, with their superior factual rundown reinforcing what we attempted daily to overcome. As you are named so shall you behave. The last time I spoke with Odell he was intent on starting a paving business, and he seemed to be doing well, being law abiding.

What I like about this particular railyard is how the bitter wind cleanses and negates the possibility of anyone watching—it's colder, but at least I'm not soaked. For some reason a relaxing tranquility can inform my being in these circumstances. A Saturday morning, the limitless track beckoning. If you can pare it down to one thing that can be done well—anything, like my version of being a transient—then it becomes more in line with the prevailing optimism of the world that I'd like to experience.

The polished gym welcomed us, more than could be expected. And it's where I had recruited Salazar to join the Board. The basketball court was home for several of us, including me, and we'd make an impression, winners. All of us with talent but untapped, the potential of five players with extremely different backgrounds. Those days I'd hit my shot automatically—sort of. Boris on the fast break was impressive, and Odell had his sheer hops. We'd lose, but there was no violence. Boris practicing his T'ai Chi as the red elevator of rage wanted to ascend, Odell with his flipsy moves but no shot. Even Charlie had game—though he was primarily a football guy—our brawny lava rock resident with his slow pace and small-town high school success. Charlie was a steady presence underneath the basket and in our household—rough country, fantastic with axles, the opposite of slippery, and bearing a great sadness. He wanted his hunting privileges back so he could go track bear or whatever. Nobody messed with his silent authority. They treated him like Callahan. Filling out this perfection was Carmelita of the lost finger—doing well in the house, signing up for this class and that, and she'd come with us too for the yoga.

We're in the area of the brick towns now, on the high plateau. This freight goes north on a line that I think goes all the way to Denver. (I'll find out soon enough, once we get moving.) At the next yard I could get off and head toward land, move into a small aging hotel—like before. Could be a softer compromise, as riding on these trains takes it out of a person physically—the noise, the jerking, the dust, et cetera. At the next yard I could follow the sidewalks into the realm of a new town, the backpack always a signal for scrutiny. Past the thrift stores with their hope measured in a wall of used crutches. I could find a heated room, with a phone even, a carpet, the smell of pension checks. A shower would be nice. Maybe make contact with what I left. I have to *feel* it, though, have to be in the right frame of mind, like with those sales calls I always had to make.

What I remember now are those *phone calls.* The long, contentious ones—with my father, for example. With Maestas, as I once again tried to convince him that others aren't out to get him, the paranoid little gangster. And all of the messages that I never returned. As if existence could be squared by the well-timed return of a phone call.

Odd how suddenly it can descend, this not caring, the workplace unpleasantness, and the difficulty presented by that kind of conflict. The household extracted its price from both of us—Annette and me—so if we weren't united and she turned hostile, it had ramifications. We could be a team, and a good one at times, until the problems not so far under the surface emerged and our dynamic was gone—like my gold Murphy crest ring lost somewhere in the gravel of the Hope House parking lot.

I had all kinds of jackets on me, or so I was told, though their precise nature escaped me. A jacket is when someone puts a hit out on you. I sensed that I could be afraid, and maybe I was when the dead-eyed man came to gather up Ramona's belongings—violence being our ultimate teacher—as he stared through me to the bad donated paintings that adorned our dining room. She had to leave. But criminals are a distracted lot, by and large, and their attention easily goes elsewhere.

Whatever happened between Annette and me had left me changed and in a strange territory. The distant national supervisors were of some assistance—but not much, we'd always been a kind of lost colony to the houses back East, including Kentucky, doing it our own way out here on the frontier. Not that their help would have made a difference. I needed to leave. And Jerry had limited influence. Still, I did have my allies in the organization, on the Board, and I was ready to come to my senses, maybe. And there's my relationship with Kit. Perhaps a brick hotel with its lobby of old men should be my destination—revisiting loneliness in a different way and the room full of cigar smoke?

CHAPTER 19

There are Western towns dying in the wind everywhere; the gust outside my rented window testifies to that. This is a better direction for me, after I performed my familiar sizing up of the town, my place now not far from the railroad tracks. It kind of evokes the Monroe in Seattle. Close enough to get my bearings with each sweet, distant rumble. Out of the wind is *nice,* and the shower was sublime. The abandoned stone buildings, the display windows opening to nothing, a high school basketball schedule posted and curled by the elements, and my stuffed pack like a target that needed to be camouflaged.

The skeptical hotel clerk got the money up front. We're on our own in this kind of journey. After the ravages of the open air and grease are washed away, my interlude begins. I've always been an ambassador to some netherworld that I barely understand, conspicuous no matter what I do. My life could be seen as an argument against too much solitude. I'm a freelancing guy representing no one except an imagined constituency of the well-intentioned. There are so many noble endeavors dedicated to undoing bad circumstances, as I learned at Hope House during those United Way banquets. I could represent another such entity: the homeless, the addicted, the young.

The hotel is warm and out of the elements, and the old men downstairs don't ask questions.

"How's it going?" I had to call him, confidentially.

"Chappie, is that you? Where in the hell *are* you?" Salazar was angry.

"Oh, on the road."

"Where in the fuck have you been? We've been worried."

"It's all right. It's something I had to do. I told you I would someday."

"I thought you were kidding. The *freight trains?"*

"It's the people, bro," I replied. "It's cumulative. No way do I belong, so why enact some kind of illusion?"

"Murphy, you're crazy. You'll hurt yourself."

"Who cares?"

"We do, you silly nut."

"Okay, I get that," I continued. "That's nice, but what's the point of all this interest in me? I mean, in the larger sense? Compared to what?"

"I don't understand what you're saying."

"No matter," I replied. "How's the household doing?"

"Great. Considering we're missing the key to keeping it afloat."

"It was brutal. What went down with the Board."

"Sorry about that," Salazar replied. "We handled it as best we could."

"It just took it out of me."

"But Chapman … you won!"

"Sure."

"She bailed, remember?" he continued. "She didn't show up for the mediation."

"I remember."

"Brenda from New Hampshire had all kinds of questions, wanted to know what happened. But we basically told national to leave us alone."

"Have you replaced Annette?"

"Dude, she's gone."

"The last go-round was too much, man," I said.

"Chappie, that's just people being themselves," Salazar said. "It's not a perfect world."

"I know."

"Look, you chose to quit. No one on the Board wanted that."

"I didn't see any other way."

"You're too sensitive."

"I've heard that one before," I replied.

"So what's this all about?" Salazar asked.

"It's where I belong."

"On the freight trains?"

"Why not? It's as good a place as any. And technically I'm off them now. In a fine establishment. Up to your standards even."

"It's childish," Salazar said. "You're needed back here. You should be proud of what you've accomplished."

"Why?" I shot back. "People betray you. Our residents re-offend."

"But you've *helped* people. I know you had problems with your dad, but even he'd be proud if he were still alive."

"That's debatable."

"You've made a difference. You have. Most of us want to, but we never find the opportunity."

"I'm counting on you not telling anyone that I called."

"I understand that. I am your attorney."

"And our Board President."

"Yes, that too. I think you should consider notifying your family. Or at least your brother. Let them know you're all right."

"We're not that close."

"What about Kit?"

"She knows. She remembers this from Montana. She hopped freights with me. We had a kind of courtship on these things."

"How's she doing?"

"Not so well. Her diagnosis is still a mystery. She's going to get a second opinion."

"That sucks."

"I know. But she's a fighter. Do others know I'm gone?"

"Rumors are out there. "

'Damn, sorry for all the drama. Are you hitting your shot?"

"Draining it, Chappie. That's what I mean. What am I supposed to tell the guys at the gym? Dumb shit, they want to know what happened to you."

"Oh, I've seen that happen. It's not real. Remember when Mateo stopped coming to the gym because he had a brain tumor? Nobody ever asked about him. They don't care."

"They do the best they can," Salazar replied. "We all do. Everyone's busy with their own lives, you know?"

"Right," I answered. "And this is mine."

"So, what, you're a hobo now?"

"Of course not. It works for me out here, that's all. And it's inexpensive."

"Where are you now?"

"Somewhere. You can check the area code. It's in another state."

"You're a very unusual guy. I mean, if it works for you, whatever. I'm mainly concerned about your safety. Isn't it violent out there?"

"I keep to myself."

"That's right. And now you're all streetwise. Courtesy of Hope House."

"Not hardly."

"Well, you fool people. The other thing is, I'm genuinely concerned about the fate of our program."

"You *are* the Board President," I interjected. "You should be."

"Of course," he answered.

“There are other people involved now,” I said. “It's not like it used to be. We're sturdier, right?”

“You're missed.”

“Well … I appreciate the kind words. I'll think about what you're saying. I promise.”

“Okay, dude. Take care.”

September 21, 1987

So I made the decision to go home:

A simple home visit, starting with a seat on a crowded airplane. Reverberations already. Less than six weeks earlier, I was sleeping in a culvert, the one Kit had found to keep us out of the rain. Now I am being served a complimentary breakfast as we fly east over the sprawling Seattle railyard and the surrounding region that I've come to know—the small towns of Montana, Washington, and Idaho. Hobo camps, the old hotels. And now such value placed on attention to my needs. On menus and seating assignments and the utter outrage of baggage delayed. The language of complaint, is that what I'm supposed to inhabit now? The passenger next to me incensed at her lukewarm coffee.

Reverberations there because, as a child, I flew a lot. The family that took vacations. I'm comfortable in airports—the secret joy of going somewhere, all that adventure. What I felt emerging was more disturbing than I cared to admit. I liked it, being on a plane again. Truth in what you recognize.

Flooded with the absolute certainty of easier days. Surely that was real too?

Then home, to the reality of my perfect family. The official home of said young man. No longer subject to distortion, to the vagaries of memory.

What on earth possessed me to do this? Kit will be here in a few days. Otherwise I'd be long gone. I might as well play it out; I've come this far. Where to begin? I don't know … the element of surprise? The question permeated the past several days; I need to sort it out. My sudden presence is a surprise. Cocktail chatter halts as you enter the room, eyes trained on the young man who left. "Hi there!" I muster, with fake animation. "Long time, no see." Their faces look older, tired—not as I remember. They're clearly glad to see me again and will readily forgive my disloyalty. At least as long as I remain. In this small Midwestern town where I grew up. Where I played football. And basketball. And baseball. Where I delivered the Gettysburg Address on Memorial Day. Where I marched in the Fourth of July parade. Here, where I belong. Where not much happens anymore and a void has been left by departed sons and daughters. To aging parents assembled in this room perhaps I'm a symbol of that. Nevertheless, they do invite me back and speak to me for the first time as an adult—as if I'd never left. They ask careful questions. I'd prefer their overt rejection. Like Mr. Waldo, rattling on about his son's law career, taking such obvious satisfaction in the way young Ted has followed his instructions to the letter. Let us praise once again the safer routes, or how rewards come to those who imitate; to those who fully appreciate the *visible* and stay within its confines.

The present is something we all wish would go away, along with the not-so-distant past. Within the walls of this house,

I'll be your son again, the one adept at achievement. In exchange, I receive that unquestioned sense of belonging. That's the trade-off.

The least we could do is acknowledge what's going on now or what has been going on for the past several *years*. The mutual disappointment, the fantasy unmasked, the bitterness. Instead, I watch Father's eyes brighten for a visage not my own. Mother sees me a little more clearly, but not so much. There I am, not discouraging their myopia. What else can I do, given the circumstances? I mean, the sheer width of the chasm involved. I hedge, don't smash the good china—as long as I am in this house, I'm under the dictates of my own legacy. I was a good boy. I learned my lessons well. The evidence is everywhere, framed and hanging on the walls.

The hallway bureau, with its stack of mail and magazines. They still read the important periodicals, remain well-informed. Everything fits. I find it hard to believe that I actually came from this. I can either be silent or express my defiance.

Late afternoon lunch with Mother yesterday. Intoxicated with the possibility of bridging the gap, of trying to make her *understand*, which is always my undoing. I risked a recent dream of mine—one of my tamer ones, actually. What did I get in response? Concern for my health. "Oh, Chapman!" she said. "How dreadful it must be to have dreams like that." Later, an unexpected frontal assault. "Chapman, there's so much pain in life. I don't understand why you feel the necessity to go *hunting* for it. Maybe I shouldn't say this," she continued, "but you were the most promising of all our boys. You're capable of so much more than what you're doing now. Oh, how I wish you would get into something that challenges you! Surely there's some better way to put your education to use. It's your life, though. You're an adult." Then an awkward silence, until the check arrived. I could have harangued my mother at that point, itemized my list of grievances, but who does that? They did the best they could, as the saying goes. It's time for me to move on; that's the whole reason I'm home.

With Father, it's more predictable. He's a creature of habit, of ritual. I can fully anticipate the trajectory of our conversation. I'll join him in his daily walk, and he'll level with me on all fronts. With his dog on a long leash, he's moving swiftly for a man of his age. I'll do my best to keep up. "You draw up a list, see?" he'll say. "This is what I can do. This is who I am. You don't concern yourself with what you're not. That's a waste of time. You submit your résumé. A guy looks at it and asks, 'Can this fellow do the job? Sure, why not. Let's give him a try.'" Gosh, Dad, why didn't I think of that? "You're smart, good-looking. You were Dean's List at college," he'll continue. "The opportunities seem unlimited. Hell, I wish I was your age again." Yeah. "Before long, you'll be looking around at your friends," he will go on, "and most of them being married, you'll probably start thinking, 'I want that for myself.' To do that, you'll have to have a marketable skill. A way of making a good income to provide for your family. Like I've done." I would like to have that option, I'll respond. "What?" he will ask. That option. I would like to have it, I clarify. "Yes, well … I'm glad of that. You know, son, you ought not lean on what came from your grandfather on your mother's side. I didn't have a dime when I was your age. Though of course, it's your money. You're free to do with it what you will. Hell, I was young once. Just don't invade the principal." No danger of that, I'll say. The past three years. "Fine," he'll answer, distractedly.

Uh, Dad, I'll continue, there's something I've been meaning to talk to you about. Concerning the money. "Okay," he'll answer, "we'll get to that in a minute. I just want to tell you a couple of things more. Chapman, I don't want to sound dramatic, but I never know if this might be the last time we see each other. You never find enough reason to come home, and I'm getting on in years. But no matter. I want you to know that I savor these moments." Yes, well, I should come home more often. "That's all right, son. I understand that a man has got to make his own way. It's tougher on your mother. I just want to tell you one more thing. You know, Chapman, we all have our weaknesses. If I were to single out Chapman Murphy's number-one fault, it would be his absolute inability to make a decision." Yeah, well … "I would hope that it might be less of a problem for you in the future." Yeah, well … "And furthermore, I would hope that you kids find as much happiness in your work as I have in mine. Now, what was it that you wished to talk about?" It can wait. You sure do walk fast.

That would be how it'd probably go. Father. Forward motion. This morning I almost beat him out of bed. I can't be objective about him; he's *my father*. But he does manage to make me feel a certain way. Like with our impending walk. I can see myself struggling to keep up, hesitating more than usual, anxious to show him a side he'll like. Attentive, organized, highly motivated. None of this fuzzy-headed stuff, this vacillation. I want to please him, but how can I when we're in such different worlds? Somewhere he must sense that. I don't want to inhabit that old role of model son. We're so opposite, and yet, isn't one usually connected to one's opposite? I feel him inside no matter what I do—his opinions, his virtues, his shortcomings. That photograph of him at twenty-six. We could as well be twins.

How he must recoil at times when he gets an authentic whiff of what I'm about. What he understands is striving upward in the well-defined world, the way he did at my age. Young men like Armand Green, my old friend who stopped by yesterday when he heard I was home. Surprise, surprise. Surely Father understands Armand better than he does me. Armand, my former best friend and current worshipper of my dad (I'd forgotten about that dynamic). Garrulous, sensible, vigorous—Armand has a promising future in business. I wonder if Dad would have preferred him as a son, at least to me? I know Armand would be thrilled at the chance to be a Murphy. But that doesn't alter my desire to please Father, to give him reason to feel proud the way I used to. The prospects for that seem to be impossible. My frustration was brought to the surface by Armand's visit. There he was, sitting in the chair in front of the fireplace, talking to my father in a way I could never do. Father must feel equally shut out of my life. I should have it out with him. Later today, when he comes home from the office. The walk—it has to be *the walk.* I've come home with precisely this in mind; it's time to get it over with.

Friends like Salazar are accurate in their concern, but warmth comes to us in many forms. The lineage carries on, our wiry spirit. I *do* keep my distance. Any dilemma presented to oneself is another matter, only mirrored in the concern of Salazar's voice.

I'm cleaned up, better now, back to my voyaging. Figures in the distance present no imminent threat with their flashlights;

there's space out here for everyone, in the open air, like that railroad baron said in the last century, the one who promised an empty boxcar for any fortunate hobo. Unfortunately, I'm stuck on a grain car, with its disconcerting ledge over the wheels and the soon-to-be-deafening sound. Maybe *that* is why no one is bothering me. I'm stupid enough to ride like this.

"What about your career?" Salazar had asked, after I called him again, from a pay phone on my way to the yard.

"You've got to be kidding," I replied.

"Chappie, you're *good* at it. You're onto something."

"So how do I explain my current situation?"

"We all have personal matters that require attention."

"Do I put my life out there again for public interpretation?"

"That's up to you," Salazar answered, "how far you go with this silliness."

"It's not silly. No weirder than asking people for money. Constantly."

"You do that well. We couldn't exist otherwise."

"So I have a personality glitch," I replied. "You know, that's rewarded."

"It's more than that."

s"What is it, then?" I asked.

"People want to believe in something better. Call it idealism or what you will. You tapped into it."

"It's just a stupid halfway house."

"You have to start somewhere."

"I think I'm heading in a different direction."

"Again, that's up to you. All I'm saying is that it's very salvageable."

"I'm not so sure."

"It's more than that and you know it," Salazar said with finality.

"Okay, guy," I replied. "Thanks for having conversations like this with me. And for sticking up for me at that Board meeting."

"Are you kidding?" He laughed. "You're my boy."

Having it wrong isn't necessarily a dire fate. This is what I do to figure things out. These rituals shouldn't be so strange. It makes as much sense as what I remember from my childhood. The morning football practices and cinnamon toast and the overnight sleepovers.

"It's easy to become emotionally attached to an idea," I said, picking up our conversation, calling my friend and attorney for the third time.

"Yeah, like the notion of your rebellion?"

"Actually, I was thinking about our program."

"You could have your job back."

"Then what?" I asked.

"Each thing leads into another."

"So then … meaning?"

"You're the spiritual one here. All those churches that you went to."

"That was for the household. It had nothing to do with me."

“Which is another reason you should come back. We'll give you a raise.”

“What would others say about that? It could be trouble.”

“I can talk to our Executive Committee.”

“I don't think that's such a good idea,” I said.

“Look, dude,” he said, “we can work these things out. I don't understand this sudden change of attitude on your part. What's happened to you?”

“Too many donations of mismatched shoes, maybe,” I answered. “Or the other things that people want to shovel out of their garage.”

“It's the thought that counts, isn't it?” Salazar replied.

“It needs to be better than that.”

“You expect too much.”

“No, I don't.”

“People have been very generous to Hope House. *I'm* a volunteer too, you know.”

"I'm not talking about that. It's about how little difference it makes. On any level.”

“Change doesn't happen overnight.”

“I know that. It's the way we celebrate the puniness of it all. Wow, a twenty-five-dollar gift. Or a worn-out couch. Or thank you for unloading this state-of-the-art weight machine. And claiming triple its value on your taxes.”

“You have to work with people. Meet them where they are.”

“I've done that. I'm tired.”

"There are other ways to regroup besides becoming a transient."

"I'm not a transient. Obviously. I have issues. And this is where I go."

"All I'm saying is that you're limiting yourself. You're still young."

"Not that young."

"Well, *youngish* then," Salazar clarified. "You can work on all these things in a less dramatic way."

"I'll take that under consideration. I'll call you in a week."

"Okay. Enjoy the scenery."

"And don't tell anybody we're talking. Besides, I know that they're not asking about me anyway."

"*That* is not true."

"And hit that shot," I said. "Remember the arc. Think about a rainbow."

"Shut up."

Our residents were talented at vanishing, and they probably taught me more than I realize in that respect; similarly, they have a remarkable ability to *wait.* Were we so ineffectual as a charity? If so, where was the skepticism among the churchgoers? And my Board, including Salazar? Why would they waste their time if the whole enterprise was as limited as it seemed to be?

There's always the same dirty current ready on the perimeter, though our neighborhood was gracious enough to let us open. We had our dust-blown sanctuary, no chained pit bulls on our grounds, the visits from parole perfunctory and well-timed. Whatever currents were swirling outside our household were nothing that we had any power over. We were simply a potential refuge from the undeniable success of sin.

They protected me against the accusations—my Board—which I shouldn't minimize, especially because their volunteering was far down the list in the larger scheme of things. Rules are there for a reason, and I needed to accept that fact. We needed to have these limitations in place for our parolees, and it was a good thing for us as well. The hasty voices to be kept in line, the ongoing battle against impulse, and the floating bad current. We accepted the donations of broken furniture and worn-out clothes, and notes of gratitude were sent out on our humble stationery. My heritage of affluence carried over so easily into this peculiar version of giving. The endless succession of meetings where the visible would be celebrated and the obvious ignored—splendidly fictional and therefore immediately satisfying. Mercifully, the work week would end and give way to the real work of the weekends. Jump-starting sick cars, providing transportation to the sacred jobs, making long-distance calls about confusing warrants, and rising at 5:00 a.m. for the series of Sunday Masses with raffle tickets in hand.

On a good day we'd storm the towers, sunlit in our aspiration. The restaurant manager had given one of our residents the keys, and the parole officer lifted her anger management requirement (what was *her* name?). Foster's foundation doubled its check and all of the locks would open. We'd somehow survived an embezzlement. There were those avuncular figures who'd come my direction and offer their well-meaning advice to change my phone message, get a haircut, don't slouch when asking for thousands of dollars. Mentors. And good ones. One of them sent a letter to my dad delineating why he should be proud of my work with Hope House. The other one with the scar on his face, like that German tradition of dueling scars—an older man who took an interest in me as well, trying to help. Or my other teacher, similarly curt and familiar with the ancient art of asking for money.

Both had given me lists that would take me years to go through, a favored set of contacts capable of sustained giving. The plaques, the comfortable outdoor chairs, and baseball caps for everyone—our new logo unveiled, sad refusal left to others. All of this on a series of good days, in the vortex of becoming, gathering speed like a westbound freight.

On a good day Boris cleans himself up and heads north on the interstate, wearing his Christmas shirt and cowboy hat, thumb extended. Or Callahan circles the prison yard with his tanned and respected presence, one cigarette to last the afternoon. Maestas comes back from the dead, calming himself at his new job as a taxi driver, making easy conversation with the just-arrived tourists. Mary Lou visits her three children, holds back the tears of her own childhood, and has reason to believe that her educational assistant's license will be reinstated. Samuel finds a ride back to his original Southern home and is granted access to the full afternoon of his life. Lewis gets solace and an authentic beginning in a new city where the citizens take his word for it. On a winter holiday his blue jeep is returned to him, restored and in excellent condition. Cortez, inside once again for yet another serious felony, finally finds inner peace in a tranquil corner of the familiar cellblock. Or Eppie makes it to his social worker appointment and is persuaded not to desert his camp under the overpass for the opportunity of shoveling snow up North.

CHAPTER 20

One day Boris actually did get out of town. I had to slam on my brakes for the thin figure on the roadside.

"Kola!" he shouted, running toward the car. "Is that you?"

"What the hell are you doing out here?" I shouted, rolling down the window.

"Can I get a ride?"

"No, I'm going to leave you here."

"Thanks, man."

"Be careful with that door." He opened it, remembering, and threw his pack into the back seat.

"Nice ride, Kola," he said, surveying the familiar inside. "Befitting a professional of your stature."

"Yeah, right," I said. "First of all, tell me that you've actually finaled?"

"Two months ago," Boris replied.

"Okay. No new charges, right?"

"I'm a free Indian, bro."

"You going back home?" I asked.

"It's a long story, Kola." He sighed. That grin. "But I did well for a while there, didn't I?"

"You damn sure did."

"My P.O. kept saying I was breaking new ground for Native peoples."

"You *are* overly represented in the prisons."

"He said he'd never had one from the iron cages do so well."

"We told you it was too early to move out," I reminded him. "But you didn't listen."

"I'd like to see you stay there, in that house, that long. I'm like you, Kola. A free spirit. We need our personal space, right?"

"I'm not on parole."

"True."

"You still shooting that shot?" He mimicked my release. "I told the guys at the parole office that you had game, but they didn't believe me."

"Well, you definitely have game. If you'd quit smoking, it might help."

"Smoking?" Boris laughed. "What about the other things?"

"You look good. Hell of a lot better than the last time I saw you."

"I knew I shouldn't have moved in with her," he said, scolding himself.

"It's nothing against her personally, Boris," I replied, quickly. "We've seen how this goes so many times."

"She had a car. A place to live."

"Let me guess. Then you started to fight."

"I didn't hit her."

"Congratulations."

"We started drinking … I fell back into it."

"I have it in me, Kola," he said quietly. "I can be better than this. I'm from a long line of warriors. My uncle's in Hollywood."

"Yeah, you told me that once," I replied.

"Not that it means anything. I wasn't always like *this*."

"So what's the plan?"

"Take me as far north as you can."

"Well, as you can see," I interjected, regarding my attire, "I have appointments in Santa Fe."

"That'll work."

"I get to introduce myself to prospects that have no idea who I am. But I'm quick to drop names. I work through the Bar Directory."

"Sounds like fun."

"All on your behalf, of course. The doors need to stay open. For your brothers and sisters in the iron cages if nothing else."

"It's appreciated, Kola."

"Last week I had to kneel and pray in the car dealership parking lot, as Peter asked Jesus for guidance. Remember him from the gym? Good-looking white guy. I think he was guarding you that one day."

"Curly hair?"

"Yes, that's him. He means well. He's very religious. Fortunately, Jesus told him to donate a car to Hope House."

"Then it was worth it, right?"

"You going back to South Dakota?" I asked, changing the subject.

"I never belonged here. Still don't know how I ended up down this way."

"It all made sense when you explained it to me at the interview."

"You recognize this shirt?" Boris asked, brightening.

"Of course I do," I replied. "That was a *great* Christmas, wasn't it?"

"I lost the jacket I got, though. After a fight."

"No, not *you.*"

"I never lost my temper on the court, though, did I? I know I had you worried."

"That one time, I was definitely worried."

"He clothes-lined me, man."

"He didn't mean to."

"Okay … see?" Boris said. "I didn't react. The way I usually would."

"You wanted to. I remember."

"Do those guys ask about me?"

"Yes, they do. Peter and the others."

"Different worlds, man." Boris paused. "Isn't it something?"

"It's a mystery," I replied. "That's for sure."

Boris gave me our special handshake and I sped off to my appointment, thinking of our commonality—the whole lot of them. The bond in our household was for life. It certainly gave me a new understanding of family, which I'm still sorting out. I know we're not blood relatives—and off we'll go into our respective fractured lives, never to be heard from again. But for some of us, the world exists outside the picket fence and the traditional definition of home. The larger community calls, holds our interest, incites our passion. Hope House persists, what we experienced in our volatile household, and I don't think it's sappy to say that I carry these men and women with me as I face the personal challenges of my adult life.

Boris had planned to build a sweat lodge on the corner of our back parking lot. Together we'd chant our protection against what awaited us outside the property line; we'd pray for good days, the way each of us wanted to. Could that kind of regimen bring me back? Maybe. We'd remember those known to us who were back inside the iron cages, and we'd face our days lean and pure and ready to embody change. Bestowed would be the stamina to return my phone calls, to make the appointments, to suffer the corporate banquets, to ask relative strangers for money. For a bonus I could go inside the walls and visit our fallen alumni the way I did with Callahan about a year ago:

"You're looking okay," I said, finally alone after the wait. Clicking locks. He shrugged his shoulders, smiled, and said nothing. "I mean, you're tan and everything," I continued.

"I get my walkin' in every day," Callahan replied. "Near a half-mile."

"What? Inside? Here?" I asked. "How do you pull that off?"

"It can be done."

"You're still smoking, I see." He always reeked of smoke.

"I've cut back a little," he said, pinching his fingers together.

"Well, I don't suppose there's much to do. Did they operate on you again? In here?"

"No, I'm still good from the other," Callahan answered. "I got this swelling, though. Around my liver. You wanna see?"

"Sure." He pulled up his prison shirt, exposing a pronounced abdominal growth.

"Damn!" I exclaimed.

"It don't hurt much.Only when I bend a certain way."

"Can't you get out of here?" I asked him. "I mean, they'd let you out, right? If you had a place to go?"

"I'm thinking that's the lowdown. I go before them again in fifty-four days."

"You know we can't take you back."

"I know that," he replied quickly, as if to ease my discomfort.

"One too many chances."

"There don't seem to be a place."

"Right. These mythical other programs ..." I mused, "besides ours. What about one of our volunteers?" I was thinking aloud. I caught myself. Bad idea. "Well, I mean, you know so many people."

"I've been writin' to that one lady."

"I don't know. That's a tough situation. If it was up to *me*—but you know it isn't."

"I know."

"Can I sell you a raffle ticket?"

"Don't have no money."

"I know. On the house. Here," I handed him three. "Put down your name. We know where to find you."

"You selling much?" he asked, taking my pen.

"It's not the same without you, guy. But it's still early in the summer. Everyone asks about you."

"I'm sorry I let you down," he said, looking up from his tickets. "Especially Annette."

"Don't worry about it. She forgives you. We gotta get you out of here."

"It was stupid. I was pulled over for the night, you know. I was asleep."

"Technically, you weren't actually driving the truck." I echoed. "It's just with your sentence. And your *crime.* You know."

"It's hard to change," he said flatly.

"Look, give me some time. There's gotta be *something.* Maybe I could convince the Board." He said nothing, always gracious. He stood up.

"You take care of yourself." We hugged, and he had tears in his eyes. The guard was at the door.

I did nothing in the way of follow-up on Callahan's plight—though in fairness his file was no longer my responsibility. Plus, there was a limit to how many chances we could give a resident. Still, I'd become a source of constant words of encouragement. Our own ragtag band of parolees without a true home—we probably could've been more systematic in our approach to their complicated issues, at least during my tenure. Work became a series of well-meaning moments, and the lives behind these random instances still visit me. With Callahan it was the way that he kept silent and observed, though he was one of our best ambassadors with that quick Irish smile of his. There was the dignity of his presence in my life; he would be there, *always, 5*:00 a.m. if necessary, during our raffle season. Helpful on the periphery, wearing my father's donated clothes—the extent of my dad's contribution to Hope House, which I shouldn't minimize, as this program had stolen his son. The succession of Masses made less tedious by the spring of Callahan's weathered frame and his laconic tales. He had the wisdom of one who had taken a life. Several lives, actually.

Speaking of which, a couple of years back, when Cortez was still in a workable limbo. It went like this:

"Chappie-o," he said in his prison orange, and I instantly recognized our shared childish greeting as the steel door slammed shut behind me, another guard behind Plexiglas.

"Cortez-ino." I replied. "What in the heck is going on here?"

"I messed up," he said, his shoulders going into that familiar sag. "But I didn't do what they say I did."

"I thought this was going to be your time, man? You know, what we talked about? Your thirties?"

"I did good for a while. Maestas got clean, then I did. Things were going good. Sorry about your car, man."

"Don't worry about it. So what happened?" I tried not to scold him, especially given the enormity of his circumstance.

"Oh," he sighed, "you know. That crazy shit. It takes my soul, man. You seen me."

"Indeed I have. That was some visit you paid me."

"Sorry about that. I wasn't going to hurt you."

"I know."

"I was in a bad place."

"Yeah, but you're good at bouncing back."

"I try and shit."

"You're *good* at it. Just when I think it's over for you. A goner."

"Did you think I was a goner?" Cortez asked.

"Yeah, maybe," I answered. "But I believe it can work out for you."

"This is a bad situation," he said solemnly. "I'm already on habitual."

"Are they gonna charge you?"

"That's my understanding."

"Do you want me to try to find you a lawyer?"

"I know I'm trouble and shit." He paused, looking straight at me. "You done more for me than anyone. Even my own family."

"It's okay. I've chosen this."

"I *am* going to make it up to you someday," he said. "Though maybe not in this life."

"It's all right. Maybe I know somebody. I do know a lot of attorneys. Half of them are Hope House donors. But not down in this part of the state." He was at the southern regional intake facility.

"If I can make it out of this one …" His voice trailed off, tears beginning.

"It's all right, fella," I said, as the guard let us know that our time had expired. "I'll let you know."

"Can you put some money on my books?"

"Sure." We embraced for a moment, and I could feel the strength in his biceps and his powerful frame.

"You're something. Especially for a white dude."

"You'd do the same for me, right?"

"Yes, I would," he replied instantly, in a low steady voice. "Yes, I would."

The problem had to do with hope being vague, and how the bad momentum would kick in. We were relieved to hear of his most recent arrest, or at least I was. Cortez could calm himself now, work once again on his resurrection, make that sincere attempt. At least it seemed so back then. For many of them jail was a place where the shaking could subside and the recovery could be resumed. Others, including myself, were safer with them inside. It was one more reminder that I wasn't equipped to deal with the threatening beauty of my chosen vocation. We all deserve a chance, though, and Cortez was one of many teachers in these matters.

September 24, 1987

Yesterday, I was swiftly crossing Main Street, staring straight ahead, hoping to avoid any meaningful contact with my town's residents. Thankfully, I'm older, perhaps not instantly recognizable. If tagged, there would be the necessity of answering natural questions. "Is that you, Chapman? What have you been up to all these years? Bette Joe always asks about you …" The composite inquiry, from keepers of our town's tradition. I stay in the car as much as possible.

But as long as I am here, stuff like what transpired this morning is going to happen. All I wanted was a carton of eggs; what I got instead was a shakedown from Mr. Collins, friend and ex-business associate of my father's. He asked if I had found myself yet. And with such contempt. That's the word on me back here.

Over there, the drinking fountain where we used to meet, always in search of someone older to buy us beer. The golf course, where I had my first cigarette. Grandmother's house, where we'd gather after practice and scarf down toast and soda pop. The expansive practice fields, where in August we'd run wind sprint after wind sprint. Helmet on, cleated, gasping for air.

What, in all this, needs to be understood? It's overpowering at times, especially with Mother and Father. It was there this morning with Mr. Collins and the other night with Coach Rayon.

He didn't ask what I've been doing since college. He didn't ask if I was married yet. Instead, we talked about his recent dismissal and how it was brought on by a streak of losing seasons. He mentioned how the talent seemed to wane with each passing year. "Nothing like your brother Fred's class," he said. "Or yours. You and Armand and Nick."

Coach Bob. Coach Bob Rayon. He encouraged us to cut our hair like his, in a crewcut. We used to call him Airport, he was so flat and shiny on top. But he accepted our different versions of his hairstyle. What *about* those guys ... should I look them up? I wonder what Nick is doing these days. He had a heck of a hook shot. Armand I know about all too well. Doubtless he'll be out to the house again today. Maybe I should have gone to that reunion last year; I mean, those were good times, even if there was a downside. What a strange case I was. Everyone must have that response when they look back, though. Right?

I'd better do something before Kit arrives. I should have the matter resolved before I meet her at the airport. How much more preferable it would be to explain it to her in the past tense—in the car from the airport—than to still have it lingering unresolved. Clouding our time together. On balance, they'll probably be pleased with Kit, relieved perhaps that their son is serious about someone. It's more what she'll think about my family, what effect they'll have on her. Will she find my dad charming? My mother? Will she make me feel my betrayal of them even more?

It has everything to do with wanting to look strong in Kit's eyes. If I'm still struggling over how and when to confront Father, it doesn't help us as a couple. It has to be today, this afternoon, on his walk. I should think about exactly how to bring it up. Maybe write it out.

I've come home—full of myself and confident that this time it will be different. Especially in light of how things went with Frederick. I know myself better now, or at least well enough to articulate what it is that's been wrong with Chapman Murphy over the past several years. Maybe if I get *real* specific with him? Dish it up as I experience it, somehow convey what it feels like. Assume that he's a worldly man who could comprehend easily enough. Or that's the hope. This afternoon, damn it! Get it over with.

"Chapman, Chapman!" It was Eppie outside my office window. When was it? A couple of years back.

"I did a bad thing."

"Come on in." He was visibly upset, pacing.

"I did a bad thing. You're not going to like it."

"Look, fella, it's all right. Tell me what's going on."

"You know the money you lent me last week?"

"Let me guess. It's gone?"

"You see, you see … I owed this one person forty dollars, so I paid him most of it. Then I went to pay my rent like I said I would. I was going to, but there was this girl, see? I thought it would be a good idea, you know, to spend it on her."

"Did you have any left over for the rent?" I asked.

"I'm sorry, Mr. Murphy," Eppie was looking at my office carpet. "He needs more. The landlord. Or he's gonna kick me out. He gave me until tonight to come up with it. Please help me out, Mr. Murphy. This one last time?"

"I told you last time, I don't have it. It's not like I make that much money."

"I know, I know. But if you could help me this one last time, then I promise not to do a bad thing."

"Have you seen your caseworker yet?"

"Next week, I think. I have the card somewhere."

"All right. Here's another forty," I said, reaching into my suit pocket. "I *mean* it this time."

"Bless you, bless you, sir. I won't let you down."

All of this became as predictable as our residents' unpredictability. Even now there are probably a slew of such entreaties on my answering machine. As if I *wanted* to be a full-time soldier in any army with too many clocks, predictable speech, forced humor, and whatever money purports to sustain. As if I'd have returned a call from Jesus Himself on my machine—maybe if he was polite enough and if I was in the right mood. As if anything mattered except finding that little boy on his bike—Marcellus—and getting that young man off the drug boulevard. My own problems are there, undeniably, but a proper context is called for. I, we, can do better than this.

September 27, 1987

> Kit arrived late this afternoon. I picked her up at the airport, very aware that I hadn't done what I had to do yet. I found myself exceptionally nervous at the terminal gate. Because I was afraid of how she might react? She takes me on faith and doesn't ask certain questions. It might be enough, what I present to her. Though she must be curious about what occupies so much of my attention.
>
> "I'm gonna try to be nice," Kit said in the car. "I've been practicing."

"Don't worry about it. They'll love you."

"I'm not so sure."

"Seriously. They're relieved that I have a girlfriend."

"I bet you've had tons of girlfriends. Dragged them home like this."

"Serious ones, I mean."

"I can't see you being casual. That's my territory."

"Whatever."

"Chapman," she began, pausing to collect her thoughts. "I'm not a good person."

"Oh, come on. Don't start that again."

"You've got to hear me out. I've had plenty of time to think it over the past couple of months. I'm afraid you might not be seeing me for who I am. We're different."

"Why is that so bad?"

"It isn't as long as you see that we are."

"Sure I do, but I also see a few similarities. More than you might care to admit."

"What's that supposed to mean?"

"Nothing. Except you deny almost as much as I do."

"You should know that I don't believe in happy endings."

"That could be a problem."

"Why are you driving so slowly?"

"I have problems with authority," I replied.

"Remind me never to let you drive my car."

As I expected, Mother went out of her way to make Kit feel welcome. As soon as we made it inside the front door, she emerged from the kitchen with a platter of deviled eggs and home-baked croissants. "Oh, Kit!" she exclaimed. "We've heard so much about you. What a pleasure to finally *meet* you."

Kit looked at me, then laughed. "Likewise, Mrs. Murphy."

Father was more reserved, though I could tell that he found her attractive. Mother cornered me in the den and said, "She is positively stunning."

It's about an hour before dinner. Kit's resting from her journey. I'm thinking about when the best time would be for me to have it out with the guy. It might be easier with Kit being here. On the walk, he'll be asking me about this girlfriend of mine. Then I'll spring it on him, catch him entirely off guard. My anger brilliantly stated, the accusations laid out in impeccable form. And the resounding conclusion, ushering me into adulthood. Finally, at age twenty-six.

September 29, 1987

Sure enough, after he came back from the office, I caught him on his way out the door, with the dog and the leash, and off we went on his early evening walk through his wooded acreage.

"She's pretty," he said.

"Thanks," I answered, not quite knowing how to respond.

"Where did you meet her?"

"In a bar."

"Well, she's probably wondering what you're about."

"I suppose," I replied.

"She's smart. And I like her sense of humor. That's important, you know. But then I don't need to tell you that. You're a grown man. It's ideal when you find a gal on an equal footing. A peer. You can meet each other best that way over the long haul."

"Dad, I've been wanting to tell you something," I said, matching his swift pace.

"Yes?" he asked, reining in Moose, his golden lab.

"As you know, my life has been on sort of a different path."

"I've noticed," he said without emotion.

"For whatever reason, I've felt a need to go in a contrary direction."

"To put it mildly," he shot back. "Have you found yourself yet?"

"Look, you can ridicule that all you want," I replied angrily. "But for some of us, it's what we're presented with."

"So," he continued, "are you hopping freight trains?"

"Yes," I answered. "Partly. I don't actually live on them. All the time, that is."

"Well, that's good to know."

"I mean, they do stop. Then you find yourself in a new town."

"How do you support yourself?"

"That's kind of what I wanted to get into, but to answer your question, a range of jobs. Waiting tables. Working for the Forest Service, planting trees. Picking cherries." I probably shouldn't have added that last one.

"With your education?" he asked, not hiding his frustration. He wasn't one for softening.

"I guess it's a process," I continued. "Like anything else."

"Some process. Go to university, get straight A's, excel in football. And then off you go, into some … *netherworld.*"

"I didn't excel in football," I corrected him. "I was special teams all the way."

"That's not the point, mister." His anger was rising again.

"Look, I know it's impossible for you to understand," I continued. "I don't understand it either. But I *have* to follow where it leads me."

"Fine." We were rounding the trail where it began to lead back to the house. "Your mother takes this … *direction* of your life easier than I do. She says that you'll grow out of it."

"It's possible," I said.

"At least you have a girlfriend now. Maybe she'll talk sense into you."

"Well, she's definitely having an impact on my life."

"You wanted to ask me something in particular?" he asked. "It seems like you had something specific in mind."

"Yes. As you know—"

"I don't know anything."

"Well, so much of this revolves around inheritance. What I've got from Mom's side."

"Which you don't use. As I understand it."

"Yes. Fred manages it. He gets the checks."

"At least you're not blowing through the principal."

"I want to give it away. I'm researching some charities."

"Fine," he answered, without emotion. "What do I care? You are a grown man. It's your money. Are you thirty yet?"

"No."

"Are you asking for permission or something?"

"I just don't want you or Mom to be offended. Ideally, I'd like you two to understand."

"Listen, mister, I don't understand a whole lot about your life. So what's one more thing?"

"Okay," I said. "I needed to have this conversation with you."

"I will say that your mother's family worked hard to insure the financial security of their children. And for the future generations. You have no idea what it's like to be poor."

"No, I don't."

"My family had nothing. It was the Depression. We took in boarders—"

"Yes, you've told me."

"Okay." He stopped in the middle of the path, and our eyes met. "I'm only going to say this once. If you are ever inclined to come back home, to this town where you were raised, and this family that loves you, you are welcome here."

I said nothing. Tears were beginning to come, for both of us. We shook hands. "I'm sorry, Dad."

"Don't apologize. Just make something of your life, okay?"

CHAPTER 21

They've significantly upgraded these piggybacks since the last time I was out here—they're now streamlined, funneled. Under their rigging, the wide splay of steel, I'm a bit more exposed to the elements, but who cares? Before leaving, before I gave my notice, after Annette had failed to show up at our mediation, I went about finding them, or at least making the effort—those whom I could track down. Like Briana. She's back inside, unsurprisingly, her mangled face still an essay.

"Well, hi, Mr. Murphy," she said in her husky smoker's voice, her one eye fixed on me. "Nice of you to visit."

"No problem. We're doing some follow up." I lied. This job had always been little more than a cover. I still had my I.D.'s.

"Sorry I turned out to be such a bust."

"Don't worry about it," I replied. "It's a long road, right?"

"That's definitely true for me."

"So what happened? They're still talking about you down at the parole office. Going in there all high, with ice cream running down your face.

She was looking at me blankly. "With the other two? Remember?"

"I think I know what you're saying."

"You look nice," I said.

"I was desperate, I guess." She laughed. "Still alive, though."

"How much more time did they give you?"

"Oh, a bunch."

"Right. We keep getting those warrants delivered to the household."

"I have a thing about writing checks."

"Apparently you do."

"I just got going again, that's all. Picked up shortly after coming to the household."

"I suppose it wasn't the most drug-free atmosphere, was it?"

"It's not your fault."

"Are you doing therapy and all that?"

Her face brightened. "Yes. I've been clean now almost a year."

"Good job."

"Getting to some core issues. It's hard, you know, with my appearance."

"I'm sorry. You know we all saw past that very quickly. We think you're beautiful."

"Well, I'm learning that it doesn't matter, as long as I'm feeling okay inside."

"Makes sense to me," I said.

This row of piggybacks is lined up as one organism, slowly moving north. The guys over there are milling around, doing nothing, and there are the rogue figures in the distance, eyeing their spots on the outbound.

I'd tried to make our household familiar in my adopted city—its niche among the other programs that help people now established. Others—like Salazar—can attend to its legacy now. I've found contentment in the enclosure of this truck-trailer bed. I might do another hotel soon, though.

Before leaving I made contact again with Maestas, who'd come back from the land of the rumored dead. I found him in prison orange as well. "Nice glasses," I said.

"Like yours, no?" He grinned at the swift pace of his thoughts. "This is who I am," he continued, "stuck inside again."

"What happened?"

"It got all crazy. They fired me from the job you got me."

"They liked you. You can't tag your own employer's machinery. What in the hell were you thinking?"

"They didn't like me," Maestas replied. "That one guy had it in for me."

"If you say so."

"That was stupid, yeah?"

"So what else is new?" I asked, trying to change the subject.

"Not much. *You're* the one with the life, not me."

"New charges?"

"They dropped them. I final in seven months."

"Then what?"

"Don't know. I was thinking about truck-driving school, or the bakery program. Seeing as how I know fast food so well. Did they ever send you my paycheck?"

"They wouldn't send it to us."

"But that's the address they have."

"What the post office doesn't forward we keep. I'll double-check when I get back."

"They're pimping me. Like those other people did."

"Maestas, you're a little paranoid, don't you think? These situations, the way they always come up—"

"Whatever. You're the one with the life."

"You can have a life, guy. Better than this." I looked around the prison visiting room.

"That's what you tell all of us."

"I mean it. In everyone's case, especially yours. Have you heard about Cortez?"

"You mean the robbery charge? That's wild."

"I saw him last week."

"Guess that means we won't do that road trip."

"It'll have to wait."

Maybe I'll pretend they are here now, *all* of them, a flatbed full of us heading North. Or East. Wherever. The only unity in our lives is one of disappointment. They might as well be with me, as they're here anyway—promises were made to them—and these rolling steel bins are spacious and familiar.

Samuel was resting in the Veterans' Hospital, one last installment in his treatment. "Chief," he said from his crutches. The waiting room had no windows.

'So you didn't go to Canada? Or home?"

"Chief, I ain't got no real home."

"I know, I know. You're in the *afternoon of your life."*

"Did I tell you that?"

"Yes, you did. About nine thousand times."

"Damn, Chief. I hate to repeat myself. Can I get a couple bucks for cigarettes?"

"They let you smoke? *In here?"*

"No, outside the building. We're veterans. We served our country. It's not asking for a whole lot, is it?"

"Okay. When I leave."

"Thanks, Chief."

"So are you off parole?"

"I still have probation. But I think they'll cut me loose if I finish up this rehab successfully."

"Where'd they catch up to you? After we met up?"

"Oh, around here."

"So you never left town?"

"I got caught up in some things. Then I broke my ankle."

"Did somebody do that to you?"

"I did it myself. I got the damnedest luck, Chief."

"Is this working?" I asked, pointing to our surroundings.

"Chief, I think this time it might take. I'm runnin' out of chances, you know."

"You still think I'm a racist?"

"Chief," he laughed, "I never called you a racist. I felt that you were singling me out, that's all. Some crazy stuff was going down in the household, you know? And you'd pull *me* upstairs."

"Everybody's back in, by the way," I said. "Or on the run."

"How's Mary Lou?"

"She got five years."

"Damn."

"Lewis absconded."

"He saved my life, you know."

"You told me."

"I still don't care for him, though."

"You told me that too."

"Chief, can you go down and get me those cigarettes? There's a machine in the basement."

"All right. But only because you're a veteran."

"You're the best."

"You're too much. All of you."

Samuel could pray almost as well as Lewis—one more source of the rivalry between the two of them—tension in the house. We'd do this every night with our guests, and they'd walk away saying how engaging Lewis was. And sincere. It was charming in the moment, the way desperation can shrink a world. Samuel, on the other hand, would openly reflect upon his past, at least with me, privately, usually in my car. Earlier in his time with us he had said, "I'm in the afternoon of my life, Chief. I can no longer go on the way I been."

"What are you going to do instead?" I asked.

"You mean after Hope House?"

"Sure."

"I wanna go home, Chief."

"You mean to Alabama or wherever."

"Montgomery. I feel this deep need within."

"Sounds like a good plan." I tried to be the enthusiast. "Can you transfer your parole?"

"Not likely, Chief. Can I smoke in the car?"

"I'd rather you didn't."

"Okay," Samuel answered.

"Is your mother still alive? Or your dad?"

"Nah, both're gone. But my sister's there."

After Samuel's hastened graduation from our program, with signs of collapsing will and his adamant denials, the inevitable. His parole officer cynically presented the prospect of a one-man crime wave starring Samuel. Months later I received a call from this man who'd cried in my car, Samuel, talking about his inescapable maturity. He suggested the supermarket off the drug avenue as a meeting place—these sordid venues where my role would take me. He cried again, this veteran of many things, and with the authorities looking for him, he spoke distractedly of Canada. He mentioned a recent botched, half-hearted suicide attempt in one of those motels.

"Lewis saved me." He brightened, sensing that it might be of interest to me.

"Lewis?" I asked, surprised. "Where is he?"

"I don't know, Chief. But he fished me out of that room and got me to a hospital."

"Lewis? Good for him."

"Still don't care for each other," Samuel said. "But the brother came through."

"What on earth was going on for you?"

"I get discouraged, Chief. You know?" He paused. "I'm in the afternoon of my life." The tears were starting again.

"I remember you saying that ."

"I just wanna go home."

"Can't you turn yourself in?" I had to say these things. "You could final and then go back to Alabama."

"Can't do that. Too many memories there."

"Well then, where *is* home?" I continued.

Samuel shrugged, truly at a loss. "Canada?" he answered softly.

"You want to go to Canada?"

"They respect black people up there. That's what I been told."

"I think you need to give yourself more choices."

"Can I borrow some money?"

"I can't. You are technically on the run. A fugitive."

"You ever been on parole?"

"That's not the point," I replied.

"It's hard, Chief. If I didn't have reasons not to go back, I'd do as you say."

"You know that we care about you," I said. "Even if you are black."

"I didn't mean it that time. I'm angry."

"It's all right, I understand. I guess I can lend you something."

"Thanks, Chief."

"I'm confident you can figure it out." I tried to be upbeat, digging into my pocket. "What to do, I mean."

Samuel's probably gone by now too—it'd be a surprise if he weren't. When our folks stop resurfacing, it's often a bad thing, unless they're re-incarcerated. There was no word on him from the parole officers, and I found myself scanning the parking lots for a tall, thin black man smoking a cigarette, getting ready to ask you something. I thought I saw him twice not long afterwards. Some hesitation on my part to make contact, bracing for the request. His tears were the most memorable of those of all my hardened felons—the rivulets flowing down his regal face. So many of them had grief deep and ready inside of them, harsh men and bruised women. Maestas had tantrums like a child, Cortez's face contorted with the image of his slain father, Mary Lou after her televised meth spree, Boris with his blackened eye, and so forth. A line of faces that flows through me on this Sunday morning, the railyard peaceful in both directions, as calm as any isolated beach.

Our entire program was geared toward what *could* be accomplished—the vows to change, the hopeful omens, new clothes on the first day of school. Foreboding waited outside the property, the darker instincts that were forever with us, easily reasserting their dominance in the hesitance of intention. For six weeks, on average, they walked resolutely in the normal, untroubled world. We were always a bunch, the lot of us, at the stores, at the movies, filing into the donated T'ai Chi movement studio, the previous class trying not to stare. My suit and tie were my uniform, and our group was certainly entitled to the healing space as much as anyone else. Briana with her one eye, Eppie in his nautical cap, Cortez's provocative stare, Samuel's brooding. On a good day jobs could be won, interviews would be successful, meetings could be attended and verified. Education would triumph.

Most might take this for granted, but not me. A decade ago I'd reduced my world into anything that would avoid the higher ladder of expectation. I'd found this orchard of losers on my own, and within its confines I felt at home. They looked at me with hopeful eyes, seeing me both as tender of the sanctuary and as a kind of movie character who could grant their wishes. All because I wore a suit and remembered their names.

I should have visited Callahan before my embarkation. He's there, probably motionless in the prison yard, watching, smoking, in the facility they call Jurassic Park because of the geriatric inmates. I should've read his file, accepted his documented past. That would've been the professional thing to do. But I could never bring myself to. I knew him in the present and that's what mattered. He was with us so long in the household, watching over everything, the severity of his offense commanding respect from the other residents, and so too his easy Southern countenance. Wiry, wearing those damned golf clothes of my father's, and *entirely* my protector. Gliding up to me with my forgotten keys, or coat, ready every Sunday morning when the monetary financial sustenance issue would drive us into the churches. His respect for the world around him was monumental, stunning, from a man who had murdered more than one person. He was an old man, different from that wild serviceman, just wanting to curl up with his whiskey in the woods for another lost weekend. Back then it must've been in between his shore leaves, when the bells would ring false and badly, his inner coals glowing. Korea. Even Callahan had cried—after his second purgatory with us, we found him watching the battleships on TV, alone on his cot in another particularly beaten-down facility. We asked him why he'd abused our trust in him and the tears welled up. "I don't rightly know," he replied. "You see, I made sure everything was in order before I went to my room. Kicked that one guy out, everyone home for curfew."

"You understand that we gave you a critical responsibility?" the voice of my colleague quivering.

"Yes …" Callahan's voice trailed off. "I'm sorry, Annette." The tears were running down his face. "I let you down. I let the house down."

"Yes, you did." She truly cared about him, there's no denying that. "You stupid old man. For three beers?"

"You understand," I interjected, "at this point we can't take you back? But it's great that you found this place." I tried to ignore the urine smell. "And who knows? This can work out."

"But not at Hope House?" Callahan asked, looking at Annette. She was silent.

"It's not up to me," she finally replied softly, staring at the wall. "I need to take it before the Board."

Situations unfolded like this—coaxing our beleaguered residents not to abandon faith while facing the reality of, and justification for, the rules. Even then, inevitably, we took Callahan back, and in the process reached new levels of our programmatic definition of penance.

CHAPTER 22

"Can you give me a reason to resume my position?" I asked Salazar, calling from a pay phone yet again.

"Chappie, are you reconsidering?"

"No way. It's just a question."

"Well, I'm only your attorney at this point."

"Yes, I know."

"As I've told you, a difference can be made. *You* can make one," he paused. "You have. You're uniquely situated to do this kind of work."

"I don't see it," I replied. "I *want* to see it."

"I think you're looking at it the wrong way. There's something here for you, you know?"

"I don't see how it matters. Even with our gold-star boys and girls from the household, the occasional success, what is it that they're graduating into? What brand of tedium awaits them?"

"I bet if you asked *them,* they wouldn't see it that way," Salazar replied. "It's a pretty big deal for them. And who are you to judge?"

"Okay. So this whole thing only works for the deprived? Conventional choices being as pathetic as we can acknowledge that they are?"

"Again, they, or even I, would strongly disagree. What's wrong with *my* life, for example?"

"I'm not talking about your life. I'm saying that we can be better than we are."

"That's why you need to come back."

"No, that's not it."

"You have to get real about your expectations, dude."

"Who wants to be a part of it?"

"Chapman, there are simple pleasures in life," Salazar sighed. "For most of us that's enough."

"Well, it shouldn't be."

"You should hear yourself."

"I don't mean it in the nutball sense," I shot back. "I *know* that there will always be sadness in the world. Injustice."

"Okay. But do you know why the difference is meaningful? Significant even? Worthy of note?"

"How?" I asked.

"That's what I mean. You're not seeing it."

"What is it that's getting in the way? What's obscuring my vision? Tell me."

"I don't know. Especially since unlike most of us, you're in the precise position to see it."

"We can do better. We should do better."

"Okay then. Come back and make it happen."

"It's too little too late," I replied.

"I beg to differ, Chappie"

"Well then, *you* try it. Why should I be the one with the freaky life?"

"Because you're a better person than I am."

"Not true. But I do have a better jump shot."

"I don't know about that."

"I'll get back to you. Thanks for talking with me again."

What would bring me back? A relentless series of good days—our residents flourishing in their new lives. Durable lives not undermined by their unruly impulses so that back inside they go. Or on the run. Salazar has been nice to hang in there with these conversations. What would bring me back most of all is my increasing awareness that *work* isn't the ultimate answer, that I don't have to justify my existence in that heavenly escape. It's the loss—my absence from Kit. That's what truly matters. All that time devoted to my uplifting cause at her expense. It didn't go well for her—alone in my absence, and now with a mysterious illness. She needs me. I need her. To be there for her without this constant pull to the world outside, this fantasy of social change. I think of Kit coming back from her wild river walks with the dogs—she could walk forever back then. Out here on these trains, I miss her. What would it be like if I could actually *be* with her, in the way that it could be?

The fact that I keep calling Salazar must mean I have some emerging intention to return. And what do I learn from ancient journals of mine? Like so many things in my life, it starts with my father, our turbulent relationship and yet the reluctant love that would surface between us. He is gone now. Oddly, his presence is more real for me now than it was when he was alive. He made it clear in what turned out to be our final walk together that whatever baffling choice I made in my life, he wanted me to live it fully, to honor his memory in that way. Salazar keeps telling me that I am making a difference at Hope House. Certainly it has always been more than a *job*, and the memory of my ghost residents should be evidence of that.

Hope House *does* hang in the balance—so tenuous, this world of charity. Funding-wise for starters. Every year asking the same people for money. And then the limitations of a volunteer enterprise and the personalities that can easily upstage the important service that you are delivering. When the cheery board meetings become something else, as tensions begin to surface and the inevitable bad flowering as alliances harden.

But my nemesis … my nemeses … have moved on from Hope House, apparently (at least according to Salazar). I won. But this hardly feels like a victory lap, out here on the freights, my hair a wadded mat and the unseasonably cold wind as our train gathers speed.

Things change when your parents are gone—and in my case, especially with *Father*. I cannot explain why there was always this conflict between us, other than he seemed to resent my very being, as my adult choices—my relentless series of no's—began to accumulate, began to shape the path that would ultimately become my path. I wince when I read these diary passages, the build-up to my walk with him. So much unspoken between us. As I fell in love with my Hope House residents, I became more appreciative of all that I have been given. Jesus, born into Murphydom? Safe in our house, popular with the sleepovers, nothing but cornfields on either side of the highway, and my father a driven but respected man. A good man.

It was not his fault that he did not know how to respond to my rebellion. I came to resent all of their comfort, the superficiality of the cocktail parties, not down with the equations the world presented to me, all of these *assumptions*. He would argue that I had the room to be so picky, so enamored with the opposite, while he was not so fortunate in his youth; he grew up poor. He wanted the opposite, as he felt as confident as his rivals, the World War II young men. He wanted to make money, and he did.

I have this photo back at Kit's house (my house too?). I am sitting on his lap, the family assembled during a mother-mandated vacation in Miami, black and white, early 60s. He is holding me—easily, gracefully—showing an affectionate side that is difficult for me to place. Instead, my memories revolve around the series of motivational lectures he felt compelled to give me, his eyes blazing incomprehension, and how I kicked back as well as I could. I am his child. No matter how smart we become, how ingrained and set in our contrasting ways, that would remain an elemental fact.

And what about *his* funeral? Not as many in attendance as my mother's, their friends having passed on in the intervening years; but when the bells rang, what did I feel? Akin to the same sensation that I had at Mom's funeral, tears streaming down my face as her casket was lifted into the awaiting white hearse, the Catholic bells lifting you back into eight years old. In *his* case, though, more complicated. I insisted on speaking from the altar, in his memory, could not get through it, strangely—would have been nice to complete my remarks, to make them comprehensible to the maybe puzzled church assemblage. Their marriage lasted decades, common back then? Undeniable, his grief at her passing, choking on his words as he so wanted to follow her into the next world—we brothers held him back, following the procession as he attempted to do, awkwardly down the church aisle—his beloved companion. And all of their dinner conversations, their joking having abruptly stopped. Final. No more.

So what about you and Kit at this point? What of *us*? So strange to be able to live the we, but to say the we a different matter? Always a pair in others' eyes, and yet ourselves refusing to surrender to our plural identity. We would mirror each other's independence in these sun-baked years, fierce, not wanting to compromise, to live through another. So here you are, on the freight trains, rattling towards God knows where, while Kit faces her uncertainty alone. But then, we have always been alone in our pairing. Hope House so at the expense of our futurity, consuming, me more absent than ever. And yet, do we not have the same level of easiness as my parents enjoyed? Do we not take each other for granted as they did?

Kit has tricked me into assuming that she will be fine. Permission granted to go work things out, this strange ritual of mine, craving the basics of jolting noise, tonnage on steel rails, hearing myself think. And yet my dream of the other night with its alarm. she had fallen on our hardwood floor, difficulty in standing, no one there to help but our powerless dogs.

But it gets back to this solitude of ours, how that seemed to be the precondition of *our* union. Obvious ceremony for others, conventional definitions ditto, recognizing in each other the same taproot defiance. Not necessarily unconditional rebellion, but a quiet and firm *no* to what was expected of us. Kit has her studio, I have my ex-cons.

The *ex-cons* … my father could never accept the idea of me working with, and on behalf of, these losers. "Is this what you went to college for?" he would ask, incredulous. As I think about whether or not to return to Hope House (Salazar seemed clear in his invitation, and he is the Board President, after all), I wonder if there was anything I could have done or said to convince my father of charity's place in the world. Maybe he could have seen it if I were a priest or something. Or if it had been a priority in my upbringing. But profit was what he understood best, and he was great at it. The beautiful order of things as the free market did its magic—the intelligence of it all.

Maybe if he could have followed my journey into this nonprofit world that I had never heard of until well after graduation? My classmates were not dying to secure a staff position at the local homeless shelter. We were an ambitious, achievement-oriented lot—competitive with each other—and truly, what was the point of our Ivy League training if we were going to go suddenly in reverse? I never included Dad in my real adult life, estranged as I would increasingly become over the years, so how could he be expected to understand how I landed at Hope House?

Maybe Dad would have understood if he could have seen how good I was at raising money. Aggressive with my charitable asks, too much so at first, but gradually softening into the wisdom of subtlety. The relationships formed, the friendships—on behalf of this larger, virtuous endeavor—*that* is what I did well. Ask my board. At least until the trouble surfaced with Hilda. The numbers were real. Parties, yes, cruising the annual attorney holiday function that *everybody* went to, into the back office with the pricey champagne. Getting their business cards, working through the Bar Directory, making the follow-up calls. Animated, the relief in it not being about myself, money for a purpose. Surely my father had been on charitable boards like this, scanning the development report each month, the income/expense sheet.

But not his son doing this kind of work at the expense of the life that he was groomed for. As year by year his third son was pulled into this *subculture*, this distant world of do-gooders and parolees and in another time zone, several states away. I was Dean's List in his eyes, and a good athlete. Popular.

But I think he could recognize, and appreciate, skill—no matter the endeavor. And I was skilled at asking for money. I do not need anybody to convince me about the importance of Hope House and the service it provides. Will it be okay if I am not there? And what other kind of job could I do? Tolerate? Explain?

How about the time when I went back, after the funerals of my parents, on my own, to pay quiet homage? The cemetery pulled me in and would not let me go; I was there for hours. I recognized so many names on the tombstones, among the maple trees in this lush village resting place for the families of Alliance, Iowa. This town embraced me, loved me, the warm clarity of a small rural college town. I had gone away, far away, to find my adult life. And I realized that I had never left. Coach Rayon, my classmates that I had grown up with, friends like Armand even—they *knew* me. Whatever I chose to do with being a Murphy, they did not care. We had the bond of childhood.

What would it have been like to go up in some kind of space capsule and come into my own family without this deep rebellion of mine? To see my own circumstance in a neutral way and relax into this village of gentle abundance, to proudly declare allegiance to my clan and become my father's son? But how could I get there without the experience of the opposite, which I sought out instinctively in my traumatized parolees?

It is so strange to feel released like this, to assume my adult life with a vengeance and identity all of its own. My own.

Some things are impossible for others to understand. You either get it or you don't. How could my father, born into financial hardship, and knowing what it took for him to escape it, how could he comprehend the choices I made? The sort of people that I was visibly drawn to—the inmates, the criminals—were people to be shunned, avoided, or at the very least *ignored.* Certainly not worthy of his son's best efforts.

What was my life like *before* Hope House? Surely, I found a purpose in social action, things came together, no longer the inward lens that can trap a person, especially a young man. Our Hope House residents pulled me out of myself—maybe at the cost of neglecting other aspects of my life, such as my relationship with Kit. But my work with the ex-cons has ushered in a steep shift, something that inhabits the deepest cavern of my being. And then, in tandem with the death of my parents, I can look back on my travels with Rodney and Timothy and of course the courtship of Kit as necessary, as embarrassing, and as worthy of praise. What happens when you say *no* to the world around you? Monumental, unforeseen things; other directions open up.

So if the point of all this searching, documented in my journal of seven years ago, was to reach some kind of resolution to my then even younger life, where does that put me now? Have I accepted the world as it is, as Salazar would encourage in his sensitive lecturing?

I don't think so. But at least I have found an entry point—service to my colorful and traumatized parolees—and of course the even deeper achievement of my commitment to Kit. All of this is much clearer to me now. Yes, it has been difficult to read these old journals, aware now of youthful longing, of the uncertainty in rejecting a mapped-out path. But I believe that walk with my dad was our version of reconciliation; he wished me well, and deep down he respected my rebellion. He loved me.

And what about Kit's transformation? She is almost unrecognizable in these early journals. Change seems to be the animating force in what we have both chosen in this, our only life, whether it be in my declaring for my parolees, or in Kit's commitment to her studio. (Aren't growth and change the whole point?) The fact that as a couple we share so many of the same *issues* probably has made the gift of our connection even sweeter. Seven years ago I would avoid conversations with others at all costs, would hug the alleys of my adopted Luxor, Montana, some kind of deep shame involved. Now I go up to complete strangers and ask for two thousand dollars to help the ex-cons, for the lovable folks who burglarized your house last week.

My dad would approve of this change in his next-to-youngest son, except of course for my choice of client population. He always wanted me to live fully in the world—to become a verb even, as he did with his Iowa business success. And we were a noticeable family in the St. Ignatius Catholic pews each Sunday.

But what about success for my beloved parolees? How would we define that at Hope House—especially in the face of all the relapses, the re-arrests, the inevitable falling down? Every one of my original five relapsed, as did almost about everyone else who ever came through our celebrated Hope House doors.

To that I say, "Oh yeah? And how would *you* fare when required by the state to leave behind all that you have known and somehow magically become a devotee of caution? Of actually following the rules that you never understood anyway?"

I am pragmatic, am like my dad there as well—I prefer the world of the real. Clearly *these people* need time to figure it all out. If Hope House is an introduction to an entirely different world, it is a success in itself. What they choose to do with what we present to them gets into the realm of individual choice. But at least the outlines of viable choices begin to emerge. If there are parole violations or drug relapses to follow, it is a long life. I can see that even at age thirty-three.

So why shouldn't I go back to Hope House? Who else is going to do this?

And what about my money issue? How defiant I was back then, in my journals, determined to elude that box of affluence. He probably did not care what I ultimately chose to do with what I inherited from my mother's side—it was so cleansing at the time to work with my stockbroker brother Fred, who always thought I was *off*—as dispersed it went to various noble charities that he helped me research. I became truly on my own then, no more secret knowledge of a soft financial pillow if things got weird. Then, irony in its truest sense as the old man kept me in his will, did not punish me for leaving the rules, almost as if to test my resolve. How prescient he proved to be, as right now it is on my mind as I am technically unemployed, uncertain of my future with Hope House.

But forget the *facility* … what about Kit? At what point do I cease defining myself through work? The belonging in a paycheck, and the daily drama of keeping the darker energies outside our sacred, fenced-off area—our Hope House? When do I acknowledge that Kit and our domestic possibilities could possibly represent the sum of my ambitions? The intimate time with our dogs, and at night in her arms. This is what people do, right? And here she is, alone, facing the logic of her undiagnosed illness. That dream the other night got my attention. I need to be with her. Not out here in the open air, wind fluffing my sleeping bag, my raw hair and skin. The opposite of sharing cognac with Kit before the fire, the chimney needing to be cleaned, and the dogs with their warm fur.

What if I were to come back and make *her* my priority? Surrender to the ways of normalcy, continue to shake down attorneys and churches for their donations, but reverse the hierarchy? Actually spend dinner evenings at *home*, not staving off the latest threat to a resident's sobriety? Take a vacation with Kit, for crissakes, factoring in her increasingly uncertain walk and arranging for her comfort?

All of these questions … but not among them the fact that I would be welcome again at Hope House. Salazar has made that clear.

There is a possible answer.

It'd go like this.

"Kit?" Knocking on the door, I ask, "Are you home?"

"Don't you still have a key?" Always that swift teasing of hers. She opens the door, looks great.

"I don't know," I reply apologetically, searching my jean pocket. "I probably left it on some freight train."

"You and the trains," she smiled. "A regular hobo."

"I'm *not* a hobo. We've had this conversation."

"So are you back now?"

"Are you going to invite me in?"

"It's still your house too. Do you want an invitation?"

"I've missed you *so* much." We embrace. Tears on my end.

"You're a crazy freak."

"You are too," I say.

I hug her in a way that I never have before, showing her what I'm feeling. We're still in the doorway.

"The dogs have asked about you."

"You and the dogs."

"They have souls, you know."

"I know. We've had this conversation as well."

Silence.

"How've you been feeling?" I continue. "What'd the doctor say?"

"I don't know." She shrugs. "Still nothing that they can pinpoint. I do have good days, though."

"Do you want me back?"

"As far as I am concerned, you never left."

Like this. It goes like this. And I am heading back now,

for real.